No Plans for Tomorrow

by

Jane Drager

No Plans for Tomorrow

Cover Art by *Kim Mendoza*

The Wild Rose Press, Inc.
PO Box 708
Adams Basin, NY 14410-0708
Visit us at www.thewildrosepress.com

Publishing History
First Edition, 2021
Trade Paperback ISBN 978-1-5092-3857-6
Digital ISBN 978-1-5092-3858-3

Published in the United States of America

A flash of light caught Carmen's eye. Snapping her gaze toward the road, she muffled a curse as a silver luxury car rounded the curve.

Struggling to suppress the wave of panic for Lucy's safety, Carmen forced the girl to her feet and gripped her shoulders. "You remember the bad man from the soccer game? Lucy, look at me." Carmen shook Lucy's shoulders. "That's him, honey. I want you to run and find your father. Don't turn back for any reason. Can you do that for me, Lucy?"

Eyes wide and lips trembling, Lucy shook her head. "I won't leave you. He's gonna hurt you."

But Lucy's safety was paramount. To protect a child, she would face the devil, despite shaking limbs. She swallowed hard. "Yes, he'll try, but I don't want him to hurt you. Do you understand? You're very important to me."

The silver vehicle crunched to a stop inches from her car's front grill, filling the overlook's stoned parking area.

With her heart jumping into her throat, Carmen tightened her grip on Lucy's shoulders. "Honey, this is not a time for heroics. Please, go find your father." Whirling Lucy, she pushed on her back. "Run—now!"

Praise for Jane Drager

"Life-affirming. That's how I would describe ALL CHOCOLATE, EXTRA CHERRIES. Jane Drager has given us loss, grief, happiness, and love in a happily ever after story."

~Betty W., Reviewer

~*~

"THE RIDDLE KEY had such an intriguing title I had to read this book. It's a fabulous read and I honestly wish there were more like it. I loved the creepy house and the guesswork involved in the murder. I absolutely adored this novel."

~Tracy S., Reviewer

~*~

"I absolutely loved MEMORIES FOR A LIFETIME and was so happy it had a happily-ever-after ending. I can't believe all the twists and turns Jane made in the story. It was great."

~Margaret K.

~*~

"I never read romance, but I picked up ASK NOTHING IN RETURN and couldn't put it down. A pleasant surprise."

~Michael P.

Dedication

To all of you who pushed for this sequel to my first novel, SECRETS BY NECESSITY. I hope you enjoy it.

Chapter One

Carmen Santiago read the text message for the third time and nearly drove the car off the winding mountain road. Bad enough the early afternoon sun blinded her on the last curve, so she gripped the wheel with one hand and dropped the phone on the passenger seat. The printed words filled her chest with pride, but holy moly, she might kill herself before answering. Why she chose to look at the text was a puzzle. She never bothered with her phone while driving, but the ID displayed *NEJM*, and her heart took a flying leap. With no desire to wait another second, she aimed her vehicle into the first available turn-off, which happened to be the Billings Mountain Elementary School, and glided to a stop where dirt met blacktop and cut the engine. Her first vacation in eons would have to wait.

Phone in hand, she stepped onto the asphalt, and a blast of cool, mountain air ruffled her hair. Lordy, how refreshing. After three and a half hours on the road with one pit stop, she needed a good stretch to let some circulation flow into her butt. What better place than a yard full of children surrounded by a green backdrop of trees?

Besides, the message required a reply. She read it again. Wow. *The New England Journal of Medicine*, the world's leading medical journal, agreed to publish her findings on pediatric leukopenia. They even wanted her picture on the cover! Mom and Dad would be so proud. She'd call them tonight, but for now, she'd respond to the journal and then send a text to her partners. At long last, a bright spot to a dismal year.

Finished with her text, she refrained from doing a happy, little dance. Instead, she stretched through the open car window to slip the phone onto the dashboard. With children's shrieks filling the air, she couldn't help but turn and watch them play. None were older than twelve—typical elementary age. The younger ones ran around like crazy, screaming and laughing as they chased each other. The older ones clustered in groups with fingers tapping on cell phones. Many more kicked a soccer ball around the field adjacent to the playground. Judging by the time of day, the students enjoyed an after-lunch recess.

According to the brochure, Billings Mountain, Virginia, was a community of three hundred permanent residents who welcomed more than two thousand visitors a year, many of whom rented one of the fifteen cabins scattered around the mountain. The colorful flowers and hiking trails attracted day-trippers and photographers, and the serenity of the surroundings enticed those who opted for a quiet stay. Like her.

Sally, her medical assistant, booked her for two weeks, and her partners practically shoved her out the door. Well, so what if she hadn't taken a vacation in forever? She loved her job and had her reasons for being a workaholic. But after a year in hell, luck finally found her. Nothing could spoil her light mood. Smiling, she sucked in a deep breath, and refreshing mountain air scented with pine filled her lungs.

She'd forgotten how nature rejuvenated the mind

and soul. Concrete and highways smelled nothing like new leaves forming on trees. She sneezed. Well, okay, allergy season was right around the corner.

With goose bumps rising from the chilly air, she reached through her car window and grabbed her mauve spring jacket. Since the canvas material blocked the wind, she rarely zipped it closed. Most of the time, heat flushed her skin, which she swore was early-onset menopause. Geez, she was only thirty-six. Sucking in another deep breath, she surprised herself by not coughing the smog of Richmond out of her lungs.

During the long drive, she weighed the pros and cons of coming to such a secluded retreat. Twice, she almost turned around, but everyone at Main Street Pediatric Center raved about this quiet, mountain getaway. Quiet meant isolated, and she argued about the logic behind such a place. Why not send her where crowds gathered, like…eh, what? Flying to some exotic location was out. She needed wheels in case…*hell*. Gut clenching, she cursed herself for thinking of him. Leaning against the car, she let her gaze wander.

About ten vehicles filled the large parking lot—mostly SUVs. Yet, the area, with its expansive size, could accommodate quite a crowd. The size of the school surprised her. For a supposedly small community, the basic, one-story red-brick structure had a gymnasium on the right and The Alexandra Colter Auditorium on the left while the center section housed the classrooms. Both ends stood much higher in height and shaped the building into an inverted C. About a hundred yards to the left, a paved helipad covered part of a grassy field. On the right, a caretaker on a huge mower cut the grass adjacent to the soccer field.

Thick woods full of pine trees outlined the perimeter of the grounds, and the scent mingled with the smell of freshly cut grass. Both fragrances calmed the queasiness in her stomach. She had never gone on vacation alone, but everyone in the office insisted she take time to straighten out her head. What a laugh. Two weeks in a mountain resort wouldn't erase the memories of a bad marriage.

At the screams of laughter, she returned her gaze to the playing children.

On the drive up, she passed one overlook, which was nothing more than a field of boulders surrounded by a forest of trees, but the school was situated on a large stretch of flatland. Since she doubted the mountain leveled itself in this particular spot, then someone spent an awful lot of money to fill in the area. Stuffing her hands into her jacket pockets, she closed her eyes and lifted her face skyward to relish the warmth of the sun.

The sound of tires crunching on stones forced her to open her eyes and rotate her head. A green-and-white Billings Mountain Sheriff SUV pulled in behind her white luxury vehicle.

Oh, crap. So much for her good mood. She was probably breaking some unwritten mountain law by parking halfway onto the grass.

Back tense, she gritted her teeth. Her assistant assured her of local law enforcement should she need them, but seeing a cop approach so soon after her arrival raised a few hairs on her scalp. Because of her ex, she would never again trust a cop. Facing the cruiser, she squared her shoulders and nodded at the officer.

4

The car door opened.

Her breath stopped. *Santa Maria*! A Greek god emerged from the vehicle, a six-foot-two, eyes-of-blue hunk of man who had a movie star quality that shot her heart rate into the stratosphere. A svelte physique filled a uniform of crisp, white shirt and gray trousers, accented by the standard equipment of a clipped radio mike on his left shoulder with a coiled cord connected to the transceiver on his hip. A right-sided holstered gun and handcuff pouch completed the picture. The overhead sunshine reflected off his golden hair to create a blinding glow, and she reached for her sunglasses on top of her head. She hit only air. Before stepping from the car, she'd tossed the glasses onto the console. Since her knees threatened to buckle, she clutched the car's door frame for support.

Holy hell. Get a grip, girl. She wasn't some love-starved woman desperate for male companionship. Even though the man ignited a fire in her belly, she couldn't dismiss one glaring obstacle. Dammit, he was a cop.

"Afternoon, ma'am."

Her entire body hummed from the sound of his deep voice. The tone conjured images of cool sheets and warm hands. If beautiful white teeth flashed her way, she might melt into a pile of goo.

She shook herself for such an asinine response. Big deal, she hadn't been with a man for more than two years, but she refused to break her dry spell with an officer of the law. Swallowing hard, she pushed away from the car. "Something wrong? I know I'm not legally parked, but I only stopped to use my cell."

A slow perusal scanned her from head to toe, and

every inch of her skin flushed with heat. Many men admired her curvy figure and often commented in their lewd ways, but she hadn't the time nor energy for another man in her life—especially since the last one refused to go away.

Strolling with thumbs in his duty belt, the cop nodded in the direction of two adults staring from the schoolyard. "The teachers worry when strangers lurk in the area. Can't say I blame them with the world being so cruel. Can I see some identification?"

Serves me right for stopping. What more natural way for Enrico to confirm her whereabouts than to have a lawman do a routine identity check? Hell, she couldn't count how many times a cop stopped her all because her ex barked his orders. Forcing her locomotive heart into some semblance of rhythm, she stretched through the car window for her purse. After bumping her head on the way out and wondering why she couldn't knock herself unconscious, she extracted the wallet and fumbled through the card slots. Some day, she might sit and sort through the useless clutter.

"No need to be nervous, ma'am—unless you've something to hide."

Oh, she had plenty to hide. First and foremost, her shaky hand. Nothing revealed a nervous person like shaking body parts. But over the past year, she'd gone through the same ritual with every cop who stopped her. No, sir—yes, sir—thank you, sir. This late in the game, she should be used to this type of harassment. Fighting like mad to appear calm, she handed over her license.

He scanned the data. "Carmen Santiago, M.D." Meeting her gaze, he cocked a brow. "I have the name on today's arrival list but no mention of a doctor." He returned her license. "What's your specialty?"

His voice conveyed a friendly tone as opposed to the hostile voices she'd come to associate with law enforcement. But in no way would she drop her guard. Just because this guy activated a yearning for some male companionship didn't mean she trusted him. Careful not to make any skin-to-skin contact, she used two fingers to take the card from his hand then threw the license, wallet, and purse onto the driver's seat like the objects were on fire. *Oh, yeah, he asked my specialty.* Swallowing a lump that was part anxiety for his presence and part regret for coming, she stuffed her hands into her jacket pockets. "Pediatrics."

He changed his stance from cop-mode to man-mode, which—by her definition—meant on-the-alert to relaxed. Obviously, she wasn't on his most-wanted list...yet. But she'd been fooled before. Every man had a price, and Enrico always found it.

Smiling, he nodded toward the schoolyard. "No wonder you stopped to watch the kids. Is this your first visit to Billings Mountain?"

"Yes." She forced out that one word. Damn, the man was eye candy. Bright white teeth sparkled behind his lips, and the combination of beautiful teeth, blue eyes, and earthy cologne devastated any further thoughts. *Mama mia.* If she wasn't so nervous, she'd fan herself.

Gaze twinkling, he clipped his thumbs into his duty belt. "I'm sorry if I alarmed you. Visitors come and go, and not all of them are legit. The residents report anything suspicious."

"Good to know." She plastered on a smile. "I'll

head to check-in. Am I far?"

"The office is up the road about a mile. You can't miss it." He crossed his arms over his chest.

Muscles bulged beneath his shirt, giving her a glimpse of a lawman without a bullet-proof vest. *Nice*. As a doctor, she appreciated a man who took care of himself. As a woman, she loved the shape and contours of well-defined muscles.

He cleared his throat. "I'm Sheriff James Thomas, ma'am. If you have any problems, you let me know."

She snapped her gaze to his face and caught the slight smirk at the corner of his lips. *Oops*. Busted. But really now, her depend on a lawman? *I don't think so.* Not with her history. She opened her car door. "Thank you, Sheriff. I'm sorry if I distressed anyone."

Jumping in with the grace of an uncoordinated toddler, she shoved aside wallet and purse before starting the car. Nerves threatened to overwhelm her common sense, and she resisted the urge to floor the gas pedal. With her luck, the tires would throw stones at his handsome face, and he'd have a real reason to toss her in jail. *Dios mio. What the hell did I get myself into*?

****

James stared until the white vehicle disappeared around the next bend. Damn, he felt sucker-punched. When he drove in and caught a glimpse of her head tilted skyward, he lost all thought at the cascade of dark hair falling down her back. Then, when she focused a pair of almond-shaped eyes on him, she…wow! No woman had stolen his breath in years. Yet, beauty aside, at the flash of panic on her face, his cop instincts activated. Then, her hand shook so badly he almost grabbed hold to steady the tremor. Why was she so nervous? Since her name and home address appeared on this morning's guest list, he hadn't bothered with an ID check on her driver's license. Maybe he should have. A quick math calculation revealed her age as thirty-six—three years younger than his thirty-nine. Once he returned to the office, he'd input her info into the national database to see what popped up. She wouldn't be the first criminal to seek refuge on Billings Mountain.

Tearing his gaze from the roadway, he rubbed the nape of his neck to force control over his raging hormones. After years of lying dormant, his body kicked into gear with just one look at this extraordinary woman. She had curves in all the right places. Blue jeans hugged endless legs, and when she bent to retrieve her purse, the round ass peeking from her canvas jacket sent a surge of warmth through his core. To top everything, she smelled like cotton candy with a hint of chocolate. If, by chance, she wore a new kind of perfume, then he was all in. Returning to his cruiser, he paused with a hand on the door handle.

"Hey, Dad!"

His daughter, Lucy, ran across the parking lot. Turning with arms outward, he waited for the inevitable collision. As expected, she flew into his embrace and nearly knocked him over. His heart swelled, as it always did whenever she entered a room. She was the love of his life, and every day beat the last. Even at the age of eleven, she remained the spitting image of himself with her blue eyes and golden hair. Soon, boys would fall in line, but for now, he'd enjoy every second of her childhood. Sniffing, he caught the scent of oregano. Yeah, sub sandwiches were on today's school lunch menu. Lucy loved those subs. He released her and shot his one-eyed daddy glare. "You cutting class?"

"Nah. I asked Miss Weatherbee if I could say hello." She jerked her head in the direction of the roadway. "I saw you talking to that lady. Who is she?"

"One of our new arrivals."

"She's pretty."

He suppressed a smile. "How would you know? You were on the soccer field."

Gaze narrowed, she jammed her fists on her hips. "I got eyes, just like Miss Weatherbee watched you more than us."

Ah, yes, Miss Weatherbee. While cute and educated, she raised not an iota of interest. Their encounters progressed no further than polite conversation at PTA meetings.

"Is the lady married?"

He snapped his gaze to his daughter. *Uh-oh.* Matchmaker Lucy was on the prowl. Over the past two years, she connived with every eligible female on the mountain. With her list exhausted, she concentrated on guests. Lucky for him, single women rarely vacationed in the mountain cabins. Most preferred sunning themselves on a beach somewhere. If he didn't love the mountain so much, he'd apply for a job in the valley and find himself a wife. But he couldn't leave the place he called home. And what were the odds of a valley woman being charmed by the mountain? Yeah, big joke. Lowering his head, he cast his most fierce glare, which never worked. His daughter was no dummy. "Shouldn't you be getting to class?"

"Yeah, yeah, in a minute." She tucked a strand of long hair behind her ear. "You should find out what cabin she's in and go see her."

And cause another look of sheer panic? Although, Lucy's suggestion had some merit. His guest list never included cabin assignments. With fifteen rentals spread over the mountain, only Henrietta knew who went where.

The school's outdoor buzzer sounded.

Chuckling, he pointed at the children rushing into the school. "Off you go. I'll head to the check-in office."

With a big smile, Lucy fist-pumped and then ran toward the building with an overhead wave.

He must be out of his mind, but the exotic beauty had him intrigued. He might as well satisfy his curiosity before Lucy jumped into full-blown matchmaker mode.

Chapter Two

Glancing in her rearview mirror, Carmen expected the handsome cop to follow. Two curves later and seeing nothing behind her, she released a long breath and loosened her grip on the steering wheel. She hated the constant paranoia. Back home, every time she passed a patrol car, she waited for the inevitable flashing lights. On more than one occasion, their stops delayed her appointment schedule by an hour.

But this time, no cop car tailgated, and a wave of relief swept over her. Because of Enrico's backhanded tactics, any guy wearing a badge needed a golden halo over his head and perhaps a nice set of white wings on his back. And, oh, yes, a solid message from the Almighty himself declaring the badge-wearer as a man or woman of impeccable honor.

Sheriff James Thomas got the golden halo right. The bright sunlight on his hair created a glow worthy of any angel. She should ask if he hid his wings under his clothes. Chuckling to herself, she slowed the car as two hikers emerged from a forested path and crossed to another on the opposite side of the road.

Lawmen aside, would she ever again trust a man? Counseling wasted her time, especially when the problem persisted. Day in and day out, she faced a constant threat from a man determined to make her life miserable. No one understood how fear affected one's life. She worked because the children filled her with joy, but over the past year, she hardly slept—until makeup no longer hid her fatigue. Hence, her trip to Billings Mountain.

While maneuvering the car up the winding road, Carmen passed a newly built police station along with several more houses tucked among the trees. Around the next bend, a yellow globe on a pole with *GAS* in big, red letters stuck out like a sore thumb among the green trees. Two antiquated gas pumps sat on a concrete island, and beyond the pumps, two garage-bay doors revealed a guy in greasy coveralls working under a car on a lift.

Adjacent to the garage, another building displayed Jenkins Auto Parts over a wide porch, complete with two, old codgers on rockers by the entrance. The entire complex resembled a scene straight from a 1950s movie. The missing detail was a banjo player with a piece of straw dangling from his mouth. The gas prices were definitely modern day. She shifted her gaze to the dashboard's fuel gauge and made a mental note to fill the tank before any day trip into the valley.

Not far from the gas station, the *Cabin Rentals* sign gleamed with a *No Vacancy* underneath. Carmen eased the car into a four-slot parking lot and cut the engine.

Like the trees, the rancher-style log cabin gave the illusion of sprouting from the ground. Rustic yet simplistic, the simulated logs were the best she'd ever seen. Two doors faced the front. On the far left, the *Office* sign hung over one door. A big bay window with flower pots on the inside sill displayed a few posters taped to the glass detailing events at the school. On the far right, a small front porch surrounded the other door with a sign on the wall stating *Private Residence*. The cute cabin had a downright welcoming appeal that wiped the fatigue from her bones. Of course, arriving helped. She alighted from the car, sucked in a deep breath of the crisp mountain air, and entered the office.

As the door opened, a bell jangled overhead. The aromas of rich coffee and baked goods bombarded her senses, and she salivated. For the past year, she hadn't much of an appetite and dropped twenty pounds. Nibbling was the norm. Just before leaving Richmond, she purchased a milk shake at a gas station's convenience store. Worse strawberry shake ever—if she could call it strawberry. Maybe with all this fresh air, she'd revive her appetite before she passed out at a critical moment. She scanned the interior.

Pine-wood paneling covered three walls. A long, chest-high, oak counter looked skillfully constructed, and she'd bet money on someone local with great carpentry skills. Photographs of rhododendrons hung on the paneling. From her research, Billings Mountain grew well over a dozen varieties. Before coming, she purchased a good pair of trail boots to take advantage of a hike or two.

To the left of the bay window, travel brochures and places of interest filled a wooden stand, and alongside, a penny bubble gum machine enticed children with its colorful array of round balls. She hadn't seen a penny machine in years.

Behind the counter, a tall woman in her seventies walked through an open door. Her salt-and-pepper hair was cut short to the neck and styled with loose curls. A creamy chocolate complexion showed the scantest of makeup, and a smile brightened a pair of light-brown eyes. Carmen returned the smile and stepped toward the reception desk.

The woman tapped her computer to activate the screen. "Hi. Welcome to Billings Mountain. You must be Ms. Santiago. Sheriff Thomas called to say you were on your way."

Ordinarily, she'd be pleased with such efficiency but not this time. At the mention of the sheriff, she tensed.

The woman rummaged through a pile of papers and extracted one. "Here we go." She grabbed a pen. "Can I see some ID? Your cabin is prepaid, but if you eat at the cafe or make purchases at the general store and post office, we can tally the amounts and add the totals onto your credit card. Is that acceptable?"

"Very." Like a fancy resort. How nice. Since she anticipated the request, she extracted her license from her coat pocket and slid the document across the counter.

"I'm Henrietta, by the way." She nodded to the left of the desk where a coffee machine and a tray full of cookies waited. "You're welcome to help yourself any time of the day."

Carmen sniffed in the aroma of oatmeal. She was half-tempted to slip a few cookies into her jacket pocket. "Everything smells wonderful. Better than air freshener. Thank you, but you mentioned something about a general store?"

"That's right. You'll see the sign a little ways up the mountain. The Millers stock everything." Brows rising, Henrietta flashed a double-take at the license. "You're a doctor! James didn't mention that. What kind?" She returned the license.

"Pediatrician."

She gasped. "Oh, my word. For well over a year, Alexandra has been hoping to snag a pedie doctor, so fair warning when she approaches. We're getting so many kids here, and she's ready to pull out her hair. Should I keep the charges on the current card?"

"Yes, please." If her partners pushed her out the door, then yeah, they were paying for this trip in full. Served them right. She slipped her license into her pocket.

"Carmen is a beautiful name, you know."

"Thank you. I'm named after my great aunt."

A feeling of contentment swelled within Carmen. She wasn't sure why, but she took an instant liking to Henrietta. Her sultry voice and warm gaze reminded her of Margarita Santiago, her paternal grandmama, and the familiar memory warmed her more than a year of therapy. What she should have done was say to hell with this mountain retreat and hop on a plane to New Mexico, but she kept her troubles with Enrico from her family. Her parents knew of her divorce but nothing else. Sighing, she leaned on the counter and forced a smile. "Who's Alexandra? I saw her name on the auditorium wall."

"Ah, our beautiful surgeon from New York." She typed on the keyboard. "Alexandra visited our mountain five years ago, and lucky for us, she fell in love with our owner and stayed."

Carmen raised her brows. "Owner of what?"

"Billings Mountain, of course. She married Charles Billings, and they have two lovely children." Swinging an arm behind her, she retrieved a printout from the machine against the wall.

A person owned the mountain? Who the hell owned a mountain? Carmen shook herself. "But I passed houses and a school. Are they sitting on his property?"

With a deep, throaty sound, Henrietta chuckled. "Every acre belongs to the Billings family. The residents and business owners pay rent for the land, which is equivalent to paying real estate taxes." She slid the paper and a pen across the counter. "Sign here, please." She pointed to a blank line.

The door opened and jingled the overhead bell.

Carmen glanced over her shoulder. At the sight of James strolling in looking like a ray of sunshine, she tightened her grip on the pen, half expecting to snap it in two. The man followed her after all, and the urge to run nearly overwhelmed her. *I'm being ridiculous.* All her life, she stood her ground, and this past year proved her mettle. Why should a small-town sheriff rattle her? Until presented with sufficient evidence, she'd take his presence as the norm for such a resort community.

After giving James a curt nod, she returned her attention to Henrietta, all the while following him from the corner of her eye as he walked to the coffee maker. She *should* ignore him, but in passing, a good whiff of his earthy cologne hit her nose, and her knees wobbled. She silently cursed her body's response—to a lawman, of all people. Resting the pen on the counter, she slid the signed paper toward Henrietta.

The older woman knocked her knuckles on the desk. "Don't eat all the cookies, James." She grinned at Carmen. "He comes in here at least twice a day for a snack." Reaching under the desk, she lifted a key ring from a hook. "You're assigned the Mallotum cabin, which is a stone's throw from the sheriff's house." She set the key onto the counter. "Whatever you purchase on the mountain, simply show your cabin key. The amount will be sent via computer to this office."

Carmen inwardly groaned. Was this trip a bunch of coincidences, or was her close proximity to the mountain sheriff a planned happenstance? Could Sheriff Thomas already be under Enrico's thumb? That thought meant her ex had a mole in her office, but such a traitorous turn from anyone on her staff was incomprehensible. Everyone understood the hell she endured. She glanced at James who scrutinized her over his steaming cup. Dammit. Enrico's reach might be powerful in Richmond, but Billings Mountain was clear across the state.

Picking up the key, she stared at the leather strap with *Mallotum* burned into the hide. The attached metal latchkey was a surprise. With hotels around the world using plastic key cards, she truly had stepped into another era.

Stretching over the counter, Henrietta extracted a pamphlet from a cardboard holder. "You'll notice the Mallotum rhododendrons in full bloom. At this time of year, a glorious red surrounds your cabin." She slid the leaflet across the desk. "Here's a map of where things are, including hiking trails. We ask that you respect homeowners' privacy by staying on the foot path." She pointed a finger. "Head up the mountain another two miles. Our one road goes to the Billings Mansion and no farther, so you can't make any wrong turns. When you reach the Billings Mountain Cafe, look left, and you'll see the Mallotum sign. Keep in mind, housekeeping cleans on Saturday but is available for any emergencies. Otherwise, our guests are responsible for their own living environment. If you have any questions, I'm a phone call away."

Carmen had a half-dozen questions on the tip of her tongue—like who assigned the cabins? Did anyone contact the sheriff? But with James standing nearby, she asked nothing. Besides, when push came to shove, who on this mountain could she trust?

****

With mug in hand, James strolled to the bay window to watch Doctor Santiago's vehicle drive away. From the moment he entered the office, he swore she'd drop to the floor in a faint. Under the olive skin tone, her face drained of blood. What was it with this woman? What was she hiding? As a cop, he wanted answers. "Does she seem nervous?"

"Not until you wandered in." Henrietta typed on her keyboard. "I've never seen a woman pale so quickly, and you usually don't have that effect. What happened?"

Turning from the window, he approached the desk. "Damned if I know."

"I've heard of the white-lab-coat syndrome where a patient's blood pressure skyrockets. Maybe you're seeing a similar situation for law enforcement." Head cocked, she paused with a finger over the Enter key. "She's very beautiful, James, and has no wedding band on her finger." She tapped the key.

In this day and age, wedding rings meant nothing. People cheated on spouses left and right and switched partners with the frequency of changing underwear. He leaned on the counter. "She's hiding something. As soon as I return to the office, I'll do a criminal check."

Slipping the signed sheet into a folder, Henrietta

shot him a sideways glance. "Do you think a criminal check is necessary? Since you lived your entire life with women falling all over you, maybe you're uncomfortable with a woman shying away." Frowning, she stared at the monitor. "I must admit most of our guests aren't so tense. Tired perhaps after a long drive but, in most cases, they're glad to be here. Give her some time to relax." She typed.

He wasn't so sure relaxing was the answer. Since his job involved the protection of all residents and visitors on the mountain, he had an obligation to ease any gut suspicions. Besides, he'd thrown guests off the mountain before—never one so beautiful, though.

The red phone hanging on the wall behind Henrietta shrilled.

She shot him a raised brow. "Uh-oh." Cringing, she grabbed the receiver.

Without the constant need for a dispatch center, the mountain community developed their own 911 emergency system with full instructions posted on every refrigerator door. Besides being the office clerk, Henrietta worked as dispatcher who activated fire, Emergency Medical Services, or police. A red phone sat on her bedside table for night-time calls. Since true emergencies were few and far between, most residents called James on his cell. Placing his cup on the counter, he listened to Henrietta's professional voice.

"Yes, please calm yourself, Mrs. Harris. The sheriff is right here." Henrietta handed him the phone. "She's a guest."

Hopefully, Mrs. Harris wasn't calling about a cat in a tree. Taking the phone, he cleared his throat. "What can I do for you, ma'am?"

****

Carmen flitted her gaze from the road to the rearview mirror, half expecting to see the green-and-white cruiser creep around the curve. For once in her life, she'd like to meet a lawman with rock-solid integrity, the kind who defied a rich man's whim. Would James Thomas be such a man? She hoped so. But really, why would a small-town sheriff be any different from a big-city cop? In this day and age of stagnant salaries, the lure of easy money created a powerful incentive. Shaking her head, she loosened her grip on the steering wheel.

All right, enough. Sucking in a calming breath, she drove the many twists and turns in the mountain road, all the while climbing higher toward the sky. Of all the years spent in the wonderful state of Virginia, she never once drove along the Blue Ridge Mountains. According to the brochure, Billings Mountain was a separate entity of the famous Blue Ridge and nowhere near the Appalachia Trail but, if she had to guess, just as beautiful with its thick forest of trees and spectacular views. Since she lived at sea level for so many years, and the brochure listed the maximum mountain altitude of forty-one hundred feet, she shouldn't have too much trouble acclimating to the difference in atmospheric pressure. Maybe in a day or two, she'd hike some of the trails and take pictures to prove to her staff she spent two glorious weeks away from her condo.

Spotting Miller's General Store, she glided into the small parking lot and cut the engine. The single-story structure sat nestled among the trees with its weathered logs half-covered with moss. The cedar shingles on the roof looked new, but a worn, wooden screen door showed heavy use. More posters for school events hung on the windows along with specials for the week, and one sign announced art entries due no later than May Day, which—if memory served correctly—was May the first.

On entering, she stopped. The store screamed old-time country with wood everywhere—the floor, the walls, and even the shelving. Antique posters, boasting of products no longer available, hung between the windows, and, on the counter, an antique cash register stood like it hadn't moved in eons. Overhead, chandeliers, reminiscent of wild-west saloon days, lit the interior.

To the left, a woman worked behind an iron gate inside a small cubbyhole with an overhead sign *Billings Mountain Post Office.* Glancing up, she smiled and waved.

Carmen waved back, feeling a little stunned. *Wow.* The mountain residents had their own zip code. Imagine that. But if one man owned an entire mountain, he could buy whatever he wanted. *As I well know.*

Several people milled around. Some folks shopped. A few chatted with a man behind the cash register. Everyone smiled and said hello as if she'd lived on the mountain her whole life. She couldn't help but smile back. She grabbed a handbasket and perused the aisles.

Twenty minutes later, she exited the store with two bags, placed them in the trunk with the rest of her stuff, and continued her drive. Already her heart held a lightness from the few people she met—minus the cop, of course. With any luck, she'd have little contact with the man.

Along the way, various signs marked the cabin

driveways—Rosebay, Bergomot, and Arboreum, to name a few. Around the next bend, a large clearing revealed the Billings Mountain Clinic, an impressive, one-story structure built with red bricks. Five cars occupied the parking lot, and about a hundred yards to the left stood a fenced-in liquid oxygen tank. *Impressive indeed.* With strained budgets, most clinics relied on portable oxygen tanks. The facility couldn't be more than three years old, and, as with every structure on the mountain, its colors blended into the trees.

Two bends later, she passed another large clearing for The Billings Mountain Cafe, a rustic-looking building, half brick and half logs, with large windows across the front. Carmen glanced left and sighted the Mallotum sign. Turning, she bounced along a stone-covered drive until the cabin shone in the sunlight.

Her breath caught. The quiet getaway was the most adorable little cabin, its exterior constructed in gray stones with a gray-slate roof and wide, wooden porch. The open deck, with one step to the platform, contained a swinging hammock to the right and, to the left, a small, round table with two plastic chairs. Surrounding the cabin, the beauty of the red Mallotum flowers created an inviting welcome. She didn't think rhododendrons bloomed this early in the season, but here they were, displaying all their fine glory. For the first time since her arrival, every muscle in her body relaxed. To hell with the sheriff, Enrico, and his hired private eye. This mountain retreat was perfect. After coasting to the porch, she cut the engine and alighted.

The silence struck her first. Like suddenly losing all sense of hearing. Beyond the cabin clearing, thick woods created a perimeter of shadows, capable of hiding anyone or anything. If houses were nearby, the forest hid them, but several worn footpaths cut through the trees. A faint scent from the rhododendrons filled the air...no, the scent was sweet, like forsythia. Bending close to a rhododendron flower, she confirmed her suspicion. No scent. No forsythias around the cabin either, so they grew somewhere else.

She drifted her gaze toward the cliff where a vinyl bench soaked in the bright afternoon sun. Curious about the view, she meandered over. A metal rail prevented any closeness to the cliff edge. She gripped the cool metal to shake it for sturdiness. As expected, solid. Below, thick trees and bushes partially hid the main mountain road. A few rooftops peeked through but not much else.

A breathtaking view stretched forever, like a big blanket of green. A large city way off in the distance jutted from the treetops. Judging from the direction of the afternoon sun, she guessed north, possibly Lynchburg. She'd need a map to confirm. But not now. She retraced her steps to the cabin.

After grabbing her luggage from the car trunk, she approached the cabin, inserted the key into the door lock, entered, and stopped. *Oh, how lovely.* The exterior stones continued inside to give the entire space a rustic feel, and the atmosphere lifted her last remaining doubts about her trip. A small modern kitchen sat to the right with a two-seater table against the wall. A sofa and two cushy chairs faced a fireplace opposite the front door, and on the left, a king-size bed loaded with pillows enticed any weary traveler. To complete the picture, a beautiful walnut floor sparkled under her sneakers. She could spend a cool night on the sofa with a book and a burning fire in the hearth, or she could put herself in the center of that large bed and feel like a queen.

Tossing her suitcase onto a luggage rack, she inspected the bathroom off to the right side of the bed. A modern shower, sink, and toilet sparkled. *Nice.* Returning to the sofa area, she stared at the fireplace. The brochure boasted of gas hook-ups for every cabin, including the fireplace. A good thing, too. She hadn't built a fire since she was a little girl. On the mantel, instructions for fire safety stood propped against the stone backdrop with directions for switching the gas on and off.

She returned to her car to retrieve the supply of food. One item in particular was of vital importance. She never traveled anywhere without two bags of ground coffee—her saving grace throughout her torturous hospital residency. After plunking her armload onto the small table, she opened cabinets and found plates, cups, and glasses available for guest use. And a new coffee maker! *Perfect.* She brought her own—just in case.

Moving toward the refrigerator, she read the notice tacked with a magnet. So, Henrietta acted as dispatcher for any emergencies. Otherwise, the list contained the phone numbers for office, sheriff, and housekeeper. Hours of operation for the cafe, general store, clinic, and post office were typed at the bottom. If her bastard ex left her alone, she might enjoy this little mountain getaway. Somehow, deep in her heart, she doubted he'd allow her a day of rest.

Chapter Three

Her stomach growled. A quick glance at her wristwatch showed the time as four-thirty. She debated whether to make a tasty omelet with her supplies, but for the first time in weeks, she had an appetite for something good and fattening. To hell with calories. She'd lost enough weight over the past year and deserved to add a few pounds in celebration. An early dinner at the cafe might be the ticket to start her vacation with a much-needed bang.

After checking for secure window locks on the two front windows and the one in the bathroom—*thank you, Enrico, for my paranoia*—she slipped on her jacket and stepped outside, using the key to lock the door.

Even though the sun hadn't set, a noticeable chill hit her neck. The breeze flowed through the woods like a blast from an air conditioner and forced her to snap her collar closer to her neck. *Brr.* She hadn't packed a heavier coat should the temperatures plummet, but if necessary, she'd layer an assortment of casual clothing. After all, April in Virginia meant warm days and cool nights. Leaving the car parked and locked beside the cabin, Carmen strolled down the drive.

The walk to the main road took all of two minutes. Once reaching the edge of the drive, she slowed her pace and gaped at the number of cars in and around the cafe's parking lot. The vehicles weren't parked in any of the slots but more along the main road and some even between the trees. Occupying two of the slots, the sheriff's SUV had its hatchback open. A large crowd of men and women surrounded James who bent over something on the trunk floor. His deep authoritative voice spieled instructions to those around him with an occasional pause for a brief comment into his shoulder mike.

One by one, groups of three dispersed into the woods.

From the serious crease in his brow, this activity was not all fun and games. Carmen approached one of the women standing off to the side. "What's going on?"

The woman, wearing an orange fluorescent jacket, scanned Carmen from head to toe then nodded toward James. "We have a lost little boy. Three years old. Wandered off while his parents fussed with their hiking equipment, right here in the cafe parking lot. Are you a day-tripper or guest?"

Dear Lord, a three-year-old lost in a forest tied her gut into a knot. She shook herself. "Guest. Just arrived."

"Then, welcome to Billings Mountain."

"Peggy! We're here."

The woman craned her neck and waved. "My teammates are calling. Gotta go." She joined two others, and all three approached James.

After years of experience in pediatric wards in three states, Carmen understood the natural curiosity of young children. People were quick to blame parents, but children had a mind of their own, and they often disappeared while parents fussed with something else. Predators fed on their inquisitiveness, and the outcome was rarely favorable.

She drifted her gaze to James. He relayed instructions to one group after another like a man who organized a search a thousand times. Should she offer her assistance? If hurt, a three-year-old might need her expertise. Any other time, she wouldn't debate the issue and jump right in, but James was a cop. She endured an entire year of constant harassment by officers more interested in money than upholding the law.

Yet, the profession still had good lawmen, right? Somewhere in the universe, she'd meet one…someday. She waited until James relayed instructions to the last group and, swallowing a hard lump in her throat, she approached. "Can you use an extra hand?"

Turning from the hatchback, he shot his brows halfway into his forehead. "Hi." A voice spoke over his radio. He clicked his shoulder mike. "Roger that." With a felt pen, he marked off a section on a large map spread across his SUV rear floor. He faced her and smiled. "We don't ask our guests to help unless they know the woods. Thanks anyway. As you can see, we're organized."

His earthy cologne swirled around her, and she swooned. *Dios mio.* What in the world? Here he was being all polite and professional, and she suffered from weak knees and heart palpitations. Something about James pumped her heart like a piston on overdrive. How could a man wearing a badge affect her so quickly? She couldn't possibly be attracted, right? Okay, maybe. All right, more than maybe. But she couldn't trust him just because he was good-looking and sounded all upstanding and honorable.

Resisting the urge to check her pulse, she cleared

her throat. "Never hesitate to call me if you need a pediatrician, Sheriff. So you know, I don't have my cell phone with me, but I'll be here in the cafe for a while."

"That's mighty nice of you, ma'am." Meeting her gaze, he leaned forward. "By the way, my name is James. We aren't formal here."

Having him so close unnerved her in a strange sort of way. A different time and place and, of course, a different profession, maybe she'd pursue this…interest. Stepping back, she gave a curt nod and headed for the cafe entrance.

Whew. If their chance meetings continued, she might not stop herself from wrapping her arms around his neck and kissing him senseless. She entered the cafe.

Grateful for the reprieve, she stopped inside the door and sucked in the abundance of aromas. Holy moly, between the pot roast and fried chicken floated the rich aroma of fresh bread and coffee. She hadn't entered any ordinary cafe. This eatery conjured images of her childhood on the ranch with Mom standing by the stove and Grandmama at the table peeling potatoes. She missed those family meals something awful. If her career hadn't taken her clear across the country…

Her stomach reminded her to hurry. She glanced around to see if anyone heard the growl.

The large dining area with tables and booths in red, walls in white, and a floor of pale blue gave every impression of a cafe built in the 1960s. Yet, modern-day touches proved otherwise—such as the computerized cash register and the fancy espresso machine. Converted oil lamps provided overhead lighting, and double-hung windows, uncovered since trees created shade from the sun, faced the road.

On Carmen's right, a long, laminated counter with red-covered stools lined the wall, broken in the center to allow access to a swinging door where pots and pans clattered. At the end of the counter, closest to the entrance, a redhead with bright blue highlights worked the cash register. She had a hefty figure, as if she tasted one-too-many entrees.

The woman glanced from the register and smiled. "Have a seat anywhere. Menus are on the table."

Several patrons occupied some of the tables and booths. One old codger sat at the counter, eyeing her like mud covered her clothes. A local, no doubt. Hopefully, he wasn't the owner of the mountain. With a nod at the codger, Carmen chose one of the booths by the front windows and slid onto the bench seat. In the traditional signal for coffee, she turned over her mug.

In the past, she'd avoid sitting near a window, but after a year of being pursued by a madman, she vowed not to hide anymore. This trip to Billings Mountain was all about liberation—mind, body, and soul. She wanted her life back, and come hell or high water, she'd succeed...or die trying.

She lifted the two-sided plastic menu from its holder and read. As she perused the selections, she debated ordering one of everything, including desserts. Club sandwich? Turkey platter? Definitely not salad.

A minute later, the redhead glided to her table with a coffee carafe in each hand. "Regular or decaf?"

"Regular, please."

Brown gaze twinkling, she poured. "Freshly brewed not two minutes ago. Take your time. We won't get busy for another hour. New arrival?"

The coffee smelled heavenly, and she leaned forward for another sniff. "Yes. I'm told to present my key." Reaching into her jacket pocket, she placed the leather strap with key onto the table.

The woman nodded. "Mallotum. I like that one the best. The committee's design made it so pretty inside and out." She jerked her head at Carmen's menu. "Special tonight is beef stew."

"No wonder the place smells so good. I'll have the stew."

"You got it. Be right back."

Carmen replaced the menu to the holder.

Two search parties trudged across the parking lot to James's SUV. While pointing to the map, one man waved an arm in the direction of downhill. Everyone nodded in unison, and together, they crossed the road and disappeared into the woods.

Glancing skyward, Carmen caught a glimpse of the remaining daylight through the thick trees. With the amount of shadows accumulating, darkness wasn't far behind, possibly even before she returned to the cabin. With any luck, she'd have some remaining light to find her way.

Five minutes later, the redhead delivered a large bowl of stew and a basket of round rolls. "Here you go."

Leaning forward, Carmen sniffed. Beef, potatoes, and onions along with carrots and peas tantalized her salivary glands. A feast fit for a queen. "This stew smells great."

"It tastes even better." Face beaming, she adjusted her white apron. "You'll love our mountain. Best place to relax, and you, girl, look like you're way overdue."

Oh-kay. Nothing subtle about this woman. Carmen arched a brow. "Do I look that bad?"

"Tired, weary…" She shrugged. "Troubled."

The woman was psychic. Lately, Carmen felt the weight of the world on her shoulders. Between Enrico and work, she hardly set aside time for fun. She released a sick laugh. "All of the above." She sipped her coffee and let the heat seep into her bones. "Have you lived on the mountain long?"

"All my life." She extended a hand. "Marion Darnell, by the way. I own this cafe."

Carmen shook the offered hand. "Nice to meet you. Carmen Santiago." The woman had a strong grip to go with her hefty figure.

"You from Virginia?"

"Yep. Richmond." She dropped her hand. "I'm booked for two weeks." Movement outside the window caught her attention.

More searchers returned.

Marion cleared her throat. "I can see where your mind went."

Startled, Carmen whipped her gaze back to the woman. "What?"

With a smirk, she nodded toward the window. "He is one hunk of man."

"I wasn't looking at him." Dear Lord, she felt her cheeks flush at her outright lie. Was her nose growing, too? She coughed. "I was wondering if they found the child."

"Right." She curled one side of her mouth. "Do you have kids?"

Whenever someone asked the question, a familiar tightness gripped her heart—like a vise squeezing out every ounce of blood. How many times in life must she admit to being denied her dream of family, kids, and the white picket fence? She forced a smile. "No kids."

"Me neither. Since we don't have too many eligible bachelors around, doesn't look like I'll get any." She pointed toward the window. "He's one of our eligible men. Too bad he's not interested. Lord knows I've tried."

Meaning James. With his handsome features, women probably fell at his feet. Sighing, Carmen returned her gaze toward the window. "He is a nice-looking man."

"Nice? Honey, have you had your eyes checked? You won't meet a more upstanding guy. Lucky for us, he chose to stay, even though he'd earn big bucks in some city with his criminology degree." She clucked her tongue. "Ah, well, a woman can throw a fortune down a wishing well and hope for the best. Enjoy your meal."

Marion headed for the old man at the counter.

When her brain registered the size of the bowl before her, Carmen gasped. If she ate the entire contents, she could skip tomorrow's breakfast and possibly lunch. But one bite of the succulent beef hooked her. She ate with gusto. After sopping the last morsel of broth with a roll, she leaned back and placed a palm over her stomach. Yep, full and distended. She should have saved half the stew for later, but she hadn't tasted anything so good in years.

Placing her elbows on the table and with coffee mug close to her nose, she sipped while watching the activity in the parking lot.

Several more search parties returned, looking

defeated.

Once again, James hovered over the map with a finger pointing to various locations.

Nodding, the searchers jumped into vehicles and sped away, some ascending the road and others descending.

Carrying the regular coffee carafe, Marion flitted from table to table to refill cups before approaching Carmen. "You have a good appetite." She poured.

"The stew was delicious, but please, take away these rolls before I finish them." She pushed the breadbasket toward the edge of the table just as a car door slammed. Returning her gaze to the window, she sighed. "Doesn't look like they found the child yet."

Marion grunted. "No one will give up, especially the sheriff. The child's biggest threat—besides exposure—is a black bear. Those critters roam the mountain, and a small child is a tempting meal."

A child being mauled by a dog was one catastrophe, but a bear used longer claws and stronger jowls to inflict damage. A small body wouldn't stand a chance. Carmen shuddered. "I wish I could help."

"No need, honey. Our volunteers are experienced with search and rescue. They'll find him."

Let it go. She was a stranger and had no right to interfere. Straightening in her seat, she smiled at Marion. "So, how do we settle the bill?"

Resting the coffee pot on the table, Marion whipped out her order pad and pen. "I'm sure Henrietta explained how we tally the charges." Making a quick notation, she placed the slip on the table. "When you're ready, come to the register and sign the receipt. Then, I'll email a copy to Henrietta. Simple, right?"

"Very. Thank you."

Marion grabbed the bowl and coffee pot. "We made some great apple pie to go with the coffee."

Puffing her cheeks, Carmen held out a hand, palm outward. "Thanks, but I'm straining my jeans. Next time."

"Okay. I'll hold you to that promise." She headed toward the kitchen.

While sipping the best coffee she'd had in months, Carmen again shifted her gaze toward the handsome cop. Marion spoke highly of Sheriff Thomas, and a tinge of hope settled around her heart. Countless people had given high praise for many officers of the law only for her to discover a different side once the greenbacks waved in their faces. Honor and integrity—two meaningless words for some in law enforcement. Could James be the exception? Lord, how she prayed to meet such a man, but she mustn't be swayed because he was the most gorgeous male she'd seen in a long time.

Gulping the last of her coffee, she stood and fished through her pockets for change. Successful, she dropped several bills on the table and approached the cash register.

After fussing with a paper clip on a bunch of receipts, Marion smiled. "I'm all ready for you." She punched some numbers into the register and ripped off the spewed paper. "Here you go. Just sign on the line." She slid a pen across the counter. "I hope you enjoy your stay."

Carmen signed where indicated. "I'm sure I will. Thanks, Marion." She turned toward the door.

"Hold on a sec." Marion set a large, covered foam cup on the counter. "Can you take this to the sheriff?"

Oh, hell. She hoped to slip by the man. "Sure." What could she say? *No, I'd rather avoid the handsome cop?* Her comment would go over like a lead balloon. To keep the peace, she smiled and took the cup.

Once outside, the air changed from aromatic food to scented pine—the former, warm and cozy, and the latter, cool and fresh. With the sun well below the treetops, parts of the forest hid any trace of light, erasing shadows and turning everything an eerie black. Quite a transformation in the space of an hour.

James had thrown on a black jacket and clipped his mike to the outside shoulder. He also switched on his hatchback light to see the map. Since the police approached her and not the other way around, she could handle this simple errand and, squaring her shoulders, stepped toward the cruiser. "From Marion." She extended the cup.

Brows high, he turned. "Hey, thanks, just what I need." Taking the container, he removed the lid and ingested several quick sips.

Carmen studied the open map covered with black crosses. "You've expanded your search."

"Had to. As a rule, small children don't wander far. They stop because the thick woods scare them. I'm half afraid someone or something carried him away." Jaw tight, he sat on the edge of his trunk. "I have my deputy checking every car leaving the mountain."

She cringed. "Does child abduction happen often up here?"

Swallowing another mouthful, he shrugged. "Not too often, but we had one a couple months back. We caught the bastard."

She stuffed her hands into her jacket pockets. "So,

he's in jail?"

"Eventually."

Brow arched, she met his twinkling gaze. "What's that mean?"

"Oh, you know, he fell a few times and broke a few bones. Right now, he's in a special rehab center. As far as I'm concerned, child predators are the scum of the earth." He clicked his mike. "Roger that." Standing, he marked off another section of the map.

The man smelled damn good for being on duty all day. A pine scent mixed with his earthy musk. Intoxicating as hell, like he rolled in pine needles. Unfortunately, her body's response floored her. *Pullease.* As if she had the slightest interest in a new man when she couldn't rid herself of the old one. She forced a smile. "Good luck, Sheriff."

"James, ma'am, and let me give you a little mountain tip. If you're out at sunset, always carry a flashlight. The woods get dark, and you won't see the hand in front of your face. Your cabin kitchen has one available."

Yeah, dummy me. She'd lived so long in Richmond with streetlights every hundred yards, she never gave a flashlight a second thought. "Thank you, Sheriff. I'll remember."

"James."

At his smile, she sucked in a quick breath. His gaze sparkled, and, like magic, the fatigue disappeared from his face. Without question, she needed to stay clear of this enticing man.

Chapter Four

Looking both ways for traffic, Carmen hurried across the road and down her lane in a desperate attempt to escape the feelings James stirred. Why did she feel like a schoolgirl around the man? She wasn't some inexperienced teenager with a crush on the handsomest boy in class. For crying out loud, she was thirty-six years old, divorced, and well-established in her career. Was she so hard up that the man caused flip-flops in her belly?

When she was halfway to the cabin, she released a long breath and slowed her pace. Damn, her knees wobbled as if they just plopped from a jelly mold. *What is wrong with me*? She traveled to Billings Mountain to rest. Period. How could she be attracted to a lawman, the same profession that ignored her pleas? She should treat him with contempt, like snarl whenever he came close. He'd get the message and avoid her at all costs.

All right, relax.

Sucking in another calming breath, she released it and lifted her gaze skyward. The tall trees hid any sight of the setting sun, but orange rays colored the sky, giving her enough light to see. Awesome quiet surrounded her, except for her shoes crunching on the drive's stones. Thoughts of lazy days in the desert floated into her mind. So long ago. She missed her family and the support they offered. After her divorce, she should have listened to her inner voice and relocated to Albuquerque. She'd be a stone's throw closer to Mom, Dad, and Juan. With family nearby, she wouldn't have endured a year in hell.

As she neared the cabin, she slowed her steps as her gaze focused on the front porch. One of the plastic table chairs stood positioned alongside the hammock. Even more alarming, the center of the canvas bed sagged with a heavy weight. Warning bells clanged in her head, and a breath stuck in her throat. She scanned the dark forest for movement. *Dammit. Too friggin' soon.*

Closing her eyes for a second to control a powerful urge to run, she swallowed and stepped onto the porch. Whatever indented the hammock might not be pleasant, but this form of harassment would be new for Enrico— unless his hired help came up with the idea. Cringing, she leaned over to peek and then whooshed the contents of her lungs as she stared at a sleeping three-year-old boy.

Well, James was right. The child hadn't wandered far.

The poor little guy looked none the worse for wear. Dirt and pine needles covered him from head to toe. He wore a lightweight jacket and blue jeans with a cute pair of boots, so he was well-protected for a trek in the forest. His curly dark hair flew in every direction, and tear tracks smudged the dirt on his cheeks. Her heart ached to think how frightened he was. She checked for blood stains and then palpated his limbs for any injuries. The waning daylight didn't help matters. She glanced at the porch light. If she turned on the fixture, she'd only frighten him.

Rather than waste time by activating her phone and then punching in the sheriff's number, she lifted the boy into her arms.

He released a soft moan and nuzzled closer.

The odor of baby powder and—oops—urine hit her nose. Offering gentle words of comfort, she retraced her steps to the cafe. *Oh, for the love of...* If her brain was in gear, she should have run into the cabin for her phone *and* a flashlight. Twenty minutes from now, she wouldn't have any light to see. She quickened her pace and reached the road.

James was nowhere in sight. The majority of the cars parked along the road had also disappeared. In all probability, he moved his command post to another location. *Just my luck.* Shifting the boy's weight onto one arm, Carmen opened the cafe door and entered.

With a loud gasp, Marion flew around the cash register. "You found him!"

Not like Carmen felt like a hero, but a certain degree of satisfaction filled her chest. "Can you call James?"

"Oh—gosh, absolutely." She extracted her cell phone from her trouser pocket and punched in numbers. "Carmen found the boy! They're here at the cafe."

Within minutes, the cafe door slammed open as people scurried from the woods and crowded the cafe's dining room, all shouting joys of relief.

James arrived with a couple who rushed through the door and spotted the boy in Carmen's arms.

The woman with red, swollen eyes stretched her arms outward.

Feeling a strong sense of relief that she helped end the night on a happy note, Carmen handed over the boy who hadn't stirred despite the chaos. The father—a splitting image of the child—grasped Carmen's hand and shook until all feeling left her fingers. She received hugs and kisses from strangers, pats on the back, and offers for pie and coffee, but as soon as possible, she escaped. The atmosphere was a trifle too disconcerting for her liking, especially when a man in the crowd could be her ex's hired hand.

With just enough light to see, she returned to the cabin, but before stepping onto the porch, she glanced skyward. Stars twinkled overhead with faint wisps of clouds floating underneath. The night promised to be clear. Given another lifetime, she'd sit on the bench and pick out constellations, like she and her brother, Juan, did on hot, summer nights. But not tonight—or any night, for that matter. Shaking her head, she returned the plastic chair to the table and entered the cabin.

No sooner had she turned on the interior lamps when bright headlights lit the front windows. Quick as a flash, she tensed. Placing her back to the wall, she peeked through the floral curtains. The sheriff's SUV. Stretching her neck from side to side to ease the tension, she flipped on the porch light and ambled outside.

James cut his headlights and alighted with a wide smile stretching his lips. "You ran off too fast. Everyone's celebrating."

"Sorry. I've had a long day." Truer than she realized. Nerves forced her out of bed at dawn. Then, she talked herself into keeping her promise to her staff, packed, then hemmed and hawed until she had no choice but to get in the car and leave. Now, here she stood, in front of this handsome sheriff, and her body tingled for an entirely different reason.

James thumped one booted foot onto the porch platform. "The boy will be taken to the clinic for a thorough exam. I suspect you gave him a quick once-over?"

She shrugged. "Old habit."

Did his blue eyes twinkle at every woman, or was she the lucky one to receive his mind-blowing glow? Between the gleaming gaze and the sparkle in his smile, the man could light an entire landscape. He banished some of the darkness in her soul—not enough to trust him but adequate to relax some of her muscles. His tenor voice soothed the flutter in her gut, and broad shoulders enticed her fingers to touch—a man easy on the ears and eyes. For sure, something about this man...

Well, I'll be damned. She was sexually stimulated. No man had activated her libido in a very long time. *Who woulda thought.* Despite the constant wariness toward a lawman in close proximity, she smiled at James, probably her first genuine smile at a man since her divorce.

He lifted his brows. "You have a beautiful smile, Doctor. You don't show it often enough."

Her smile faded, and she snorted. "Not lately, but thank you." She stuffed her hands into her jacket pockets.

"Care to explain?"

Hell, no. How could she describe the man who made it his mission to wipe the smile off her face? She had a hard enough time convincing her staff. She leaned toward him. "I think Alexandra Colter Billings makes for a more interesting story. It sounds like a doozy."

Chuckling, he dropped his foot to the ground.

"Charles and Alex share a regular fairytale romance. I'll be glad to give you all the sordid details over breakfast in the morning—at the cafe."

He added the last part with a cough.

Whoa! The suddenness of his invitation took her aback. She learned early how Enrico's contacts operated. Because of her ex's legendary jealous streak, no one crossed the line by flirting. Inviting her for breakfast was akin to a death wish.

For the first time in months, hope seeped into her heart. From a cop even. Could he be one of the good guys? Lord knew, she needed such a man. What she didn't need was an awakening of a part of her that slipped into a black abyss so long ago—the age-old feelings of want and possibilities. When push came to shove, she couldn't go around forever distrusting men. Her Spanish blood thrived on love, and right now, her hormones screamed for some action.

Gathering her courage and flashing him another smile, she met his gaze. "All right, Sheriff Thomas. You're on for breakfast."

****

Carmen slept like a rock without once waking to check her surroundings. A first. She hadn't expected to hit the pillow and zonk into la-la land, but Lord Almighty, the uninterrupted sleep felt wonderful. The silence in and around the cabin helped…except for the hoot of an owl. Even the creature's raucous cry brought a smile to her lips before she drifted off.

By morning, she stretched in the center of her king-sized bed and, after much effort, forced her legs over the side. Without the slightest nudge, she could get used to the mountain's serenity, but the thought caused a heavy sigh to escape. The area was way too isolated for her liking—especially with her crazy ex still in the picture. Since Billings Mountain didn't have a gate to stop intruders, Enrico could drive in. Then, what would she do? Would anyone hear her calls for help? The idea of Enrico catching her alone sent a chill straight down her spine. *Yeah, this vacation is a big mistake.* She should never have agreed to come to such a beautiful place.

With all these thoughts swirling through her head, why, of all people, had she accepted a breakfast invitation from a cop? Even if James wasn't under Enrico's thumb—now—didn't mean he wouldn't be later. For the time being, she'd keep her hormones in check.

While a pot of coffee brewed, she dressed in blue jeans and sweatshirt and marveled at the indescribable freedom of such comfortable clothing. Her ex called them lowlife clothes and refused to allow his wife to wear such rags in public. For three years, she tolerated his shit. Throwing on her jacket, she checked her cell phone for messages. Grateful to find none, she slid the device into the jacket pocket.

Holding a hot mug of coffee and barefoot, Carmen moseyed outside into the cool April morning. She hadn't gone barefoot since med school, and as soon as her feet hit the dirt, she wiggled her toes in the cold, sandy soil. Why had she allowed Enrico to stifle so much of her life? He denied her the simple pleasures of her youth—like walking outside in bare feet. *Well, no more, pendejo.* Even though the soles of her feet were as tender as a baby's bottom, she headed for the cliffside bench while feeling every stone and pine needle along the way. The sensation felt absolutely wonderful. Coffee cup poised near her mouth, she paused to look out over the valley.

An early fog covered the world below. The sight of so much white gave her the sensation of floating on a cloud. Normally, by sunrise, she'd be at her desk, attending to the pile of patient test results. So, watching a fog dissipate became a new experience. For the first time in years, her heart unloaded the persistent heaviness. The day was beautiful with the air crisp and the morning dew intensifying the scent of the forest.

Maybe her partners had the right idea after all. Doctor Andrea McFadden to be precise. She recommended this hideaway and talked the other partners into pushing Carmen out the door. *Here's to you, Andrea.* Carmen raised her mug and sipped. Turning toward the bench, she slid sideways onto the slats, stretched her legs in front of her, and used both hands to hold her mug. She sucked in another large breath and closed her eyes.

"Hello."

Santa Maria! With her heart jumping straight into her throat, Carmen whirled on the bench seat, nearly spilling her coffee all over her jeans.

From behind, a child approached. Judging by her size, she couldn't be more than eleven with extraordinary beauty for such an early age. She wore blue jeans and spring jacket with hiking boots and backpack. Her long blonde hair and blue eyes were so distinctive, the little girl might as well wear a sign reading *Sheriff's Daughter*. Carmen smiled. "Hi. Where'd you come from?"

She threw a thumb over her shoulder. "Through the

woods. Me and my dad live in the next house up the mountain. He's the sheriff." She gripped the straps of her pack. "I'm sorry I scared you."

Yeah, well, what's a heart attack or two? Carmen patted the center of her chest, willing her organ into a calmer rhythm. "That's okay. What's your name?"

"Lucy."

"Well, hi, Lucy." Marion mentioned James's availability but never said anything about children. Where was the mother, and how about siblings? Was James widowed or divorced? Either way, the news wouldn't be devastating, but Carmen had a certain degree of curiosity about the man. All right, a lot of curiosity. "Are you off to school?"

"Yeah. I like to walk this time of year." She shifted on her feet. "My dad drives me when the weather's bad."

Carmen scanned the thick woods. "Aren't you afraid of getting lost?"

The girl walked around to the front of the bench. "I can't get lost. I grew up here, and the woods are my favorite place. I know all the shortcuts."

Wow. Back in Richmond, mothers panicked if their child wandered outside the front yard, but woods were a different story. *Lions, tigers, and bears, oh, my*. Controlling a shudder, Carmen forced a smile. "The school is—what—two or three miles away? Isn't that a bit far to walk?"

"Nah. I'll meet with Angie and Michael, and we cut through the forest to the school." She propped a hip against the bench seat. "What's your name?"

"Carmen."

"I like that name." She pointed to Carmen's feet.

"You always walk barefoot?"

Carmen wiggled her toes. "When I can. I was raised on a ranch in New Mexico. Have a seat." She bent her legs to give Lucy room.

Eyes wide, Lucy slipped her butt onto the bench. "With real horses and stuff?"

"Yep. Horses and cattle. My mom and dad worked for the ranch owner."

The little girl pouted. "We don't have horses or cattle here. Mr. Watson has chickens. They lay brown eggs. Are you married?"

Carmen almost spewed her sip of coffee. With her thumb, she wiped the dribble off her chin. "No. How about you?"

Lucy jammed a fist onto her hip. "I'm eleven, silly. Besides, I can't marry until I become a doctor, like Alex, my bestest friend in the whole world." She clamped both hands onto her backpack straps. "She's Mrs. Billings now. She married Charles."

And the romance story waiting to be told. Lucky woman. Although Carmen had her chance with a man and his money. Look how *that* turned out.

The familiar wop-wop-wop of a helicopter echoed through the woods. Carmen glanced skyward, half expecting to see the machine fly overhead. Like any city-slicker, copters didn't faze her anymore. Between Richmond International Airport and fighter jets from the naval base along the coast, she tuned out all sounds of aircraft. The loud vibrations never failed to excite a child, though.

Lucy jumped to her feet. "Something happened. The copter is heading for the landing pad at the school. See ya later, Carmen." She ran into the woods.

Before the dust settled, the girl disappeared. Five minutes later, Carmen's cell phone vibrated in her pocket—a text message from James. *Need to cancel breakfast. How about lunch, say one o'clock?*
Fingers hovering over the keypad, she stared at her phone. All she had to do was say some other time. Should she? But really, if she wanted to break away from her boring routine, she wouldn't do it by sitting around feeling sorry for herself. James offered a simple lunch date, and she fully intended to enjoy his company. What could possibly go wrong?

Chapter Five

Help me, Lord, I'm starving over here.

James placed a palm over his belly to quiet the roar. If this morning's pace kept going, he'd run out of steam before checking into his office. Hissing through his teeth, he waved the car through the roadblock.

Days like this one belonged in a training manual, the how-not-to-pull-out-your-hair chapter. Lucy started his morning off with a bang. She hadn't a thing to wear to school...so she said. She always wore jeans and T-shirt, so what the hell changed? After he convinced her to wear her newest pair, he received a call from Mrs. Vandermeyer who locked herself out of the house— again.

Hurrying Lucy to finish her breakfast, he packed her lunch and tossed everything into her backpack before pushing her off to school. Damn, he hated to rush the kid. Not as if every day began with chaos, but he liked taking care of his daughter, and she was fast approaching independence. Two more years, she'd be a teenager. *Heaven help me.*

Since today began as a test-his-patience day, he prepared himself to take each call in stride. As happened in the past, the world fell apart at the seams. His next emergency came from Alex with a warning about an incoming copter. Helicopters required the presence of police because gawkers stood too close to the helipad. His job was to prevent injuries from flying debris. Even more important, the pilot needed colorful smoke flares to judge wind direction. Otherwise, the copter could crash into the trees.

While waiting by the helipad, he received his next call which canceled any hope for breakfast. He made a quick call to Carmen, and she agreed to reschedule for lunch, but by then, he might turn into skin and bones, a mere whisper of a man. As soon as the copter cleared the pad and the gawkers dispersed, he headed for the inevitable traffic jam by the gas station. Finished, he debated between his office, waiting at the cafe, or a quick trip to Henrietta's.

His stomach growled in answer. What better place than the check-in office? Henrietta always brewed a fresh pot of coffee and kept a plate full of cookies. A quick check at his watch told him he had one hour before meeting Carmen. *A snack will hit the spot.* Saying a silent prayer for a reprieve, he arrived at the office, hurried through the door, and aimed straight for the refreshment center at the end of the counter. As always, the place smelled like a bakery.

Seconds after the jingle of the overhead bell, Henrietta strolled through the doorway connecting her living quarters to the office. She carried an open cardboard box, which she clunked onto the desk portion of the counter. "What was the copter about?"

He swallowed a mouthful of cookie with a sip of coffee. "Fergie had a heart attack. Alex told him his high-fat diet finally plugged his arteries." He shoved in another cookie. The flavors of oatmeal and brown sugar burst on his tongue.

Henrietta shook her head. "His wife eats the same

diet." She nudged the box flaps out of her way. "How's she getting to the hospital? I know Betsy won't fly in the whirlybird."

"Lou Plotts is driving her into the valley to meet with her son." He checked his wristwatch. Barring any more interruptions, he should meet Carmen on time.

"Lou's a good neighbor." Pausing with her elbows resting on the box, she frowned while narrowing her gaze. "Don't talk with your mouth full. My Heimlich maneuver is a bit rusty, and I don't want you to choke to death on my clean floor."

"Yes, ma'am."

He was so glad Henrietta changed her plans to leave the mountain. When she sold the general store to the Millers, she intended to live in a senior housing complex near her daughter in Roanoke.

The cabin rental committee had a better idea. With the help of Charles Billings, they built her a beautiful rancher with the office attached—handicap-friendly, even though Henrietta still kicked up her heels. The fifteen rental cabins kept her busy, along with day-trippers who stopped by for brochures or directions to the trails. The pace of the office was a heck of a lot slower than running a general store.

She shifted her gaze to the cookie tray and pursed her lips. "You're gobbling like a starving Neanderthal. Didn't you eat this morning?"

"Missed breakfast." He swallowed a gulp of coffee. *Best damn brew on the mountain.* "While I waited for the copter, Jenkins called. His gasoline delivery arrived early. You know what a traffic hazard that big tanker causes."

"Then, go to the cafe and eat something."

"I will. Got a lunch date with Carmen." He shoved in the rest of his cookie.

She raised her brows. "Well, about time. You've been without a woman for too long."

As if a man couldn't be complete without a woman by his side. Feeling itchy, he shifted on his feet. "Yeah, well, don't get any ideas. She's a guest. I'm giving a sort of thank you for finding the boy."

"Right." With a smile curling one side of her mouth, she fussed with the contents in the box.

Yeah, he didn't believe himself either. All night, Carmen flashed in and out of his mind, and he caught zero sleep. He spent hours staring at the cracks in his bedroom ceiling. Why was this dark-haired beauty jump-starting his sorry heart? Was it her plump, kissable lips? How about the body curves perfect for a man's hands? Her eyes certainly captivated him—dark and mysterious. Yet, twice, her gaze held a look as if something—or someone—ripped out her soul.

Resisting the urge to pick at the cookie crumbs, he refilled his cup and strolled over to Henrietta.

The older woman glanced at the cookie tray. "You left one."

Glancing over his shoulder, he shrugged. "That was in case you didn't bake anymore."

"Uh-huh."

She chuckled in her low, sultry tone.

The door flew open. A Hispanic man entered and stood in the doorway, as if he was an actor pausing for effect. He wore black wool trousers and a white silk shirt, unbuttoned at the collar to reveal several gold necklaces. From the sleeves of a black, leather jacket, a gold watch peeked out on his left wrist, along with a pair of diamond-studded cuff links. A similar diamond-studded wedding band circled his left ring finger. He wasn't tall, at a guess, five-foot-ten, but he had weight with a chest like a barrel.

Shutting the door, the man scanned the interior, then James, before smiling at Henrietta with a mouthful of white teeth. "I'm Enrico Cruz. I understand my wife, Carmen, is here."

His heart thudded. Emotions swirled within his chest, and the cookies turned into a hard lump inside his stomach. Carmen mentioned nothing about being married. Thinking back, when he asked her to breakfast, he assumed her newness on the mountain caused her hesitation. If she was married, she had the perfect opportunity to tell him to go take a hike. But dammit, she said nothing.

Fighting the urge to storm from the office to give Carmen a piece of his mind, he loosened his grip on his coffee cup before he crushed the foam into pieces. Despite the discreet glimpse from Henrietta, he'd be damned to let his anger show. Instead, he sipped his coffee. *Blah.* The brew now tasted like mud.

Clearing her throat, Henrietta gave Enrico Cruz a strained smile. "We don't have a Mrs. Cruz registered, sir."

One brow twitched while he twisted his lips to the side. "Then she's using her maiden name of Santiago. She does that a lot when she travels."

James inwardly groaned. Whatever happened to the good old days when a woman took her husband's name? Even Alex hyphenated her name once she married Charles. He understood the hassle of updating paperwork, including medical degrees, but wasn't a man worth the effort? Then again, marriage failure rates should be considered. Hyphenated names were far easier to correct.

Henrietta shuffled some papers on the counter. "I'm sorry, sir. Billings Mountain policy is to maintain guest privacy. I'm sure she has a cell phone you can call."

He waved aside the comment. "I tried already, but she won't answer." He leaned on the counter. "The other day, we had a little spat. She took off in a huff and...well—we were supposed to come together." He reached into his rear pocket and extracted his wallet. Pulling out a hundred dollar bill, he snapped it taut and slid it across the counter. "We need to kiss and makeup. I can't apologize if she won't answer my calls. You understand, right?" He winked. "Tell me where she is."

With a cocked brow, Henrietta glanced at James.

Enrico Cruz had the brass balls to bribe Henrietta in front of an officer of the law. The man was either a total moron or bribed out of habit. *Interesting.* Stepping closer, James stretched to his full six-foot-two height and, with one finger on the bill, slid it toward Cruz. "We don't break the rules for anyone, sir. I suggest you try your wife again and receive permission to visit."

Pursing his lips, Cruz retrieved the bill and folded it into his breast pocket. A smirk lifted one lip as he scanned James from head to toe.

James returned the perusal but without any expression.

Cruz tugged on one of his cuff links. "I'm surprised such a small community has its own law enforcement. I can't imagine you have much to do."

With a half-smile, James leaned against the

counter. "Just the way I like it."

"You fall under the jurisdiction of the county or state police?"

"Neither. I'm paid by the community."

The smirk lifted higher, and he pointed to James's chest. "From your sheriff's badge, you're the man in charge." He coughed. "I'd like to talk to you privately. How about in your office?" He cocked a dark brow.

The hairs on the back of James's neck stood on end. Something about the guy bothered him. He was way too smooth and a tad too cocky. Could Cruz be the reason why Carmen had no light in her eyes? Even more important, had she come to the mountain, knowing Cruz would follow, and made a date with James anyway? *I need answers.* James glanced at his watch. "I have a few things to do. We can meet at my office at two o'clock."

Cruz shook his head. "Now is a better time, Sheriff. I'm a busy man."

James didn't give a damn if he was President of the United States. Something wasn't right, and a discussion with Carmen rose to the top of his list. "Sorry, sir. Two is the best I can do."

Gaze narrowed, Cruz pressed his lips into a thin line. "All right. Where can I hang out in the meantime? I'm pretty much in the boonies here."

Brows high, Henrietta leaned onto the counter. "The *boonies* is our home, Mr. Cruz."

Well said, Henrietta. James forced a smile. "I suggest you go into the valley and buy yourself something to eat. Frankie's Place serves decent sandwiches."

"Sandwiches aren't quite my taste."

Yeah, Cruz looked like an escargot man with a side order of caviar. Hell, as rich as Charles was, he still enjoyed burger night at the cafe, not to mention blue jeans and flannel shirts. He shrugged. "Suit yourself."

"Come on, Sheriff. Surely, this town has something close by."

"Nope." Not technically anyway. The cafe was at least two miles up the road.

A flush colored Cruz's fat cheeks while a pair of dark eyes blazed.

Well, well, the man had anger issues. What did he expect, the residents of Billing Mountain to bow at his feet?

Cruz huffed out a breath. "We'll talk later." With a brief nod at Henrietta, he left.

Good riddance. Pompous ass. James stared at the door.

Leaning back, Henrietta snorted. "That was interesting. I gather he likes to bribe people to achieve his goals."

"Seems so." He shifted his gaze to his near-empty cup then again to Henrietta. "Did Carmen book a reservation for two?"

"Nope, and she didn't make the reservation. Her office made it for her as a party of one. I can't believe they'd exclude the husband unless Carmen made a special request." She paused to stare into the box. "She doesn't wear a ring."

James twisted his mouth to the side. "According to Alex, a lot of medical professionals don't wear jewelry when they work. Some even wear a watch on a chain around their neck."

"I don't know, James. She isn't working now."

He swirled the contents in his cup. "Regardless, I'm not a marriage counselor. I don't intend to place myself in the middle."

"Are you canceling lunch?"

For his own sanity, he should. Whatever happened between Carmen and her husband was none of his business. But he took an immediate dislike to Cruz, and as sheriff, a certain curiosity surfaced. "I'm not canceling lunch."

"Good." She dug into the box and extracted a handful of pens with the Billings Mountain logo then dropped them into a Billings Mountain pencil holder on the counter. "I noticed you failed to mention our lovely cafe."

James gulped the last of his cold coffee. "Carmen's due to meet me in—" He glanced at the wall clock behind the desk. "Twenty minutes. I'll tell her he paid us a visit and let her decide what she wants to do. Either way, those two better not cause any trouble on this mountain."

****

Well, no cancellation for lunch.

After spending another hour on the bench, Carmen rose and stretched. She just wasted a fabulous amount of time and felt not an iota of guilt. She'd do the same tomorrow and every day for the remainder of her stay. Too bad nighttime was out of the picture. She'd love to sit and watch the stars twinkle overhead. But with Enrico and his cronies in the picture...

The story of my life. She returned to the cabin to prepare for her 'date' with James. Feeling a crunch between her toes, she glanced at her feet and chuckled at the dirt covering her skin. If she strolled into the cafe without shoes, she might be banned from ever stepping through the doors again. A quick wash and dry in the bathroom solved the dirty feet problem.

Then, while slipping on a pair of socks and sneakers, she allowed her thoughts to drift to her most asinine decision—her lunch date with a cop. A damn cop! Yes, all right, a good-looking one, but he still represented the professionals who ignored her when she needed them most. *I should have my head examined.* Shaking off her lack of better judgment, she locked the door, jammed the key into her jacket pocket, and headed for the cafe.

Six cars filled the parking lot. The police cruiser wasn't one of them. She entered the cafe.

Marion waved from behind the long counter. "Sit anywhere, Carmen."

More people sat in the restaurant than the number of cars in the lot. Several tables in the center remained empty, but she'd rather pick a less conspicuous spot. Once James joined her, gossip wouldn't be far behind. So, no center table. She chose an empty booth against the far wall with a good view of the entrance.

In between working the cash register and refilling the coffee machines, Marion attended to the patrons seated at the counter. Another food server flitted from table to table, balancing a tray on one arm and delivering plates or drinks as she passed. The girl was surprisingly efficient. If she rolled on skates, she'd zip by the tables without stopping. Judging from her size and bone structure, she could be no more than twenty with jet black hair cut short, black fingernails, and black clothing except for the white apron. The Goth phase, no doubt, but not true Goth with her lips sporting hot-pink lipstick.

The girl glided toward Carmen's booth. "Can I get you anything to drink while you look at the menu?"

Donna was on her name tag. Carmen smiled. "I'm waiting for someone. How about unsweetened iced tea?"

"Sure thing. Be back in a sec."

Quite a few of the patrons had backpacks tucked under their seats. Several small children sat with their parents, squirming to escape. Booths were ideal for trapping a child against the wall, but children, being curious, always managed to bother the patron in the booth behind them.

Like now. A little girl with two ponytails on top of her head peeked over her seat at an old guy who struggled to contain his smile.

While she waited, Carmen inhaled the aroma of fresh apple pie. Maybe this time, she'd get a slice to go and enjoy it by the fireplace. Although, something else smelled pretty good. Bacon?

James entered, looking as handsome as ever in his starched uniform. She'd bet any amount of money he had laddered abs underneath his shirt. After spotting her, he weaved through the tables, but something in his expression took her aback. With jaw muscles twitching and gaze cutting her in two, he wasn't what she'd call a guy meeting a woman for a date. Her gut twisted.

Fists tight, he towered over her. "You're married."

Santa Maria. Her mouth fell open, her stomach fluttered, but she played the cool card and rolled her eyes. "Hello to you, too. Can't you sit first?" She glanced at all the heads turned toward them.

Then, just as quickly, they turned away.

"Answer the question."

"For the record, that wasn't a question. You stated. But no, I am not married, and thank you for your wonderful discretion." Nothing like telling everyone her business. "Please, sit."

Nostrils flaring, he slid onto the opposite seat. "I don't like being fooled."

"We haven't discussed our marital status, Sheriff." She leaned on the table. "I'm divorced. What about you?"

"Single."

"Uh-huh." Sitting back, she crossed her arms over her chest. "I met your daughter."

He cocked a brow. "I'm still single." With one finger tapping on the table, he glared. "I just met your husband."

Aw, hell. Enrico was on the mountain. Carmen dropped her arms and shifted her gaze in every direction, half-expecting her ex to waltz through the door. And why not? Did she really believe he'd leave her alone for two weeks?

Donna returned with the tea and placed the glass on the table. "You coming or going, Sheriff?"

"Get me a sweet tea, Donna."

"Gotcha." She left.

James straightened in the seat and drummed his fingers on the table. "Someone isn't telling the truth. Did he contact you?"

She huffed. "Not since my last phone number change." She sipped her tea. A tad on the bitter side. She met James's hard-as-nails gaze. "Enrico and I have been divorced for a year. He refuses to accept what he calls a dangerous precedent—as in a wife divorcing her husband despite his strenuous objections."

"All right." Lips pursed, he nodded. "I'm aware of our state law regarding a one-sided divorce. His non-acceptance explains why he wears a wedding ring, and you do not. I imagine the situation created a legal quagmire."

"Not really. I walked away with my personal belongings. I wanted nothing else from him. We never consolidated our bank accounts, primarily because he refused to allow me access to his money." Breaking eye contact, she stared into her tea. "Enrico was never one to share, James, but money wasn't the reason for the divorce." She glanced his way. "He refused to share *me,* even with a colleague." Toying with her tea glass, she cringed. "So, when did he arrive?"

He rubbed the back of his neck. "I stopped at the check-in office for some coffee when he strolled through the door. He told me some cockamamie story about a spat, and he was here to apologize." He dropped his hand. "Did you tell him where you were?"

She snorted. "He has a PI tracking me. I've changed my phone twice and use my car's GPS only when necessary, but he still finds me."

Pursing his lips, he leaned back. "Some vehicle navigation systems stay active despite being turned off. If that's the case, the PI can pinpoint your exact location. Why would your ex stop at the office?"

Because he has something up his sleeve. Like bribery. Did he try already? God help her if he succeeded. How would she know one way or the other? If James played good-cop-bad-cop, he could fool her. *And here I am having lunch with the guy.* Since she had no idea what Enrico said to James or even if Enrico's PI

61

was within earshot, she wouldn't volunteer any information just yet. Trust was earned, not given, and so far, cops remained at the top of her do-not-trust list. *So much for an enjoyable lunch.* She tapped her nails against her glass. "Where is he?"

"Mountain policy is to protect guest privacy. I sent him to the valley to eat, but he wants a private meeting. I told him I'd be in my office at two o'clock."

Yep. Private meeting. Once Enrico cornered James, he could be very persuasive. Why had she assumed everything would be okay if she traveled clear across the state? Sighing, she leaned on the table. "*Cuidado,* James. The translation means be careful. He is a man who gets what he wants."

Donna returned with his tea. "Ready to order? Lunch special is BLT."

She lost her appetite, but maybe for supper... "Sounds good."

"Sounds good."

For some reason, ordering in unison broke the tension, and he smiled.

The sparkle returned to his eyes, and a devastating glow perused her face. Could James be different? Somewhere along the way, she'd meet a man with impeccable integrity. She'd like it to be James. If not...ah, well, she'd been dealt bad hands in the past and learned to cope.

He plucked a few napkins from the table dispenser and placed two by her glass. "How long were you married?"

"Three years. They were the most horrible years of my life." She rubbed a finger around the rim of her glass. "After we married, Enrico changed. He became more possessive and controlled every minute of my day." She shrugged. "Because of him, I wasn't doing my share of the pediatric partnership." After a furtive glance toward the door, she returned her gaze to James. "I probably should have my lunch to go, in case he walks in. I doubt he left for the valley."

His shoulder mike crackled.

"Sheriff."

James clicked the call button. "What's up, Harry?"

"Got a gentleman here who wants to see you. Name's Enrico Cruz. Says it's urgent."

James cocked a brow at Carmen but tilted the mike closer to his mouth. "I told him two o'clock."

"He said he won't leave until he talks to you."

Carmen grinned and mouthed the words, I warned you.

James hung his head.

"You still there, Sheriff?"

Rolling his eyes at Carmen, he keyed the mike. "Yeah, I'm still here. I'll see what I can do." Releasing the mike, he gulped a large mouthful of his iced tea. "I'm leaving only because I have sympathy for my deputy who is back from a court appearance and needs a break. So, I'll meet your ex and hear what's so important."

She'd like to be a fly on the wall to see how much money Enrico slapped on the table and whether James resisted temptation. The prospect of easy cash motivated an awful lot of people, and a man with a child to support could fall prey to Enrico's devious manipulations. Gut twisting, she tapped a finger on the table. "Enrico flaunts his wealth, James. He also dictates, so your suggestion to go to the valley fell on

63

deaf ears." She locked onto his gaze. "As I said before, be careful. Enrico is a persuasive man."

Releasing a long breath, he slapped his palms flat on the table. "Then, we'll both have our lunch to go. Let's catch Donna at the counter." He stood and tugged on his duty belt. "Be honest, Carmen. Are children involved?"

"Luckily, no." She stood. "He was all for a big family prior to the wedding. Several months into our marriage, he reneged with the excuse of spending more time together. I should have listened to my heart and divorced him then, but stupid me, I felt flattered with his selfishness." Carrying her iced tea, she led the way to the counter.

After relaying their order change, Carmen and James waited by two empty counter stools. Her mind raced with all the possibilities about to surface. Would Enrico add another cop to his roster, or would James be the exception? Throat tight, she turned toward James. "Do you know how hard it is to be a pediatrician and not have kids? By denying me children, Enrico broke my heart." Leaning close to James's ear, she kept her voice low. "He stopped sex to be sure."

Chapter Six

Stopped sex? What the hell kind of moron refused to bed a beauty like Carmen Santiago? He—whoa! Swerving, James hit the brake to avoid a woodchuck crossing the road. The fat marmot shot him a look that showed more annoyance than fear. "Yeah, go ahead. Meander like you own the damn road." If he hit the critter, he'd be cleaning up roadkill, and scraping squished viscera from the asphalt would just about top his day.

Cursing at the two people who brought a domestic dispute into his territory, James pulled into the small police station parking lot. Yanking the take-out box from the passenger seat, he stepped out and then slammed the cruiser door. A silver luxury vehicle occupied the slot next to Harry's cruiser. James noted the Virginia license plate and current inspection sticker before stomping into the office without so much as a hello to Enrico Cruz.

Deputy Harry Cartwright stood near the coffee maker with a cup in hand, staring wide-eyed through wire-rimmed glasses.

Yeah, surprise, surprise. James rarely lost his composure, but men—and some women—like Cruz thought the world owed them favors. As sheriff, he'd dealt with their tantrums and their unreasonable demands but always kept a cool head. Carmen and her ex brought a different problem to his peaceful mountain. He wasn't some damn divorce counselor. For Pete's sake, Billings Mountain was a small, private community whose owner *allowed* visitors onto his property. For the most part, guests respected the rules and regulations, but one of these days, the shenanigans of some guests would force Charles Billings to erect a locked gate.

Oh, hell, calm down. James wasn't sure what bothered him more—Enrico interrupting his date or the fat guy's unresolved issues with his wife. Getting stuck smack dab in the middle of their squabble didn't help either. "Go get some lunch, Harry."

The deputy glanced from Cruz to his boss, slipped his mug onto his desk pad, and left.

James threw his container onto his desk. No separate office, of course. The station was one big room with a desk for Harry and one for himself with a door behind them leading to a holding cell, bathroom, and storage closet. After taking a moment to control his temper, he turned to the visitor and glared. "What do you want, Mr. Cruz?"

Grinning, Enrico wagged a finger. "Very wise to send away your deputy. What we discuss should remain private." Stuffing his hands into his trouser pockets, he strolled around the small office. "My wife and I have a history and not a pleasant one."

This oughta be good. "Go on." James slipped his butt onto the corner of his desk.

Turning, Cruz wiped the grin from his face. "I have every suspicion Carmen plans to kill me for insurance money."

Aw, damn, his day shot straight to hell. After

pinching the bridge of his nose, he folded his arms over his chest and released a breath through tight teeth. "You've made quite an accusation. Do you have proof?"

"Positive proof, Sheriff. She took out a life insurance policy on me for two million dollars, naming herself as sole beneficiary."

His heart sank into his gut. Murder for money was the most predominant motive in history, and two million was a significant chunk of change. People killed for a lot less. Lips pursed, James studied the man. "Has she harmed you in some way or made any threats?"

He lowered his chin to his chest. "Not yet, but I know she's planning something."

This sort of shit happened in the city, not here on Billings Mountain. James possessed neither the will nor the power to arrest someone because he or she *might* do something. He scanned Cruz from his patent leather shoes up to the black curl of hair falling onto his forehead. "If you knew your life was in danger, why follow her to the mountain?"

Cruz stopped by the front window and shot James a sideways glance. "You're a smart man, Sheriff. You know why."

What were they playing, Truth or Dare? James hated games, but if what Cruz said was true and Carmen planned to kill him, then Cruz followed her to...*holy crap*! The hairs on his scalp stood on end. Resisting the urge to jump to his feet and toss Cruz from the office, James took a deep breath and narrowed his gaze. "You plan to kill her first." A statement, not a question. His gut wrung so tight, he swore he'd never eat again.

Turning from the window, Cruz tapped a finger on the side of his nose.

How the hell had Carmen stayed with this man for three years? If Virginia's laws hadn't allowed a one-sided divorce, she'd still be stuck to this bastard. Lips pressed into a thin line, James slid his butt off the desk. "You're looking at Murder One, Mr. Cruz. You can't expect a self-defense plea if you followed her here."

"I beg to differ." He returned his hands into his trouser pockets and strolled in a circle. "She lured me here on purpose, and I, like the faithful husband, obeyed. She talked about reconciliation, and she found the perfect spot to air all our differences." He chuckled. "What better place than a quiet, little mountaintop with scant population?" He shook his head. "She must think I'm a total moron."

If what she said is true about the sex, then yeah, you are a moron. He kept his face expressionless. "What are you reconciling?"

Cruz waved aside the question. "A minor spat."

"She told me you were divorced."

"She'd say anything to stay on your good side." Reaching across the desk, Cruz rotated the framed photo of Lucy. "Nice looking kid."

Cruz was one smooth operator. He thought nothing of revealing his plan to an officer of the law. James clenched his jaw. "Did you report your suspicions to the local authorities?"

He grunted. "Sure, but they can't do anything. Crazy laws, right?"

In all probability, no one filed an official report. What the hell was he supposed to do now? Did Cruz really talk to the authorities or was the man throwing a lot of bull at a small-town cop? James wanted to kick his desk, but he'd only hurt his foot. Instead, he jammed his thumbs into his duty belt and eyed Cruz through narrowed lids. "If she lured you here, why stop in the office to find out where she is?" A light bulb lit, and he cursed. "You saw my patrol car."

Cruz grinned. "Why waste a perfect opportunity?"

Yeah, if he suspected a trap, he'd rather have a cop on his side. *Dammit to hell.* James straightened Lucy's photo, wishing like hell he had a handkerchief to wipe away Cruz's touch. If the bastard so much as turned in Lucy's direction… With a chest ready to explode, he sucked in a calming breath. "Do you have children, Mr. Cruz?" He avoided any glance in the man's direction.

"Alas, no." He released a heavy sigh. "During our engagement, Carmen was all for a big family. After the wedding, she refused to have anything to do with children. She says she's with them all day and needs the peace and quiet of a childless home." He snorted. "Ironic, isn't it? A pediatrician who doesn't want her own kids. She even withheld sex."

Same story, different versions. Who spoke the truth? Could James be wrong about Carmen? Suppose she was some two-bit pediatrician with a list of lawsuits a mile long, or worse, what if she was a chronic liar? He prided himself on being a good judge of character, or did infatuation cloud his vision?

Facing James, Cruz furrowed his brows. "I'm a wealthy man, Sheriff. I can make your life very comfortable."

What the hell? The implication of his words hit like a brick. Dropping his hands to his sides, James struggled with every ounce of self-control not to swing

69

at the man's smug face. "You want me to look the other way?" Not once in his career had someone the audacity to bribe him, and the tension flowed straight to his fists. Really, what had he expected? Since Cruz slipped a hundred dollar bill toward Henrietta, he'd think nothing of adding a few zeros for the sheriff to keep his scheme quiet.

Releasing a breath in one big whoosh, James stuffed his hands into his trouser pockets in an effort to keep his fists unfurled. Otherwise, he might throw a few jabs at the man's ugly puss, and he wanted to hear Cruz's plans. A man couldn't talk with a busted jaw. He cleared his throat. "We have a close-knit community, Mr. Cruz. Keeping something quiet is impossible."

"I'm sure you'd find a way." He stopped before a wall map of the mountain's many trails. "I imagine you have a lot of cliffsides where one can slip and fall?"

Ah, so we come to the nitty-gritty. Cruz planned to stage an accident. Brass balls indeed. Hands slipping from his pockets, James stretched to his full height and leveled a glare on his visitor. "You admitted a murder plot to an officer of the law with bribery thrown in for good measure. What's stopping me from tossing you into my holding cell?"

Cruz laughed. "No proof, Sheriff. Your word against mine."

Well, damn. Clever man. He tucked his hands under his armpits to hold them stationary. "You are mistaken if you believe I will let you anywhere near Carmen Santiago."

"So, you doubt her plans to kill me?"

"As I said before, your presence on Billings Mountain will make a court of law rule self-defense in her favor. If she lured you here, what proof do you have? A voicemail message? A written note?"

Cruz glared. "None."

"Then, why should I believe you?"

The man's face flushed a deep red. "Confront my wife, Sheriff. She's a conniving bitch. I'll bet any amount of money she has a gun."

Why did he bother to leave his bed this morning? He wasn't some hotshot psychic who read minds. If need be, he'd restrict both of them from the mountain.

The thought irked him to no end. He finally met a woman who piqued his interest, and she was involved in some domestic dispute of gigantic proportion. *My friggin' luck.* James rubbed the back of his neck. "Guns are popular with our residents, Mr. Cruz. No one will think twice if she has one." Although, a visitor with a gun raised a few questions. He tugged on an ear, a little too hard since he damn near yanked off his lobe. Shaking his head, he walked to the front door. "You should return home. I'll talk to Doctor Santiago, and if I'm not satisfied with her response, I'll ask her to leave. The two of you can settle your differences elsewhere." Would he toss Carmen into the arms of a dangerous man? *Another dilemma to consider.* He grabbed the door knob.

"Tell you what." Cruz extracted his wallet and tossed five, one hundred dollar bills onto James's desk. "Consider these a down payment for your efforts. You'll see a lot more in the future."

James gripped the doorknob so hard he swore he'd snap the mechanism in two. The integrity of his badge meant everything to his career. If he couldn't stand behind the Oath of Honor, then he had no business being in the profession.

Leaving the door, he returned to his desk and stared at the bills. He hadn't a damn witness to this conversation. Why had he sent Harry to lunch? Gathering the money, he faced Cruz. "I can't be bribed." Fighting a strong urge to jam the money down Enrico's throat, James stuffed the bills into the man's shirt pocket. "Get out before I do something I'll regret."

Cruz sneered. "I'm rarely refused, Sheriff."

"Well, today, you found a man who can't be bought." Returning to the door, he jerked the knob. "Leave the mountain, Mr. Cruz. I'll deal with your wife."

Lips spread into a wide grin, the man wagged a finger. "Remember. My word against yours." Winking, he left the office.

James refrained from giving the man the third finger salute. Instead, he slammed the door hard enough to rattle the two front windows.

Swinging his arms to ease the tightness in his chest, he returned to his desk and stared at his take-out container. He had no appetite. Someone was full of shit, and he needed hard facts. High time Sheriff James Thomas put his investigative skills to work.

Having no desire to waste a good BLT, James sat at his desk, grabbed hold of the sandwich, and took a large bite before tapping the keyboard to awaken his computer. After several hours of steady research, he found what he needed and more than he expected, but what he didn't find concerned him the most. While tapping a pen on the desk, he stared at his notes.

The Virginia medical board confirmed Carmen's license along with several certifications in pediatrics, including surgery—all in good standing.

The Richmond public records listed Carmen's divorce as finalized one year ago for domestic abuse. For some reason, the cause didn't surprise him, but nowhere in his search could he uncover any police dispatch for a domestic dispute to the home of Enrico and Carmen Cruz. That missing piece of info raised a red flag. Lawyers needed evidence of abuse in order to file a petition for divorce. *Hmm.* Knowing Enrico's habit of bribery, did he dig up a dirty cop to make the reports disappear? Yet, how did Carmen succeed with her one-sided appeal?

With an idea springing to mind, James again searched public records and hit the jackpot. A restraining order popped onto the screen, filed by Carmen Santiago against Enrico Cruz, still in effect from seven months ago. Okay. Obviously, Carmen held proof of domestic violence to win her divorce and restraining order. Because Cruz lied about being divorced, all available data leaned in Carmen's favor as the one telling the truth, but James still had too many unanswered questions. Like the insurance policy. Did one actually exist? He should have asked Cruz for documentation. Although, following her to the mountain was in direct violation of the restraining order.

But what if she did invite him? No, that scenario made no sense. Also, James couldn't dismiss Enrico's accusation of a gun in her possession. Without a weapon's serial number, no way could he confirm ownership of a gun on the basis of name alone. A name-based weapons database created a handy shopping list for a crook. James clicked the button on his shoulder mike. "Harry, where are you?"

"Leaving the Billings Mansion."

"Any sign of Cruz's silver car?"

"Haven't seen it, but I'll keep an eye out. Problem?"

"A big one. I'll explain later. As a precaution, do a quick check at the Mallotum cabin. Carmen Santiago drives a white luxury vehicle. Make sure Cruz's silver car isn't parked anywhere near her cabin."

"Will do." A brief pause. "You must have some story to tell. Harry, out."

Billings Mountain hadn't seen a whole lot of excitement over the years. He and Harry dealt with skirmishes but nothing drastic. After the fiasco involving Charles's ex-girlfriend and an unsuspecting Alexandra, the cabin rental committee voted to install metal rails near every cliff side as a precaution. The rails destroyed some of the scenery's beauty, but better an obstruction to the view than to have another visitor tossed off the mountain. Something in his gut told him the community was about to experience another serious threat to its peace. With every intention of getting answers from Carmen, he turned off his computer and stood.

The front door opened. Lucy bobbed through looking all rosy cheeked. His beautiful daughter never failed to grip his heart. God, he loved her, and soon, she'd have boyfriends and dates. He'd sit home on pins and needles until she returned. As sheriff, he'd check out the boy, plus his parents, aunts, uncles, and grandparents. If anyone had so much as a parking ticket...well, his thoughts could be a bit premature. Smiling, he outstretched his arms. "How's my girl?"

Dropping her backpack by the door, she ran in for a hug.

The scents of flowers and sunshine and—if he wasn't mistaken—freshly cut grass swirled around Lucy. He held her at arm's length to inspect her clothes. Smudges of dirt and loose grass covered her jeans. "You've been practicing." If Lucy hadn't broken her leg on a patch of ice over the winter, she'd be on the soccer team again. The break kept her in a cast for eight weeks. The poor girl went bonkers. "How's the leg feel?"

She shrugged. "All right, I guess. My knee aches when I do twists and turns."

"You know what Alex said. The exercises help build the muscles." He ruffled her hair. "Give yourself time. You can sign on with the summer league."

"Yeah, I know. I'll be ready by then." Scooting around his desk, she hopped onto his chair and swiveled. "You got anything planned for dinner? Today's Tuesday, you know. Burger night at the cafe."

He almost laughed. Lucy loved Marion's burgers. In fact, everyone did. People packed the dining room like sardines in a can. "Yeah, okay. We'll get burgers." Her suggestion saved him from thinking about dinner. He wasn't the world's best cook but managed to feed his daughter a proper diet.

"Great." She jumped to her feet. "I'm heading over to Jennie's house. We're doing homework together. Is that okay?"

"Sure. You want me to pick you up?"

"Nah. I'll meet you at home. I have to change for dinner. I'm a mess."

He cocked a brow. "Since when are you concerned

about how you look?"

"Since Tommy and Jeffy said they'd see me at the cafe." She headed for the door.

Uh-oh. It has begun. He was second fiddle to Tommy and Jeffy. Hell, she was hardly out of diapers. Maybe he should put birth control pills in her morning orange juice. Hiding a smile, he waved. "I'll see you later."

"Thanks, Dad...oh!" She reached for her backpack but stopped. "Can I ask Carmen to the soccer game tomorrow night?"

The question took him aback. What the hell hit her? "Our guest in the Mallotum cabin? You've never invited a visitor to a game."

"I like her, but she's sad. We need to make her happy."

"Make her happy, eh?" In his opinion, any woman married to Enrico Cruz needed a constant flow of anti-depressants to survive. As much as he'd like to see Carmen smile more, he'd rather Lucy steer clear. Far too many questions lacked answers, and he'd rather talk to Carmen before Lucy extended any invitations. He rubbed the nape of his neck. "I don't know, honey. She might not want to be disturbed." Not to mention his possibility of throwing the doctor off the mountain. He met Lucy's pleading gaze. *What a sucker I am.* He smiled. "All right, ask her, but wait until tomorrow. And don't be disappointed if she refuses."

"Thanks, Dad." Yanking her backpack from the floor, she opened the door and waved. "See ya later."

Through the window, he watched her run uphill and into the woods.

He wasn't the only one to see the sadness in

76

Carmen's eyes. No woman should look as if the weight of the world rested on her shoulders. *Time to fill in the gaps.* He headed for the door when his shoulder mike crackled.

"Sheriff."

Harry always addressed him as Sheriff while on duty and particularly in front of visitors. "Yeah, Harry?" He closed the office door behind him.

"Cruz's car is parked at the cafe. You want me to go inside?"

His back stiffened. Damn that insolent asshole. Despite an officer of the law telling him otherwise, Enrico did whatever he pleased. *I definitely need to talk to Carmen.* "Have a seat at the counter, Harry. I'll talk to Mr. Cruz personally."

Fighting the urge to floor the gas pedal, James guided the cruiser uphill, all the while cursing under his breath. People visited Billings Mountain for the peace and quiet, not to murder each other. "Diplomacy," he muttered while gripping the steering wheel. "I must handle this guy with all the diplomatic finesse of a polished politician."

Easier said than done when his hands itched to strangle Cruz's fat neck.

Five minutes later, he glided his SUV into one of the open slots in the cafe's parking lot. Naturally, Cruz's silver car occupied two spaces. The man disregarded all rules. Adjusting his service belt, James entered the cafe.

"Sheriff! Come join me."

Enrico waved to James as if they were best buds. Of course, he occupied one of the booths by the front window for a good view of the road. With a quick nod at Harry, James ambled to the booth, well aware of the amount of people surrounding them. "This is not a social meeting, Mr. Cruz. I found the restraining order."

With a sly grin, he dabbed the corner of his mouth with a paper napkin. "Aw, well, what can I say? She's crazy."

The hairs on the back of his neck bristled. Oh, how he'd love to punch out those pearly-white teeth. Rather than chance a swing at Cruz's smug face, James clamped onto the table's edge and leaned forward. "I ran your name through my database since you had no qualms about bribing the sheriff." He spoke loud enough for everyone to hear. To hell with discretion. This arrogant SOB sent crawling critters along his skin. "You need to leave, Mr. Cruz."

"Why?" He scanned the nearly full cafe. "She's not here. I have a right to eat."

"But you're hoping she'll walk in. Then, you will be in direct violation of the restraining order." Before he broke off a piece of the table, he dropped his hands and stepped back.

After pushing his plate to the side, Cruz laughed. "The charges are bogus, Sheriff. She paid someone a handsome sum of money, but I retain the best lawyers in Richmond to fight whatever she throws my way."

"I'm sure you do." Money bought a lot of things, including crooked attorneys. "You might also discuss with your wonderful lawyers the consequences of stalking. I strongly suggest you return to Richmond."

Chuckling, Enrico stood and tossed a twenty-dollar bill onto the table. "Where can I find a decent hotel?"

So much for his returning to Richmond. James pinched the bridge of his nose. He should ignore the bastard and walk away. *Give me strength, Lord.* Frustration levels near maximum, he dropped his hand. "We have several motels in the valley, but if you want something fancy, you should drive to Lynchburg."

Narrowing his gaze, Enrico hissed. "You sent me to the valley to eat when you have a fine establishment right here. Why should I believe you about the motels?"

Since James towered over the man, he leaned close. "Even if you drive our main road from one end to the other, you won't find a hotel, a motel, nor a bed and breakfast. We are a private community, and I have every right to restrict your access."

Enrico flashed his gaze. "All right, Sheriff. You win—for the moment. We'll meet again."

"I hope not. I hate stalkers, Mr. Cruz."

James escorted Cruz to the door and waited for him to drive away. Frowning, he turned to the counter where Harry and Marion stared, both wide-eyed.

Harry nodded at the door. "Who's he stalking?"

"He's Carmen Santiago's ex, and she holds an active restraining order. One thousand feet. I wasn't about to tell him he was actually within the zone."

Marion huffed. "No wonder she looks so downtrodden. He probably won't give her a moment's peace."

Straddling a stool, James flopped onto the seat and rested his elbows on the counter. He used both hands to scrub his face. He hadn't a whole lot of patience with men like Enrico. Abusers and stalkers were on his personal shit list. Drumming his fingers on the counter, he stared at the door. "Carmen already told me he doesn't recognize the divorce. Between the two of them, they've raised more questions that threaten the safety of our mountain community. I might ask her to leave."

Marion gaped. "You'll give that ass exactly what he wants. She's safe here."

Shifting on the stool, Harry faced him. "I agree. We can protect her, and she'll have a chance to catch her breath."

They were both right. Given the word, the community would rally around Carmen without a second of hesitation. Glancing from Harry to Marion, he nodded. "Before I make a decision, I'll see what her plans are. Harry, I want you to confirm Cruz's exit from the mountain."

"And if not?"

"Cuff him and call me. We'll see how good his lawyers are." James smiled at Marion. "Lucy and I will return for burger night."

Marion grabbed a dish towel. "Bring Carmen with you. She needs a few friends, and I'll be more than happy to be one."

With a bastard for an ex-husband, Carmen needed protection—but not until she answered some probing questions.

Chapter Seven

James turned onto Mallotum Drive with a horrible sense of foreboding filling his gut. With the news about the insurance policy, Enrico dropped a bombshell, one which James had no clue how to handle.

Did Carmen lure her ex to the mountain? But that scenario made no sense. She had a restraining order against the man. Even more important, did Cruz tell the truth about the policy? James had no way to find out until a claim became public knowledge. If he had his brain screwed in right, he should have asked Cruz for proof, but how many people walked around with sensitive documents in their pocket?

The worse part of all this uncertainty? He finally met an intriguing woman only to have her ex raise doubts concerning their relationship. *Just my damn luck.* He tightened his grip on the steering wheel.

Nearing the cabin, he caught sight of Carmen's silhouette at cliffside. She sat on the bench, feet up, and coffee mug in both hands, looking like she belonged with the panoramic view. With her dark hair blowing, she created a picture that robbed his breath. God, she was beautiful. He cursed Enrico's presence and the problems between the two.

The crunch of the car tires on the stones announced his arrival.

Acknowledging with a wave, she rose and

meandered toward the cabin with the mug in her hand.

She walked on bare feet, even with the spring chill in the air. A nature girl. He never would have guessed. No matter how much he wanted to explore his attraction, if his questions weren't answered, he had every right to ask her to leave.

Keeping his expression neutral, he stepped from the vehicle. "Can we talk?"

Her face remained equally neutral, and without a word, she waved toward the porch.

Her hair tempted his fingers. The strands looked soft, and he itched to tuck a wayward curl behind her ear. A man could get lost in her gorgeous hair.

So much for professionalism. With a determination to lock himself into sheriff-mode, he followed her onto the porch.

She cocked her head. "I take it this isn't a social call?"

"No, ma'am."

A deep, low-pitched chuckle rose from her throat, and she pointed to the porch chairs. "If you're calling me ma'am, I guess it isn't. Have a seat. Want some coffee?"

"I'd love a cup. Black."

While he waited, he settled onto one of the plastic chairs, feeling as nervous as a boy on his first date. For crying out loud, he was a seasoned professional with a criminology degree and twelve years as the mountain's law enforcement. Beautiful women never rattled him. He rolled his shoulders to ease some of the tension.

Carmen returned with two mugs of steaming coffee. After handing him one, she slipped onto the second chair and faced him while holding her mug with both hands. "What did Enrico say?"

Too much and not enough. James preferred facts, not ambiguity. He sipped his coffee—nice and hot, the perfect temp to take away the chill of the mountain. He met her gaze. Her eyes held an all-too-familiar wariness. On the day of her arrival, the look raised suspicions, but after meeting Enrico, he'd bet her distrust stemmed from the money flowing from Cruz's wallet. Placing his cup onto the table, he faced her. "Your ex raised an awful lot of questions. I just spent the last two hours digging through court documents and police records and discovered the restraining order. I sent him away."

Lifting her mug, she blew the steam rising from the fluid. "He doesn't believe in the legality of a restraining order. As far as he's concerned, I'm his wife, and no one can keep him away." She met his gaze. "Did you notice he had no violations listed?"

Yeah, he noticed and thought Enrico was being a good boy, but his presence on the mountain told a different story. He fingered the handle on the mug. "I ran across police reports logged with a number but listed as unavailable. Since Cruz threw money on my desk without considering the consequences, I suspect he's done the same to other cops to make the reports disappear." He cocked a brow. "Am I right?"

Dropping her gaze, she snorted. "Cops, lawyers, judges, and anyone else to serve his purpose. He has so many people in his pocket I'm surprised his pants don't fall." Lowering the mug to the table, she stared into the liquid.

"How many times has he violated the restraining order?"

She huffed. "Eight. He never spent more than an hour in jail."

Yeah, funny that. Eight reports were inaccessible, obviously to hide all traces of the arrests, including the names of the officers involved. *Dammit to hell.* He hated uncovering shit like this. Rumor or truth, both ruined the public's trust in law enforcement. Sighing, he flopped back. "For the record, I don't like Cruz. He's an arrogant SOB." He learned early in his career to reserve judgment, but Enrico defied a direct order to leave the mountain. His actions spoke volumes as a man who dictated rather than obeyed. Well, not anymore, and not on this mountain. James tapped a finger on the side of his mug. "Enrico claims *you're* the one who doesn't want children."

Head snapping, she flashed him a hard gaze. "Why would he say something so stupid? Everyone knows I want my own kids."

Judging from the flush rising onto her cheeks and the white-knuckled grip on her mug, he believed her. The majority of women who *didn't* want children rarely reacted with such fury. He reached across the table to squeeze her arm. "Enrico doesn't strike me as the fatherly type."

Sitting back, she gaped. "You believe me?" She shook herself and lowered her gaze. "Sorry. I expected you to take his side." Releasing a long breath, she leaned against the table and toyed with her mug. "Now that I'm divorced, I'm contemplating adoption, but I'll never get approval with Enrico one step behind me."

Every muscle in his body tensed. She just mentioned a motive for murder. Was Carmen desperate enough to kill her ex in order to stop his interference in the adoption process? What better reason to eliminate Cruz and get rich in the process? He'd heard of weaker motives, but for now, he'd keep the news of the insurance policy tucked away. Coughing to unclench his jaw, he struggled for an air of nonchalance. "Why should he object?"

"Because he can." She propped an elbow on the table and rested her chin on a fist. "For three years, Enrico strung me along and made promises he never intended to keep. I think he hoped I'd grow too old to reproduce." With a sick laugh, she dropped her fist and stared into the distance. "I was so damn blind. I went into the marriage with idealistic expectations." Lifting a shoulder, she met his gaze. "You know, family, two-point-five kids, a dog, and a house with a white picket fence. I expected our marriage to evolve along those lines." She stared at a squirrel digging a hole in the dirt.

Well, I'll be damned. She's trying for a pity angle. No matter what, he wouldn't let her sad gaze and pouty lips sway him. He sipped his coffee. "I'm sure your marriage wasn't *all* bad."

She lifted her chin. "No, it wasn't. In the beginning, Enrico was kind and attentive until he changed into a control freak." She shifted her gaze over his shoulder. "He controlled everything about me— what I ate, how I dressed, and who I socialized with. I turned into a typical trophy wife and hated every second." She tucked a hair strand behind her ear before meeting his gaze. "I accepted his domineering nature because I was part of a busy pediatric practice, and any decisions involving home life were up to him. When I talked about limiting my hours and having children, I discovered his true colors. He refused to be seen with a fat wife."

Dear Lord Almighty. The man was a complete ass—assuming she spoke the truth. But he met Enrico, and his gut agreed. Leaning back, he drummed his fingers on the table. "Your divorce papers listed domestic abuse as the reason." He narrowed his gaze. "I found no charges against him."

A smile played on her lips.

Something slammed his chest. How could a smile affect him when her gaze still held the sad look? Maybe he should have his eyes checked.

She rotated her mug. "You're thorough, James. Those records disappeared, too. My concrete proof of abuse derived from the one time he put me in the hospital. By some miracle, he couldn't touch the medical records because I had staff privileges in the pediatrics department. If those records disappeared or were altered in any way, I'd have gone straight to the state medical board." Shifting on her seat, she folded one foot under her butt.

"Over the years, he never hit my face. Most of my body marks were from his grip. But the time he put me in the hospital, he left too many bruises, a cut lip, and two cracked ribs. Legally, the hospital had an obligation to report the assault, which they did, and Enrico should have been arrested."

"But he wasn't."

"Hell, no." With a fiery gaze, she hissed through tight teeth then held up a finger in a wait gesture. After rotating her shoulders and releasing a slow breath, she lifted her chin. "I can't tell you how many times I hit a brick wall when attempting to get that man arrested. Once discharged, I had to move fast. I requested copies of my medical records and went straight to my lawyer, Roxanne Travali. That day, she initiated divorce proceedings. Enrico fought every step of the way." She fussed with her pant leg. "He's a regular Jekyll and Hyde. Nice in public but a devil in private. He says we're married until he divorces me, regardless what the decree states."

Her shoulders slumped.

Well, he understood who crushed her spirit. Anger pulsed within him. No man should treat a woman like property, and he'd be damned to let any assault take place on this mountain. Still, he had far too many unanswered questions. Gulping the last of his coffee, James slid his mug onto the table and rapped a knuckle on the table surface to get her attention. When she looked up and met his gaze, he smiled. "I want you to know I stuffed his bribe into his breast pocket."

Her gaze scanned every inch of his face. Whether she believed him or not, he couldn't tell. Her face showed no emotion. Perhaps she heard the words before, only to have her faith evaporate. After Enrico's shenanigans, how could she trust any man in uniform?

A tightness settled in his chest. He felt so damn helpless. He'd like to wrap her in his arms and fill her mind with assurances, but what possible guarantee could he offer once she left the protection of the mountain? The men and women who swore to uphold the law thumbed their noses at the vow. Respect, trust, and integrity—all shot to hell. He cleared his throat. "I want you to understand something, Carmen. A long time ago, I vowed never to dismiss any mention of domestic abuse." Leaning forward with elbows on his knees, he focused his gaze on the porch floor. "I have a daughter. What you don't know is I never had a chance to marry Lucy's mother." Shooting her a quick glance, he leaned back and twisted his mouth to the side. "Cindy and I grew up together. We attended the same schools and dated off and on but were never anything serious. I left for college to focus on my career, and Cindy married another classmate. She discovered too late about his abusive behavior. Despite my arguments, she stuck with him and claimed his temper was all her fault."

She pursed her lips. "A classic response."

"Too classic." He scratched his ear. "Cindy's husband was an emotional abuser, so I never saw physical evidence to substantiate an arrest. I pushed her toward divorce, and in the interim, we grew closer. When she became pregnant with my child, she took two more years to file for divorce." He sucked in a shuddering breath. Reliving the memory was painful. So many regrets. All the woulda-coulda-shoulda scenarios crept into his thoughts.

He looked into Carmen's gaze. Her dark eyes held a softness that jarred his heart. If he wasn't careful, he'd melt right through the floorboards. Since he failed to help Cindy, he for damn sure would help Carmen.

"Go on, James."

Just the way she said his name sent warmth through his veins. He stared into the forest. "One fine morning, Cindy's husband drove the car over the cliff with Cindy and Lucy on board. He and Cindy died outright. We found Lucy dangling from her car seat with her back broken. Luckily, she didn't have spinal cord damage. She was two years old." He kicked a tiny pebble and watched it roll off the porch. "I hate how my hands are tied with emotional abuse." Sighing, he faced her.

A light shone in her gaze, a dull light but nonetheless, a glow so long missing.

With her brows drawn together, she ran a finger along the rim of her mug. "Lucy made a remarkable recovery."

"She had great care in Roanoke."

A slow smile quirked on her lips, and she shifted on the seat. "Today could be the first time I have a lawman on my side."

He wagged a finger. "Don't count your blessings yet. I need to clarify a few things." Gaze narrowed, he leaned on the table. "Tell me why you took out a two-million-dollar insurance policy on Enrico Cruz."

****

In the midst of sipping, Carmen choked and sputtered. What the hell kind of conversation did James have with Enrico? Coughing into her hand, she stared at the man who changed into all lawman. "What policy?"

"The one where you're sole beneficiary."

Her mind raced. Had she suffered a memory lapse? What was he talking about? Did someone slip a document in front of her, and she signed without reading? Could she—*holy shit*! She tightened her grip on the mug. Enrico secured himself a perfect self-defense plea for their 'official divorce'. She'd been waiting for this day and worked steadily with her lawyer to put her documents in proper order. But why did Enrico come to Billings Mountain with a restraining order in place? She'd have bet money he'd do the deed in Richmond.

Nothing made sense, not even the wave of calm

settling in her bones. She should be shaking with terror, but their final confrontation day was way overdue. He threatened to end their marriage in his way, not the legal way—in other words, with her in a coffin. Now, the big question. Would James believe her? Placing both elbows on the table, she steepled her fingers and studied James. He had a grim, watchful expression, as if debating whether to slap on a pair of handcuffs. "I know nothing about an insurance policy."

Lips tight, he folded his arms across his chest. "Do you have a gun?"

"A gun?" Ah, Enrico again. Sucking in a deep breath, she released it and dropped her hands to the table. "No, I don't have a gun. If you don't believe me, you can search the cabin, and since you don't have a warrant, you have my permission." Damn, she might feel calm, but her hands shook. She drummed her fingers on the table before returning her gaze to him. "Maybe I *should* have a gun. Enrico won't obey the restraining order, and no cop will arrest him. Spending my remaining years in jail might be a hell of a lot easier than my life is now."

Her voice cracked. Well, all right, so she wasn't so calm. Coming to Billings Mountain placed everyone in danger, and no one deserved the wrath of Enrico Cruz. She cleared her throat. "The staff at my pedie practice has no idea how tenacious Enrico is. They booked this vacation to help me relax, but I knew he'd show. Over the past year, he's followed me to every major event." Not like she expected James to show sympathy. She'd consider it a blessing if he allowed her time to pack her bags. In hindsight, she should have listened to her inner voice and stayed locked in her condo for two weeks.

He muttered a growl. "Two million is one hell of a motive, Doctor. If you banked on his following, you've succeeded, but I doubt a jury will allow you a self-defense plea if you lured him here."

Lured him? Holy Mother of God. Enrico told James one hell of a story. Lifting her chin, she gave him a long look. "I never opened any policy on Enrico. More likely, he's setting the stage to kill me." She narrowed her gaze. "For the record, Mr. Sheriff, I don't give a damn what you think." She lifted her chin higher. "I take back what I said earlier about having a lawman on my side."

One blond brow cocked, but he said nothing.

If she insulted him, well, too damn bad. Her heart squeezed with the realization of her own words. Her hope shattered, she contemplated her next move. To leave, of course. From the day her divorce was finalized, her days were numbered. Knowing this fact, she planned accordingly. Along with her personal papers locked away in her lawyer's safe, Carmen included a sealed letter to her parents, explaining the details of a marriage made in hell. She even worked out at a fitness club, in case she had a chance to wring Enrico's fat neck. *Oh, hell, I'm getting a headache.* With one hand, she rubbed her temples. She should tell James to get out so she could pack her bags. But with Enrico in the vicinity...

Dropping her hand, she held his gaze. "Enrico isn't on the mountain to give me a big hug, James. He's here because he already has local connections in place. You can lock him in a cell for whatever reason, but he's still granted his one phone call."

Gritting his teeth, he slammed an open palm on the

table. "You and your ex placed me in one hell of a position. As an officer of the law, I can't permit a premeditated murder to occur."

"Premeditated on his part, not mine." She tossed the remainder of her coffee onto the dirt and scared a blue jay in the process. "I'll pack and leave."

With lightning speed, he stretched across the table to grab her hand. "He'll follow."

The heat of his hand stopped her. No doubt from holding his coffee cup. Or maybe she was desperate for some skin-to-skin contact. Jerking her hand from his, she snorted. "Of course, he'll follow. He likes his torment games. I'm sure he'd rather I put a bullet in my own head—although, I'd have to buy a gun first."

"No, he has plans for your *accident*."

She snapped up her head. "My what?"

"You heard me."

"Then you have a reason to arrest him."

"Er…no." He cleared his throat. "No witnesses. His word against mine. Since we're such a small community, my deputy and I have no need for body cams."

"You don't wear protective vests either."

He shook his head. "We carry them and slip them on when needed…which isn't often." With a huff, he flopped back in the chair. "We'll figure out something. In the meantime, I'll keep an eye on his whereabouts." He stood.

With hope returning into her heart, she stared at this tall, blond man. "Don't you want me to leave?"

"Hell, no." He tugged on his duty belt. "You're safer here."

But could she trust him enough to stay? What if

Enrico already had James in his pocket? *Oh, God. I don't know what to do.*

****

Pausing with a hand on the cruiser door, James stared into the woods. What was with this woman who tied him in knots? Sure, her ex frightened her. What woman wouldn't be afraid of a stalker? Although outwardly calm, she couldn't hide the fear clouding her eyes. From a legal standpoint, the restraining order gave her a heads-up. If Enrico violated the stated distance, he'd find his sorry ass sitting on a crappy jail mattress. Rotating his head, he glanced back at the cabin.

Carmen stood on the porch with her gaze focused on the ground and hands in her jacket pockets.

Her mind was likely a million miles away. Was James Thomas being a sap, perhaps suckered in by a woman in peril?

His history with Lucy's mom replayed in his mind. If Cindy hadn't forced him to keep his distance, she'd be alive today. Maybe, subconsciously, he wanted to avoid the same mistake with Carmen.

At least, in Carmen's case, he had three glaring facts at his disposal. One, her divorce decree revealed domestic abuse as the reason. Two, the restraining order, taken out after their divorce, told of a woman desperate to keep her ex from approaching. Best of all, Cruz's bribe gave James insight into the man's character. Enrico used money like a flytrap and had no qualms about revealing his plan to stage Carmen's demise. The man had guts. James learned a valuable lesson—never, ever have a private conversation with Enrico Cruz unless a recording device was in play.

Leaving the car door ajar, he strolled back. "I

meant what I said, Carmen. You're safer here."

A blank stare faced him. "Not for long." Shaking herself, she cleared her throat. "I'm booked for two weeks. After that…" She shrugged.

He lifted one booted foot onto the porch step. "Our guests come to enjoy their stay, not live in fear. I'll do my best to keep him away." Noting the sun had set below the treetops, he glanced at his wristwatch. "I've an errand to run before I change for dinner. Why don't you join me and Lucy for burger night at the cafe?" He cocked his head. "We never had a lunch date."

With a gaze studying his face, she bit her lower lip.

Still too cautious. Not that he blamed her. What he didn't want was for her to bolt and confront her ex without support. He leaned forward. "Marion makes the best burgers around. We even get people driving from the valley on burger night."

A slow smile stretched onto her lips.

Out of nowhere, a glow settled within her gaze and turned her into an absolutely breathtaking woman. His heart took off like a galloping horse. If possible, he'd keep the glow in her eyes indefinitely. He grinned. "Well?"

Like magic, the glow faded. A haunted look took its place. He silently cursed.

She shook her head. "For everyone's safety, I'll keep my distance."

Friendship was what she needed and time to believe him to be a man of his word. Not wanting to push, he pursed his lips and dropped his foot from the step. "Thanks for the coffee. If you change your mind about tonight, meet us at the cafe." He headed for the cruiser.

"James."

He turned to see her behind him. With him in his boots and her in bare feet, she barely reached his neck, and his breath stuck in his throat at her close proximity. He'd seen many beautiful women over the years, but none struck him as a combination of exotic and down-to-earth at the same time. The old adage *'Where have you been all my life?'* sat on the tip of his tongue. Hell, the phrase was such an overused pickup line, how could he say the words out loud?

She stretched on tiptoe and placed a kiss on his cheek. "Thank you."

Her cotton candy perfume swirled around him. Would she taste as delicious as her smell? "For what?" Damn, his voice squeaked. He coughed.

"For being kind."

He'd rather she planted those soft lips a little more centered on his face, like on his hungry mouth. Driven by impulse without a concern if he overstepped his bounds, he slipped two fingers under her chin and lifted her lips to his. He slid across them with no tongue and no pressure. A simple taste to serve as an appetizer. Damn if heat didn't pool in his groin.

After pulling away, she searched his face with a puzzled gaze.

Having no desire to analyze what passed between them, he winked and slid into the cruiser, feeling like a schoolboy who kissed the most beautiful girl in class. Come hell or high water, he'd earn her trust.

Chapter Eight

With the weather too beautiful to stay indoors, Carmen washed both mugs then grabbed one of her medical journals. Figuring she'd spend an hour reading before darkness forced her inside, she lounged at the table on the porch. But instead of concentrating on the articles, she flipped through the pages as if she held a fashion magazine with nothing but advertisements and photos.

Her thoughts drifted to James and how his lips brushed across hers. The contact created a warm, fuzzy feeling inside her chest—a sensation she embraced to rid the cold chill of Enrico being on the mountain. Since her divorce, she practiced caution with any man who approached, and James was no exception. After one colossal mistake marrying Enrico, she hesitated big-time before every dinner invitation or even a social gathering. Her ex had a way of putting the fear into her date.

She hoped James was different. Would he force Enrico to keep his distance, or had his words been merely to pacify? He was, after all, a man with a badge. History necessitated that he earn her trust, but despite the internal conflict, a smidgen of hope filled her heart.

Aw, hell. How could she relax and concentrate on her journal when her mind shot in every direction? James. Enrico. James again. Was she really safe here?

Should she pack up and return home to hibernate in her condo? Throwing the magazine onto the table, she flopped against the backrest and dropped her hands over the arms of the chair.

The blue jay returned and squawked at her presence. "Tough. I'm staying." And yes, she was staying. She made up her mind to stick around, and all because the jay's beautiful coat of feathers reminded her of a certain pair of blue eyes. When James kissed her, she almost clamped onto his neck to hold him in place.

"Carmen!"

The frightened voice jerked her from her thoughts. Bolting upright, Carmen snapped her gaze to the left side of the cabin.

Lucy flew around the porch and up onto the steps.

In Carmen's medical opinion, a backpack ladened with books was far too much weight for a child's spine. She argued incessantly about the subject and even wrote a paper for a pediatric journal, but would anyone listen?

After a quick glance at the darkening forest, Carmen raised her brows. "Did you just come from school?" Geez, she hoped not. If her child walked home this late, she'd be a basket case. But Lucy's pale face and wide eyes put Carmen on full alert. She reached for the girl. "What's wrong, honey?"

A twig snapped, once again drawing Carmen's gaze to the left.

Seconds later, a man wandered into view.

He slid to an abrupt halt alongside the porch. With dark hair peppered with gray, he arched one bushy brow high onto his forehead, as if seeing Carmen came as a complete surprise. He wore the traditional hiker's outfit of flannel shirt and blue jeans with a small backpack, but her gut said he was no ordinary hiker. Muscles tense, she touched the girl's arm. "Lucy?"

Eyes wide, she pointed. "He's following me."

Squaring her shoulders, Carmen stood and glared at the man. "Can I help you?"

Never moving his dark gaze from Lucy, he sauntered toward the front of the porch, stopping several feet from the step. "Sorry. Guess I followed the wrong trail."

With every nerve firing at once, Carmen used a hand to sweep Lucy behind her. "The office has trail maps."

The man drifted his gaze to meet Carmen's. "Guess I missed the office."

"So, instead, you followed a little girl."

He shrugged. "She looks like she knows her way through the woods."

Carmen glanced over her shoulder at Lucy. "When did you notice him behind you?"

Edging closer, Lucy clamped her small hands onto Carmen's jacket. "Just before the Mitchells' house, but I think I heard twigs snapping before that." She tugged on the jacket. "I was thinking too much about my homework."

And the snapping twigs never registered. Carmen gritted her teeth. "Was anyone home in the Mitchell house?"

"I knocked, but no one answered. I got scared and ran here."

Carmen didn't need a neon sign to figure out the man's intentions. Even if she was wrong, she sure as hell shared Lucy's unease. "You better leave, sir."

Lucy darted her head around Carmen. "Yeah, my dad's the sheriff."

The man grinned. "Kids say the darnedest things."

"Her dad really is the sheriff." *Wow*. From his amused expression, the man didn't believe her either.

"Can't say I blame you for being overprotective. She's a gorgeous little girl." He scanned Carmen from head to toe. "You're a looker yourself. I'd say you passed on the beauty genes."

The man was so full of shit, and her back stiffened.

Lucy nudged Carmen's hips. "He's creeping me out."

Yeah, me, too. She brushed Lucy's arm. "Do you have a phone?"

She dropped her chin to her chest. "The battery died. I forgot to plug it in last night."

"Then, go into the cabin and use mine. It's on the kitchen table. Code 1221. Call your dad."

Lucy ran inside the cabin.

With his gaze glued to the cabin door, the man lifted one booted foot onto the step. "Look, I don't mean no harm. I photograph children for department stores, and your little girl would be a sensation in our summer catalog."

Yeah, right. A photographer wouldn't stare at his subject as if she was his next meal. Stretching to her full height, Carmen folded her arms over her chest. "You should have a business card to show me."

He patted his pockets. "No card. Sorry." Again, he drifted his gaze to the door. "You can make a lot of money on your little one."

Modeling, my ass. At a guess, the man arranged

private sessions for deranged clients. If he so much as took one step in Lucy's direction, she'd beat the crap out of the creepy intruder. She didn't give a damn if he claimed to be a famous photojournalist. Her years in practice taught her how to recognize a pedophile, and he was no more a talent scout than her assistant's dog.

"At least, let me talk to your daughter."

Dear Lord. A shiver just shot up her spine. She gritted her teeth. "The decision isn't hers to make."

A bronchitic cough drew her gaze to the edge of the porch.

"You heard the lady."

An older man appeared, cradling a shotgun in his arms. If his scraggly beard was white, he'd make a good Santa Claus, complete with potbelly...except for the toothpick dangling from his mouth.

Carmen released a breath she hadn't realized she held and nodded at the bearded man.

Catching her gaze, the old guy winked. "The missus and I came home to see him enter the woods right behind Lucy. We knew he wasn't following no trail. Gladys already called the sheriff."

With eyes growing wide, the stranger bolted for the woods.

The old man sighed. "Now, that was a dumb move. No way in hell will he make it off the mountain. He's heading uphill."

With lights flashing, a cop car raced down the drive, creating a cloud of dust as it screeched to a stop near the trees.

A stocky man with glasses and a police uniform jumped from the vehicle and, following the direction of the older man's gesture, took off in pursuit.

James arrived ten seconds later and slammed his brakes closer to Carmen's car. With a jaw like granite, he jumped from the vehicle and caught Carmen's gaze.

After an okay nod from Carmen, he disappeared into the trees.

Lucy hurried through the door. "Go get 'em, Dad!"

Jamming fists onto her hips, Carmen scowled at Lucy.

Lucy kicked a twig off the porch. "I guess I didn't pay attention."

"I guess not." Dropping her arms, Carmen squeezed the back of Lucy's neck. "You have to be careful, honey. The world is full of bad people."

The old guy ambled to the porch steps, hand outstretched. "I'm Frank Mitchell. Me and the missus live one house below this cabin. Since most of the kids walk to school, the neighbors along the footpaths keep an eye on them. So, thanks for helping out."

Carmen shook the rough hand. "Anytime." After dropping her hand, she slipped an arm around Lucy's shoulders and hugged her to her side. "You have good neighbors, but if I wasn't here, that man would have followed you right to your door. Was anyone home waiting?"

"Mrs. O'Reilly."

"Good, but keep alert next time."

James and his deputy emerged from the woods with the stranger in tow, handcuffed and covered with pine needles. With a gaze full of fire, the sheriff carried the intruder's backpack in his left hand. Judging from the white-knuckled grip on the strap, James might swing it at the man's head at any second.

After popping the hatch to his SUV, James threw

the pack into the rear and slammed the hood.

She expected glass to shatter and fly all over the yard.

Lucy cringed. "Dad's really mad."

"I don't blame him." She'd like to string up a few child predators in Wild West fashion. Too bad those days had passed.

After the deputy drove away, James walked over to Frank Mitchell and shook the man's hand.

With a nod and wave toward Carmen, the old guy retreated into the woods.

James approached the porch. "Thank you." Then, he shot a narrow-eyed glare at his daughter. "Why didn't you see him? You know how you're supposed to keep your eyes and ears open."

Lucy leaned into Carmen. "Sorry, Dad. I got distracted."

"Well, get in the car. I'll take you home." Reaching across the porch, he hefted her backpack onto his shoulder. "As punishment, I should keep you home tonight."

She stomped her foot. "Aw, Dad, it's burger night."

Frowning, he shot her a one-eyed glare. "Yeah, well, we'll continue our discussion at home. Let's go."

Lucy whirled and wrapped her arms around Carmen's waist. "Thanks. You're the best."

Carmen returned the hug.

Lucy released her hold and ran to the cruiser.

With a shake of his head, James met Carmen's gaze. "I'm glad Lucy stopped here."

"I'm glad I was sitting on the porch. If I wasn't, I'd have missed her—and him." She followed Lucy's movements until the little girl closed the cruiser door. She shifted her gaze to James. "He doesn't strike me as a first offender."

He cocked a brow. "I'll let you know what we discover on his background check." With his gaze focused on his cruiser, he adjusted the pack's strap. "If anyone steals my little girl, I might kill them without an ounce of regret. She means everything to me." Clearing his throat, he forced a smile. "Thanks again, Carmen." He headed for his car.

Before stepping into the vehicle, he paused by the door and locked onto her gaze.

His warm gaze scanned her, and her breath hitched. Over the years, she'd seen gratitude from the eyes of many parents but, never once, had her heart skipped erratically. *Santa Maria, I'm doomed.*

****

The next day, after driving Lucy to school, he stopped to join the morning crowd at the cafe. Taking his usual spot on the counter stool by the wall, he perused a menu already memorized just for something to do. His mood sucked. As punishment for not paying attention to her surroundings, James kept Lucy from burger night and fed her a grilled cheese sandwich. According to Marion, Carmen never showed, and something inside him felt relief. After all, he invited her. Knowing the patterns of domestic violence, he understood her reluctance. An abusive husband ripped out her soul and left an empty shell. James blamed her sadness on the failure of the justice system and the weak laws governing spousal abuse. Even as a lawman, his hands were tied.

But yesterday, at the sight of her first genuine

Jane Drager

smile, he watched a portion of her walls crumble. She had a beautiful smile, and he damned near hit the dirt. And her kiss…Lord, he thought about her all night. For the first time in years, a woman kick-started his pulse and sent it skittering. How in the world could he get some alone time with a woman without activating the mountain gossip mill?

"What are you so reflective about?"

At Marion's voice, he jerked. "I'm annoyed with Lucy."

"You're lucky Carmen was sitting outside." While holding a coffee carafe, she nodded at the menu in his hands. "You want your usual eggs and grits?"

"Yeah. Throw on two slices of bacon." He replaced the menu to the holder.

"Be back in a few." She refilled his coffee cup and moved on.

Naturally, Marion heard everything from Harry when he stopped by for his morning stack of pancakes. He had no intention of reprimanding Harry for opening his yap…again. In this case, his gossip served as a reminder of their dangerous world. With elbows on the counter, he sipped the steaming cup.

Strategically speaking, he perched his butt on the best seat in the house, which put him in direct view of the entrance and the entire dining area. About ten feet away and cut into the wall was an opening to the kitchen where the cook slid platters onto the stainless steel counter. The aromas of eggs, bacon, and coffee always filled him with gratitude for his life on Billings Mountain. Simple pleasures, like how everyone knew your name and watched out for the neighbors. Yesterday's incident with the man following Lucy proved his point. Even Carmen, a stranger to the mountain, protected Lucy like the child was her own.

Carmen had been right. The guy served six years for pedophilia, all seven-to-ten-year-old girls. If James had his way, he'd beat the perp to a pulp and then throw him to the bears. As it happened, the man violated probation and was in transit to the penitentiary. Thanks to Carmen and Frank, two ordinary citizens put another criminal behind bars where he belonged.

As usual for the cafe, a steady influx of morning customers flowed through the door. Quite a few of the patrons carried backpacks and wore hiking boots. If they ordered the cafe's breakfast special, they received a free thermos of piping hot coffee, as long as the hiker provided the thermos. Marion's neighbor, Lizzy, worked as hostess in the mornings when crowds jammed the cafe. At ninety-two, she was a peppy little woman.

Because of the early hour, most people yawned or rubbed their eyes. Some looked perky enough to go dancing. Like the one Hispanic male sitting alone in the booth by the window. He gave every impression of a man who'd been awake for hours. A pre-dawn hiker, no doubt. He wore the typical attire of blue jeans and plaid flannel shirt covered by a pale gray jacket.

Catching the sheriff's perusal, the Hispanic responded with a curt nod, slid from the booth, and tossed a few bills onto the table.

James half expected the man to saunter up to him, but instead, he walked straight to the register. No backpack nor hiking boots—just sneakers, which wasn't unusual. Quite a few people came onto the mountain to enjoy the breathtaking overlooks along the road.

"Eggs over-easy."

Marion slid his plate toward him and served two others down the line.

The busy proprietor performed her usual hustling behind the counter, between serving meals and helping Lizzy at the cash register. Donna, the half-Goth girl, zipped around the tables while Mrs. Willis—another neighbor who worked during the morning rush—blew like a whirlwind clearing tables. Every morning, a line formed by the door as locals and visitors alike took advantage of Marion's generous serving portions.

A ruckus by the front door drew his gaze.

Enrico Cruz elbowed his way through the crowd. Catching sight of James, he flashed a brilliant smile and strolled over. "I'm here for a bite to eat." He slipped onto the vacant stool next to James.

Wonderful. Nothing like an arrogant SOB to start the day. James swallowed the last of his bacon. "You should wait in line like the rest of the people, Mr. Cruz."

"Nonsense. They're mostly couples, and this is the last stool. Lucky me."

Yeah, and unlucky me. He gripped the handle on his mug and sipped. Before he snapped the ceramic in two, he lowered his cup to the counter. With a steady gaze, he watched Cruz wipe the counter with a napkin. "You realize I'll arrest you if Ms. Santiago walks in."

"Don't worry. I'll make sure she sees me."

He rolled his eyes. "The purpose of the restraining order is to keep you away."

Snarling, Enrico shifted on the stool. "In my opinion, a thousand feet is ridiculous."

Give a gold star to Carmen. Smiling, James lowered his gaze to his empty platter. "I'd say your ex had a good lawyer." One who wasn't part of Cruz's entourage. Waving a hand in the air to catch Marion's attention, he pointed toward his cup.

Marion strolled over with a coffee pot in her hand. "You're wasting your time, Mr. Cruz. Carmen's been in and out already." She refilled James's cup.

Jaw twitching, Enrico pursed his lips. "Where'd she go?"

Grunting, she used a wet cloth to wipe the spilled drops on the counter. "She wanted a mall. Nearest one is in Lynchburg."

James almost spewed his mouthful of coffee all over Marion. Why would she tell Enrico Carmen's plans? In the valley, Carmen would be a sitting duck. At least here on the mountain, the woman had people watching her back. James glared at Marion—for what good it did. The damn gossip just smirked.

Frowning, Enrico flipped the cup in front of him.

"Sorry." Marion glanced at the cup. "If I serve you, I'll have a riot in here. You cut in front of a lot of people." She wagged a finger in front of his face and tsked. "Very rude, buster. You either join the line or return in three hours for lunch—that is, if the sheriff allows you." She tapped a finger to her lips. "Come to think of it, I'd rather you stay away. Your patronage is not welcome here."

Face tight, Cruz slammed a palm onto the counter. "Do you hear her, Sheriff? I'll sue."

To hide a smile, James lifted his cup to his lips. "The cafe is hers to do with as she pleases. If she asks me to throw you out, I will."

With cheeks flushing a deep red, Enrico glared at Marion. "I don't know why you hate me so much. I'm here to stop Carmen from killing herself."

Marion gasped.

Several other patrons within earshot followed suit.

Funny how Cruz elevated his voice when he told lies. At least, James hoped he lied. He had no proof one way or the other. Resting his cup onto the counter, James faced him. "What makes you think she'll kill herself, Mr. Cruz?" *Besides having an asshole for an ex.*

He tapped the counter. "Her mental state, of course. She's been battling depression for years."

Since Marion's jaw muscles twitched while she gripped a hot coffee carafe, James held up a finger in warning before she dumped the contents onto Cruz's head. She would, too, and damn the consequences. After toying with the handle on his cup, he glanced at Cruz. "Ms. Santiago seems fine to me."

"Well, of course, she does. She's a great actress. And besides, a doctor has access to lots of medications." After a quick scan around the cafe, he twisted his lips to the side.

Clever bastard. He gave everyone who overheard a reason for Carmen's untimely death. James slid his empty plate to the side. "Being married to you would cause any woman to spiral into depression."

The man gaped. "I'm the best thing in her life, and that's a fact."

"So, why did she divorce you?" James purposely elevated his voice to one-up the asshole. Two could play this damn game.

"Humph. She was drugged out of her mind."

Standing, Cruz leaned across the counter and sneered at Marion. "The next time I'm in here, I demand to be served."

Snorting and with a fist jammed onto her hip, Marion closed the gap by leaning on the counter. "You can demand all you want, honey. This is my place, and I serve whomever I please."

Enrico leveled a piercing glare at Marion and left.

The entire restaurant exploded with applause.

Grinning, Marion took a bow then turned to James. "Do you believe him about Carmen?"

After swallowing a large gulp of coffee, he shook his head. "Not a chance." He lowered his cup. Unfortunately, Cruz's comment seeped through a lot of ears. People heard about mental disorders all the time, thanks to the multitude of drug commercials on TV. If Carmen suddenly fell over the cliff, no one would think twice. Death by drug-induced inebriation—a classic accidental fatality. He felt like a man stuck between a rock and a solid wall. "Has anyone been in here who somehow doesn't belong?"

Brows raised, she scanned the crowd. "All the cabins are rented, so I don't know a lot of people. Do you have someone in mind?"

"Carmen said her ex has a PI following her."

Frowning, Marion chewed on her inner lip. "We had a couple of men eating alone, but no one suspicious."

The loner by the window flashed through his mind. "What about the Hispanic guy who just left? He wore a light-gray jacket?"

Marion shook her head. "Sorry. Too many people coming and going."

"Well, keep your eyes and ears open, will you?" Glancing behind him, he leaned against the counter. "Why did you tell Cruz about her shopping in Lynchburg?"

She clicked her tongue. "For your information, Mr. Sheriff, Carmen arrived early for pancakes. I asked if she had any plans for today. She said just the hammock with a good book. Considering Cruz and the possibility of her being followed, I'd say you have a valid reason to check on her from time to time."

Brows high, he shot back. "You lied!" Then, he chuckled. "I love it."

She winked. "I know a bastard when I see one." Moving along the counter, she poured coffee in whatever empty cup she passed as she worked her way to the register.

Okay, now what? He had to keep an objective head and think with his mind and ignore his heart. He didn't like Enrico Cruz nor appreciate how he lumped Carmen into a suicidal wannabe. The turmoil of not knowing what to do gnawed at his gut. High time he talked to the one woman with an objective mind.

Chapter Nine

James entered the Billings Mountain clinic with the hope Doctor Alexandra Colter-Billings wasn't too busy. The limited number of cars in the parking lot never gave a good indication of activity within the facility. The majority of patients were hikers, and they hobbled in on sprained ankles or screamed bloody murder from poison ivy or sumac.

Five years ago, when she rented one of their cabins, she fell head-over-heels in love with Charles. The heir to the mountain fell even harder, and everyone saw why. Alex had spunk. For such a small woman at five foot one, she had the fierceness of a tigress, the heart of an angel, and the brain of an online encyclopedia. On the personal side, she was naïve as sin, and everyone on the mountain fell in love. James had the honor of being best man at their wedding with Lucy as flower girl.

Once the automatic doors closed behind him, he looked around and rubbed his nose when the smell of chlorine bleach hit his senses. The reception desk sat empty—a good sign. Mrs. Carmichael from across the road worked when an influx of patients overwhelmed Alex and her nurse—mainly in summer when hiking season reached full swing. He peeked through the double doors leading into the four-bed emergency room to see Nurse Becca wrapping a hiker's ankle.

Becca cocked her head and smiled. "Hi, James. Can I help you?"

"Is Alex busy?"

"She's in her office."

After the birth of their first child, Alex convinced Charles to build a small clinic so she wouldn't have to do so many house calls. Charles went above and beyond with the building's plans. Besides the ER with its array of X-ray equipment and lab machines, the facility contained a two-bed ward for patients recovering from minor surgery and, in some cases, emergency surgery. Alex still made house calls but also scheduled clinic office hours. Her personal office stood away from the patient-care areas, and he headed down a short hall.

Finding the door open, he peeked in to see her intent on a computer screen. Her long, dark hair fell in waves around her shoulders and reminded him of Carmen. The similarities struck him. While Alex had brown, expressive eyes, Carmen's eyes reminded him of hot fudge. Both women were doctors, both beautiful, but only Carmen got his heart pumping. Shaking away the thought, he knocked on the doorjamb. "Busy?"

Glancing up, she smiled. "Never for you. Come in."

She always wore scrubs and a lab coat while at work. Today, her lab coat hung on the rack by the door. Despite giving birth to two children, her petite frame hadn't changed.

"Have a seat." She waved toward the two chairs in front of her desk. "What's on your mind?"

Astute. He never stopped at the clinic for a social call. Most of their conversations took place at the cafe or whenever he and Lucy visited the mansion. "I'm having a hard time being objective about something."

She rolled her chair away from the desk and lifted both feet onto the leather seat. "Does this have anything to do with our guest in the Mallotum cabin?"

Damn mountain grapevine. News traveled faster than warp speed. Frowning, he flopped onto one of the two chairs in front of her desk. "How much have you heard?"

With a twinkling gaze, she grinned. "That her ex followed her here, and nobody likes him."

Chuckling, he leaned back against the plush leather. "I'd say you heard correctly."

"So, what's the problem?"

He lifted his right ankle onto his left knee and fussed with his trouser hem. "I'm getting conflicting stories—the he-said-she-said scenario. I don't know who to believe."

Narrowing her gaze, she pursed her lips. "About the depression?"

Wow. She heard everything. He fidgeted. "I studied mental illness as part of my criminology degree, but as far as recognizing the condition in someone without a gun or knife in their hands, I'm a bit dumb. Well, yeah, okay, a person is sad all the time and doesn't want to leave the house or talk to people. How can I prove what Cruz said is true, and how can I tell if Carmen is popping pills to function?"

Brows drawn together, she released a long breath before meeting his gaze. "You can't. You can keep an eye out for any medication bottles, but I doubt she'll keep them in the open. Does she look depressed?"

He shrugged. "She looks sad, but any woman

would with an ass like Cruz on her tail." While tapping the side of his boot, he shot Alex a glance. "Her ex claims she has a gun. If she's suffering from depression and has a weapon, I'm dealing with a major problem."

With a fixed gaze on the far wall, Alex rocked her chair. "When a restraining order doesn't work for a woman, a gun is the next logical step." Shifting her gaze to meet his, she wagged a finger. "As law enforcement, you'll disagree, but during my years in New York, I met quite a few nurses who bought a gun to protect themselves from an abusive ex. Restraining orders won't keep a cop at the door."

He'd be the first to admit the system sucked. He huffed out a breath. "I've never felt so helpless."

She curled one side of her lip. "When you have personal feelings involved, you struggle to be objective."

Yeah, Alex was too damn astute. He cringed. "I should deny every word, but I can't."

"Nor should you, but let me make another point." Gaze steady, she tapped a finger on the desk. "Are you sure Enrico isn't saying things to swing everyone onto his side? Carmen is a well-respected pediatrician from one of Richmond's largest practices." Grinning, she rocked. "Henrietta told me we had a pedie doctor on the mountain. I checked her out." She cocked her head. "But you have more, don't you?"

Alex had a way of listening and hearing words not spoken. Her advice was always sound, and he loved her calm demeanor. But he was about to test her calm. Dropping his foot to the floor, he leaned his elbows onto his knees and locked onto her gaze. "Cruz claims she took out a two-million-dollar insurance policy on him, listing herself as sole beneficiary and then lured him here."

Eyes and mouth wide, she stopped rocking. "You're serious?" She shook herself. "Wow, some motive."

"My thought exactly. But that's not all. He plans to kill her first."

Alex dropped one foot to the floor with a thud and stared. "He told you all this?"

"Yeah, hard to believe he had the nerve." His gut erupted into one big fireball. If he developed ulcers over this problem, he'd be mighty pissed. He gripped his knees. "Cruz wants to stage an accident and bribed me to look the other way. I haven't a damn witness to our conversation." He squeezed until the knee joint protested. "I don't know what to do. Her ex is a man with paid officials in his pocket. If I throw him off the mountain, he'll wait like some vulture in the valley. Plus, Carmen said he has a PI following her. I suspect he's already here."

She whistled. "That's not good." She hugged her knee. "You can't protect her forever, James. She's scheduled to leave in two weeks."

If Cruz had his way, the bastard would make sure she went home in a box. James cursed under his breath. "Like I said, it's their word against mine. They could both have guns."

Alex winced. "Can you prove such a policy exists?"

"No, and Carmen denies buying one."

Shaking her head, she stood and moseyed to the front of the desk. Resting her butt onto a corner, she folded her arms over her chest. "You know emotional abuse is hard to prove. A person experiencing the torment can display depression symptoms and, of course, a sense of isolation. I haven't met her yet, but from my research, she doesn't sound like a woman going off the deep end." She tugged on an ear. "Professionally, she's well-respected and won last year's Pediatrician of the Year award. This coming July, she is the keynote speaker at a symposium in Washington D.C. Pediatric doctors are coming from around the world. So, I doubt she plans to kill herself anytime soon." While biting her lower lip, she drummed her fingers on her forearms.

Alex's information combined with his own research painted a clear picture of Carmen Santiago's mental stability. Enrico Cruz was the unstable one. Thanks to Alex, James no longer felt like punching a wall.

After a minute, she met his gaze. "This Enrico guy is setting the stage for self-defense—although, coming here was a stupid move with a restraining order in place." Dropping both hands to her sides, she gripped the edge of her desk. "I can tell you one fact for certain. Enrico will not approach Carmen's cabin. In my opinion, the confrontation must look like she is the aggressor. Otherwise, his arguments won't work." While biting her lower lip, she pushed a stapler to the side. "You know the law better than any of us, James. You can throw Enrico off the mountain, but you can't stop him from following Carmen wherever she goes."

Oh, he knew the law and cursed every ineffective piece of legislation. Cops might as well wear their own handcuffs. Straightening in the chair, he spread his arms. "I honestly have no idea what to do, Alex." With a knot forming in the back of his neck, he rubbed the muscle—for what good it did. "I can't sit around and let him harm Carmen."

"I'm sure he'll violate the restraining order. Then, you can arrest him."

A headache threatened. He rubbed his temples. "From what Carmen tells me, he's always out within hours."

"Maybe she'll enjoy herself and extend her stay." Smiling, she waggled her eyebrows.

James chuckled. "Like you did?" He'd love to see Carmen stay an extra week or two. With the extended time, he'd figure out what to do with her ex—not to mention explore why this woman caused so many emotions to slam him like some battering ram. Hell, he spent years raising Lucy on his own. What changed?

Grinning, Alex leaned forward. "You can't fool me. People are already talking how you look smitten."

He gaped. "I'm not smitten!"

"Aren't you?" She poked a finger onto his chest. "Then perhaps you should listen to your heart."

Damn people should mind their own business. Sure, Carmen was a gorgeous woman, but he wasn't smitten, not by a long shot. As sheriff, his duty involved the safety of their visitors. Period.

****

With a contented sigh, Carmen lifted her bare feet onto the bench and sipped her coffee. Bright and early this morning, she awakened fully rested and couldn't wait to start her day. After completing a few yoga stretches on the hearth rug, she strolled to the cafe for a big breakfast. As soon as she entered, she salivated. Blueberry pancakes—her favorite. She ordered a plateful along with lots of maple syrup and crispy bacon. To hell with rotting her teeth or clogging her arteries. If Enrico had his way, she wouldn't live long enough for either to develop. As the morning crowd poured through the door, she returned to the cabin, made her own pot of coffee, and lounged at cliff side.

A loud screech drew her gaze upward, and her breath caught. An eagle soared overhead with its white head reflecting the bright sunshine. She hadn't seen one since her lazy days in New Mexico, like—oh, wow—nineteen years ago.

The creature flapped strong wings, glided, and then flapped more.

So graceful. Could a nest be nearby? In no time, the little fuzzball babies would grow into the majestic symbols of freedom. She raised her mug in salute.

The eagle eyed her and flew away.

Knowing her ex planned her imminent demise, she wasn't sure why she hadn't packed her bags and fled. If the clever bastard listed her as a death beneficiary, then he set her up for a big fall. The glitch to his story involved her restraining order. A jury would question why she invited him to a remote mountain on the other side of the state. Although, knowing Enrico, he finagled some sort of documentation as proof of her intentions. No, something wasn't right. Desperation on Enrico's part forced him to leave his kingdom of paid officials. All she had to do was find out why.

Crunching tires on stones snapped her gaze toward the driveway. Every muscle went on high alert until the police cruiser rolled into the clearing. Whew. With Enrico in the vicinity, she nearly bolted into the woods, bare feet and all.

Seconds later, James alighted from the vehicle holding a covered foam cup. He held up an open palm. "Stay where you are, Carmen."

Santa Maria, the man looked good. His pressed uniform of white shirt and gray slacks fit a lean but powerful body. He wasn't body-builder big, but distinctive muscles bulged from his thighs, shoulders, and arms. His belt buckle and badge sparkled, and he carried the gun on his right hip as if the weapon was a part of his body. Long legs took him to the bench with little effort.

"Morning." He stopped at the edge of the backrest.

Ordinarily, she'd tense in the presence of a lawman, but James chipped away part of her reserve. His disarming smile and deep voice soothed her nerves, and his lips…well, that part of his anatomy was another story. Despite her growing ease, she couldn't ignore the constant warning bells clanging in her head. Trust was something she couldn't afford to give. Not yet.

She checked her watch. Yep, still morning. "Hi. What brings you here?"

"Your ex stopped at the cafe for breakfast." He opened the tab on his cup lid and took a sip. "Marion refused to serve him."

What a delightful piece of news! If not for James's serious gaze, she'd laugh. Instead, she raised her mug. "Good for her. I'll bet he was pissed."

"I'd say apoplectic. Before he left, he boldly announced about your depression."

She spewed her coffee onto the dirt. After wiping the drip on her chin, she gaped. "My what?"

Frowning, he studied her. "Are you depressed, Carmen?"

A lump formed in her throat. *Clever bastard, indeed.* Enrico set the stage for her demise, whether by accident or suicide. Wow. Would he or his PI do the dirty deed? The latter possibility concerned her. She had no idea who the PI was, or how about a mountain resident under Enrico's thumb?

Again, something wasn't right. Bribing officials was Enrico's specialty, but he would never set himself up for blackmail by having someone else push her off a cliff. With her mind racing through so many variables and getting nowhere, she shook her head. "No, I am not depressed." Drawing her feet closer to her body, she patted the bench seat. "Sit down, James."

James slipped onto the vinyl slabs. "I didn't believe him. Neither did Marion." He leaned onto his knees with the cup held by both hands, his jaw twitching. "Sometimes I hate the way laws are written. He can say whatever he wants whether true or not." Rotating his head, he met her gaze. "Slander is your best defense."

She grunted. "Suing him will be a waste of time. He'd use one of the judges he has in his pocket."

Straightening, James shifted on the bench to face her. "I have a suggestion. Stay a while. He might give up and go home."

"Ha! Not a chance." She passed a hand through her hair. "If anything, Enrico is persistent. He'll follow me to the ends of the earth." A chill shot down her spine. She stared into her mug.

The breeze blew his cologne her way. One sniff of his earthy scent took all her strength not to shift her position to rest her head on his shoulder.

"Carmen?"

"Hmm?" She wiggled her toes.

"I'd like you and I to get more acquainted."

Curling one side of her mouth, she shot him a quick glance. "A slippery slope, James. Enrico still considers me his wife." Was this another ploy for her to drop her guard? She had no guarantee that James was upright and worthy of her trust. Ever since her divorce, a simple traffic stop scared the hell out of her. Although, none of the officers flirted like James nor invited her to lunch or burger night. Was this a new tactic or genuine interest? *How the hell will I know*?

"I'll never take a bribe, Carmen."

Gazes locked, she swore she saw straight to his soul. Dammit, her gut said trust him. Unable to ignore the lift to her heart, she smiled. "Then, I truly have a lawman on my side."

Chuckling, he bobbed his head. "Seems that way. At least, I can offer you protection while you're here."

While I'm here. The urge to stay forever took root, but where would she live and work? A community of three hundred residents wouldn't give her the necessary influx of pediatric patients to survive.

James gulped the last of his coffee and rested the empty cup on the ground. He then grabbed her mug, placed it alongside the cup, and stood with a hand extended.

The smile on his lips combined with his heated gaze caused her heart to flip. Holy moly. The intensity was enough to melt her bones. But really, she had to be out of her mind to start anything. Like a magnet pulled her, she took his hand and stood, but as he drew her close, she placed a palm on his chest. "Maybe you haven't thought this through."

"I can think of nothing else, Carmen." He slipped

both arms around her. "I'm teetering on the edge of right and wrong, but a man can't go wrong if a woman is in need of a hug." He tugged her flush against his chest.

Holy Mother of God. Her breasts pressed against a rock-hard chest. Without him realizing, he extended her needs far beyond a hug. Hell, she could write a list. Every one of her cells sucked in the comfort of his warm embrace. She'd gone so long without a man holding her. Muscles relaxed. Her mind cleared, and without hesitation, she slipped her arms around his waist to lock him in place. All her troubles over the past year evaporated. Enrico and his cronies could go to hell, because if possible, she'd stand here all day and relish James's marvelous scent. Right or wrong, she lowered her head to his shoulder.

Within minutes, his male hardness rose against her belly, and the pressure alone activated a strong yearning to see him naked. Would he take the embrace further, like inside the cabin? *Oh, yeah, I'm willing.*

"This is nice, Carmen."

Nice? Too mild a word.

A minute later, he released his arms. With both hands, he cupped her cheeks and tilted her head. His dark gaze scanned her mouth.

She licked her lips. "If you're waiting for my permission, you don't need it."

He smiled. "I'm marveling at the most beautiful woman I've ever seen." He lowered his lips to hers.

Dios mio. He tasted like heaven on earth, with lips soft and sensuous—and hungry. The kiss intensified. His tongue separated her lips and probed, and she responded with a probe of her own. He felt so damn right, and she'd be a fool to push him away. He created a pool of moisture in an area of her anatomy where the Sahara had formed. Nice to know the drought ended.

He lifted his head. "You taste good."

"So do you." She'd like to taste a lot more than his lips. Should she invite him into the cabin?

He raised her hands to his lips and kissed her knuckles. "I'm still on duty."

So much for asking him inside. Her saving grace. She needed time to analyze the sensations churning within her chest. Lust, she understood, but something else had surfaced. Shuddering at how close she came to dragging him to her bed, she buried her face against his chest. "I don't make a habit of jumping a man without a first date." Smiling, she looked up. "Our half-fast lunch doesn't count."

"Then, I'll make arrangements for a first date." Taking hold of her shoulders, he kissed her nose.

She rubbed her hip against the bulge in his trousers. "I hope you're not heading to the elementary school."

Lifting his face skyward, he laughed. "You're beautiful." He dropped his hands. "I'll check my duty schedule and give you a call."

As he drove away, she smiled. Her heart felt so light she almost skipped to the cabin, all the while watching the dust cloud created by the cruiser. Once on the porch, reality set in, and she frowned at the dust. "*Cuidado*, James."

The man dared to kiss Enrico's *wife*.

Chapter Ten

Carmen completed another round of yoga on the hearth rug to clear her mind of James's glorious lips. Not like any of the exercises helped. With every movement, she envisioned him stretching alongside with their heat combining into one. The wild thoughts gave her a workout beyond all others. Even the memory of his tongue touching hers ignited every square inch of her body. God help her in the heated throes of passion with skin-to-skin contact. Finished with the yoga, she stuck her head into the refrigerator to survey some dinner options. Since the coolness felt great against her hot cheeks, she took longer than usual contemplating her selection.

A soft tap on the cabin door jerked her from the fridge, and she whirled. She'd missed the footsteps on the porch. Had she gone deaf, or did someone sneak to her door to avoid detection? Heart racing like some runaway freight train, she shot a quick glance at the rooster clock above the stove. Three-fifty in the afternoon. When a second tap sounded, she debated whether to grab a knife from the kitchen drawer, but Enrico would never knock. He'd pound. The man loved to invoke fear. Sucking in a calming breath, she tiptoed toward the front window and peeked around the curtain.

Lucy stood alone by the door with hands gripping her backpack straps.

Releasing a breath, Carmen answered the door. "Lucy, hi. What a nice surprise. Want to come in?"

Lucy clutched the straps on her backpack. "No, thanks. Dad said I shouldn't enter anyone's cabin unless he's with me."

"Very wise words. What's up?" She leaned against the doorjamb.

"We're having a big soccer game tonight at the elementary school. Everyone's gonna go. Wanna come?" She chewed on her lower lip.

Mouth agape, Carmen had no idea how to respond. Did Lucy ask because the residents practiced some unwritten rule to involve guests in local activities, or was Lucy being friendly because she lived near the Mallotum cabin?

Lucy shifted on her feet. "I think you need the company."

What the... Feeling like a guppy with an open mouth, Carmen coughed and pushed away from the jamb. "What made you say that?"

"No one should be alone. And you look like you need a happy pill."

Still with the tight grip on her pack straps, Lucy crossed her feet at the ankles, her gaze shy but steady.

"A happy pill, huh?" Carmen couldn't contain her smile. This little girl was adorable and tugged on Carmen's heartstrings. Over the years, she'd met quite a few children adept at recognizing adult emotions and, all too often, found herself on the receiving end of their observations. Like now. No matter how high the walls, children clamored to knock them down. Chuckling, she stepped onto the porch. "Are you on the team?"

"Not this year. I broke my leg real bad before the

season started, but I'll be in the summer league. Can you come?"

She rocked on her ankles.

Wow. If Carmen crisscrossed her ankles like Lucy and attempted one iota of movement, she'd fall flat on her face. *Ah, the joys of youth.* She smiled. "I don't mind being alone, Lucy." At this stage of her life, she preferred isolation, but judging by the pleading look in Lucy's gaze, the girl had determination written all over her face. *Hmm.* Peering with one eye, Carmen folded her arms over her chest. "Did your father send you here?"

She shook her head. "I asked his permission. He said yes." She hefted her backpack.

"Oh, he did, eh?" How eagerly did he say yes? Carmen sighed. "I don't know anything about soccer, Lucy."

"I'll teach ya. Please? It'll be fun."

Wide, blue eyes scanned Carmen's face.

Dear Lord, what should she do? Half of her wanted to participate in life again while the other half considered the consequences. She was a woman with a large stone around her neck—namely Enrico.

"My dad will be there. He's on duty, though."

Great. If she agreed to attend the event, she'd sound as if her interest centered on James. With two fingers, Carmen pinched the bridge of her nose. Given another point in her life, she'd love to make new friends, but with Enrico nearby, he'd find a way to spoil any fun.

"Aw, come on, Carmen. You're too sad."

How in the world could she refuse such an earnest invitation? Wondering what the hell Lucy did to her brain cells, Carmen gave the little girl a lopsided grin. "All right, I'll come. What time?"

She stretched her lips into a big smile. "The game starts at six. We got lots of those big lights. So, look for me in the bleachers. I'll save ya a seat."

"Okay then. I'll meet you there."

Lucy flew off the porch and disappeared into the woods.

While closing the door, Carmen sighed. She must be out of her mind for agreeing. But she had to admit to an insatiable curiosity about this small mountain community. The people expressed a closeness so foreign to city slickers. Even though she grew up on a ranch, she transformed into the typical city dweller with head down and limited eye contact. After her divorce, she turned into an isolationist with hardly any social activities. Carefully constructed walls protected her heart, but one little girl and her handsome father forced an opening. Should she cut her losses and leave before the walls crumbled altogether?

She'd never been so indecisive. Yet, somewhere deep inside, the need to enjoy living reared its ugly head. She had a choice—mope around in the cabin or stop hiding. Not like she had plans for tonight. A soccer game with a bunch of friendly people might be the ticket to an enjoyable evening.

Five minutes before six o'clock, Carmen alighted from her car and scanned the huge crowd. Vehicles of all makes and models packed the school's parking lot. People milled about, talking and laughing. Parents chased after little ones who ran to make their great escape. At a guess, the entire mountain population was in attendance, plus supporters for the away team.

Before three food concession trucks, customers gathered for snow cones, hot dogs, and pork sandwiches, along with hot and cold drinks. Alongside the trucks sat several tables full of team memorabilia for sale—red and yellow Billings Mountain Bears flags, T-shirts, and pom-poms.

One young mother blotted an orange stain from a little boy's jacket while an elderly man stood nearby staring at a similar stain on his white shirt.

Chuckling, Carmen headed for the bleachers marked with a *Home Team* sign.

Bright overhead lights lit the playing field like daytime sunlight. Two teams—one in red jerseys and the other in blue—ran around the field while kicking soccer balls for warm up. Even though the game hadn't started, pom-poms waved from the bleachers on both sides. The sheriff's cruiser sat on the grass behind the home-team bleachers. James was nowhere in sight, but considering the size of the crowd, she could walk right by and miss him. Pausing before the steps, she sucked in a steadying breath.

She shouldn't be here. Enrico could be anywhere among this crowd, waiting for his opportunity to pounce. Despite warnings from the sheriff, her ex wouldn't drive halfway across the state to sit in a motel room. So many times, she wanted to cancel tonight and hibernate. *But I'm here now, and I don't want to disappoint a little girl.* Squaring her shoulders, she scanned the bleachers.

"Carmen, here I am!"

Lucy jumped onto the bench seat and waved two pom-poms overhead, her face sporting a bright smile.

The entire crowd, including Lucy, wore red so

Carmen's mauve jacket should suffice. Raising an arm overhead, Carmen acknowledged her with a wave, swallowed whatever stuck in her throat, and made her way toward the little girl.

Two sections of eight-tiered benches faced opposite each other with the field in between, neither quite filled to capacity yet. Most of the people accumulated in groups on the grass, some in lawn chairs and others standing. Excitement vibrated the air. Without question, this soccer game had rivalry written all over it. Midway along the row, Carmen joined Lucy on the third-tier bench.

Lucy hugged her. "I'm glad you came."

Surprised at the tight clutch around her middle, Carmen hugged back. "That's because you're here to teach me about the game." Lucy's hug relaxed every one of Carmen's muscles. For the first time in eons, she didn't give a damn if Enrico appeared. She came to enjoy the crowd and learn something about soccer.

Holding Carmen's arm, Lucy tugged her onto the bench. "I'll tell ya everything you need to know."

Carmen almost laughed. The girl was so cute. As with all children, the familiar love swelled within her chest. That love drove her to become a pediatrician, and she never regretted her decision. She scanned the area for James. "Is your dad on crowd control?" Aw, rats. She shouldn't have mentioned Lucy's father. The little imp might get ideas into her head.

"Dad and Harry are both here. Harry's on the other side. There's Dad!" She waved the pom-pom.

Following Lucy's gaze, Carmen caught sight of James standing by the scorekeeper's table near the sidelines. Several women circulated around him, eyeing him like a piece of choice steak.

He waved to Lucy but locked his gaze onto Carmen. A slow smile stretched his lips.

Carmen's breath hitched. The man was absolutely the best eye candy imaginable, and despite the women surrounding him, she couldn't look away—until he winked.

Lord Almighty. Heat flushed Carmen's cheeks. Why were the overhead lights so bright? Dropping her gaze, she cleared her throat.

Lucy nudged Carmen's side. "Dad likes you."

Resisting the urge to touch her hot cheeks, Carmen shot Lucy a one-eyed glare. "How would you know?"

She huffed. "I know my dad. He doesn't look at anyone like he looks at you." She pointed to her father. "See? He's not even paying attention to the women near him. You like him, too. I can tell. Your cheeks are all red."

Lucy's comment shot more heat up her neck. *Oh, dear Lord. Deliver me from observant children.* "My cheeks are red because it's cool out."

"Uh-huh."

At the adult-sounding tone of Lucy's voice, Carmen smiled. While her ego lifted a few notches with Lucy's words, Carmen recognized the caution seeping into her heart. Children latched onto someone far faster than an adult. They also experienced rejection harder. If Lucy got attached…

A loudspeaker blasted the national anthem, dispelling any further thoughts.

Everyone stood. After the song, the crowd cheered, and the referee's whistle signaled the start of the game.

Carmen hadn't been to a sporting event since high

school, and the crowd's enthusiasm awakened memories of linking arms with fellow classmates and kicking up her heels in the bleachers. College and med school had teams, but studies consumed her time, not to mention money remained in short supply. If she wasn't studying, she flipped burgers at a local sandwich shop.

Throughout the game, Lucy explained each player's position and the strategic importance in reaching the goal.

The little girl spoke like a professional commentator, and her knowledge impressed Carmen. The two teams consisted of both boys and girls in the age range of ten to twelve with the tallest designated as goalie. Carmen loved the boundless energy of children and always encouraged parents to get them outside into fresh air. Most of the time, her arguments fell on deaf ears, but hey, she tried.

"Having fun watching the little kiddies?"

Jerking from the warm breath on her neck, Carmen bristled at the familiar cigar stench. Only one man raised the hairs on her head—the one man who lived by his own rules and used money to put lawmen in his pocket. She scanned the sidelines for James, but he was nowhere in sight. Why didn't she have his cell number? If she called 911, she'd spoil everyone's fun. Lifting her chin, she whirled to face her ex.

The damn man sat with a cocky grin, even though his dark eyes showed the devil within. One month—one whole, damn month—since she saw him last. The bastard followed her right into the coffee shop and broke into the line to stand behind her. But he didn't scare her anymore. Yes, he was dangerous, and yes, he had a nasty habit of invading her space, but she couldn't live her life in fear. She wasn't built that way. If he wanted her dead, why here? Why not Richmond where his paid officers stood ready to respond? She shot him a hard glare. "The sheriff told me you were on the mountain."

He sneered. "You can't escape me, Carmen. You're my wife, and I won't let you go."

Gasping, Lucy twisted on the bench. "You're married?"

Taking Lucy's hand, Carmen squeezed. "No, honey, I am not."

Enrico tapped Lucy's shoulder. "See this ring, kid?" He pointed to the fourth finger on his left hand. "This is a wedding band. We're married, and don't let Carmen tell you otherwise."

Lucy's mouth gaped.

Now wasn't the time to explain Enrico's law-defying nature. What Carmen needed was to find James and have Enrico arrested for violating the restraining order. But where was James? Enrico wasn't stupid enough to cause a scene...unless James took the bribe. *Oh, God.* Her heart sank.

A person jostled Carmen's left side. Since Lucy hugged Carmen's right and the row beyond was full to capacity, she had nowhere to slide to make room. Gut tensing from the pressure against her shoulder, Carmen glanced to her left, ready to give the rude individual a piece of her mind.

Smiling, Henrietta from the check-in office patted Carmen's knee.

Enrico released a loud oomph—not once, but twice.

Curious, Carmen turned.

Marion from the cafe crowded Enrico's right side while a dark-haired woman squeezed against his left. Both women waved pom-poms in his face.

The man looked like a sardine in a can with arms unable to move. Carmen bit back a laugh.

The woman with the dark hair leaned toward Enrico. "We don't tolerate abusers on this mountain, Mr. Cruz, and we don't like our guests harassed."

Enrico placed a palm over his heart. "I don't abuse beautiful women."

"Your restraining order says otherwise," Henrietta stated.

He waved a hand. "Tut-tut. We're talking about a mere piece of paper." Sneering, he shifted his gaze from one woman to the other. "You ladies are hardly in a position to toss me off the mountain."

Marion jammed her shoulder against his. "We want you to leave peacefully and never return."

Enrico narrowed his gaze. "And if I don't?"

Holy Mother of God. Enrico might kill one of them right in front of the crowd. In his opinion, women were nothing more than ornaments to be displayed on the arm of a successful man. If he had his way, he'd cut out every woman's tongue. Carmen opened her mouth to speak when a big bear of a man rose behind Enrico.

With a tight grip on Enrico's jacket collar, the man hauled him off the seat. "You should have chosen peacefully."

The entire crowd on the bench either shifted position or stood as the bear dragged Enrico down the bleachers where James waited with a pair of dangling handcuffs.

Enrico let loose with a string of expletives then

followed with threats of lawsuits loud enough for everyone to hear.

As James slapped on the handcuffs, the big man growled into Enrico's face.

Enrico's brows shot halfway into his forehead, and his skin turned ashen.

For the first time ever, her ex cowered before another man. Wow. Definitely a sight for sore eyes.

Carmen sat in stunned silence. All around her, faces beamed like they did her a huge favor. She glanced from Henrietta to Marion and then to the small dark-haired woman.

All three stretched their lips into victorious grins.

Carmen shook herself. "What just happened?"

Henrietta squeezed Carmen's knee. "Solidarity, my dear. Plain and simple solidarity."

Three virtual strangers stuck out their necks to protect her from her miserable ex. Tears glistened her vision.

Lucy tugged her arm. "Are you gonna cry?"

"I'm overwhelmed." Damn, her voice cracked.

Henrietta gestured with a thumb over her shoulder. "Thank Marion. She told us about your ex's bold statement to everyone in the dining room, and since he continues to defy James, we went to bat for our sheriff, too."

Carmen watched James and the big man disappear behind the bleachers. "Who's the brave man who dragged him like a rag doll?"

The dark-haired woman leaned forward. "He's my husband, Charles, the owner of this mountain." She extended a hand. "I'm Doctor Alexandra Colter-Billings."

As she took the hand, Carmen smiled. "So, we meet at last."

"Alex is my bestest friend," Lucy declared and jumped up to give Alex a hug.

A slew of emotions choked Carmen, and she had difficulty taking a breath. After a few short days, she had more support from the people on this mountain than the entire year since her divorce. Even her colleagues feared Enrico's wrath. Their fear isolated Carmen, but the mountain women showed a solidarity that touched a dark corner of her heart and opened the vessel to sunshine. Damn, what a feeling.

Alex tapped Carmen's shoulder. "Henrietta tells me you're a pediatrician. I'd like to talk to you about your work. I have lots of questions."

Coughing and blinking to clear the moisture accumulating, Carmen nodded. "I'm sure we can meet before I leave."

Marion leaned over and hugged Carmen from behind. "I detested the bastard from the moment I met him. His bully tactics explain the sad look in your eyes."

"Which we hope to change right here and now," Henrietta said. "No more sadness while you're on this mountain. We won't allow it." She bumped Carmen's shoulder with her own. "Don't worry. James will lock your ex in a cell for violating the restraining order."

But not for long. Enrico paid some sleazy lawyers to be at his beck and call and never spent a day behind bars. Nothing would change because of the good people on this mountain. Once released, he'd be out for blood.

Chapter Eleven

Early the next morning, while sitting at his desk,
James cursed at the computer screen. The mountain had
excellent Internet speed, but for some reason, data
moved like molasses from the freezer. If he slapped the
keyboard any harder, he'd crack the crappy plastic into
a thousand pieces. Then, he'd spend the rest of the day
digging through the junk in the storeroom for a spare
keyboard. Maybe he should break the damn thing
anyway.

His deputy, Harry, peeked around his own screen.
"You had no control over the situation. How often do
we receive a call from a district judge?"

Growling, James slammed the Enter key on his
keyboard, half expecting the rectangle to pop out of its
hole. He shot a glare at Harry. "Two friggin' hours he
spent in jail. That's gotta be a record. The guy's lawyer
must have a phone glued to his ear." Pushing away
from the desk, he ran all ten fingers through his hair.
"Carmen warned me. She said her ex makes a mockery
of our justice system."

"At least, we have one restraining violation that
won't disappear."

He grunted. "Not from our computers, but I'll
make a bet the county records department denies
receiving it."

Frowning, Harry picked up his computer mouse

and shook it. "So, we'll send the report again and again. Even via snail mail where they have to sign the return receipt." He slammed the mouse onto the desk. "I think I need a new one of these."

If his aggravation level wasn't ready to blow his brain from his skull, James would have thought of his deputy's suggestion...eventually. He shot his deputy a half grin. "Not a bad idea, Harry."

Last night, Enrico Cruz laughed on his way out the door. James struggled with every ounce of self control not to knock out a few of the bastard's perfectly capped teeth. The man had a judge call. A damn judge! His small police department hadn't a chance in hell when a cocky citizen paid his way out of trouble.

Rising, Harry poured a cup of coffee from the carafe by the wall. "This time, Charles put down his foot. We should be grateful Cruz can't circumvent another wealthy man."

"Yeah, lucky for us."

Since Charles Billings owned the mountain, he could restrict access to anyone he pleased. His explicit orders—in writing—granted James and Harry the authority to keep Enrico Cruz off his property. A plus for Carmen...for now. When time to leave, she'd once again be at her ex's mercy, and he hadn't a clue how to help her. Flopping back in his chair, he dangled his arms over the armrests. "Harry, I need you to make sure I stay on the straight and narrow with this Cruz guy."

Harry sipped his coffee. "Don't know if I can when I'd like to take him into the woods and rough him up a little." Another sip. "All right, a lot. You have to promise to look the other way, though."

Look the other way. Like Cruz implied. *And that*

reminds me. James told Harry in detail about Cruz's earlier visit, his bribery attempt, and plans for Carmen's untimely death.

While listening, Harry's eyes grew wider behind his glasses.

When finished, James rubbed the back of his neck. "I'm sorry I sent you away. Turns out I needed a witness."

"I can't believe he tried something so brazen."

"Believe it. He'll dangle the greenbacks at you, too."

Harry squinted. "Now, I really want to rough him up."

"There's more." James rocked his chair. "Carmen said he has a PI following her. We should assume the guy is already here and snooping around."

With two fingers, Harry rubbed his forehead. Then, he met James's gaze. "How can we pinpoint a PI when strangers hike these woods every day?"

"If he knows which cabin she's in, he'll hang around its vicinity. Otherwise, he will frequent the cafe then follow her from there."

"You're saying *he*. Are you sure the PI is a male?"

James snorted. "Knowing Cruz, he'd never hire a woman. So, yes, a man. I already have a pretty good idea who he is." He stopped rocking. "I saw him at the cafe. Hispanic male, trimmed black hair, mustache, late forties, about five-foot-eleven, and stocky—like you, Harry." He grinned.

Harry Cartwright once owned the lone gas station on Billings Mountain. For years, he left his mechanic duties to assist James on police calls. With James's urging, Harry attended the police academy, and after graduation, he sold his garage and became a full-time employee. While small in stature at five-foot-six, he was built like a brick shithouse from years of repairing car engines. James couldn't ask for better backup.

Simultaneously, James's and Harry's shoulder mikes crackled to life. "Medical emergency at the Taylor residence. EMS dispatched."

Henrietta's calm, sultry voice was always a pleasure to hear, even in an emergency. He never told her how sexy she sounded over the radio. He clicked his shoulder mike. "Roger that. Harry's on the way." James frowned. "See what's wrong, and call if you need assistance."

"Will do." Harry gulped the last of his coffee and left.

He might as well dig into his paperwork. Not a whole lot accumulated with their small community. Minor incidents usually—a missing bicycle or a fender bender. Even theft was rare. Neighbor disputes happened, but if the quarrel continued, Charles settled all matters through arbitration.

Thirty minutes later, his cell phone rang. Caller ID showed Alex. "Hey, everything okay?"

"Think you can get Carmen for me? Tell her I have a four-year-old with an unusual problem."

"Sure. I'll see if she's in her cabin." Good. An excuse to visit the beautiful doctor. After last night's fiasco with Cruz, he hadn't a chance to return to the school. So, he missed the entire game.

Lucy relayed the highlights—which their team won.

He hopped into the cruiser and drove off.

Cruz definitely had connections. Last night, James

hardly finished the paperwork before Cruz sauntered out the door, a free man. Under different circumstances, he'd admire the asshole, but like any cop who followed the law, he fought the mounting frustration at all the loopholes in their justice system. He'd hate like hell to be a cop in a big city. Those poor bastards couldn't draw their gun without severe reprimands.

What the hell time was it anyway? A quick glance at the car's digital display showed close to ten o'clock. Carmen should be awake, right? He hated to disturb guests. They came to rest and enjoy themselves, and Carmen needed a little fun in her life. With Cruz banned from the mountain, at least Carmen would sleep better.

On the other hand, last night, he tossed and turned while his mind raced through all of Cruz's antics. Stalking laws helped victims only if enforced, and those laws had holes bigger than a shotgun blast. Gripping the steering wheel like it would fly out of his hand, he slowed the car and turned left onto Mallotum Drive.

Her white car stood bright in the morning sunlight. Relief swept through him. Not like he expected her to pack and run, but Marion told him of the tears rolling down Carmen's cheeks at the women's show of solidarity. Damn, he was proud of his neighbors.

Alighting, he glanced toward the cliff side bench. Empty. He prayed he wasn't about to wake her. With one stride across the porch, he knocked on the cabin door. As expected, the front window curtains fluttered.

The door swung open, and his heart thumped hard. Two words flashed into his mind—barefoot and beautiful. Dressed in jeans and T-shirt with long hair mussed, she smelled like fresh flowers on a warm summer day. Intoxicating as hell. She had the ability to erase any man's troubles.

She scanned him from head to toe. "Hi. What's up?"

An appendage that sprang to life the second he set eyes on her, that's what was up. He cleared his throat. "Alex needs you at the clinic for a four-year-old. Do you mind? I don't think she'd ask if she weren't stumped."

"Of course not." She waved him inside. "Let me put on my shoes and jacket."

He stepped in. Out of habit, he scanned the interior, smelled the toast and coffee, and noted the unmade bed. Visions of her in that bed turned X-rated. He diverted his gaze. "I'll drive."

Nodding, she dropped onto the sofa and slipped on a pair of socks and sneakers. "Did Alex say anything specific?"

"Unusual problem." Whatever that meant. Doctor speak, he guessed.

He didn't know what to do with his hands. A hat would be the perfect foil. He'd wring the rim to keep from grabbing her and kissing her senseless. With limited options, he stuffed his hands into his trouser pockets.

Carmen threw on her jacket. "Ready."

Yeah, well, so was he, but his mind traveled in a different direction—like lowering her onto those soft sofa cushions. *God, help me.*

****

Police cruisers certainly changed over the years. The last time Carmen rode in one was when she was twelve. A delivery truck ran over her bicycle, and she had no way to get home. For a little girl, the experience excited her. Now, as a grown woman, curiosity overtook excitement. A laptop computer sat on a bracket and faced James. A clipboard with a pen on a string rested in a leather pouch, ready to grab. Extra battery packs, metal paper clips, and a selection of pens cluttered the open console.

"I'm glad you didn't pack and leave."

The man's voice sent chills down her spine, and she closed her eyes to let the sensation roll over her. He should learn to sing. Women would fall at his feet faster than raindrops. Opening her eyes, Carmen rotated her head. "Because of Enrico? No way. You and everyone here are filling me with a sense of awe."

More than awe. Carmen still couldn't comprehend the warmth of so many strangers. Nice people existed, and Billings Mountain proved it.

One such individual sat right next to her in the cruiser with his earthy aftershave swirling within the cabin. This handsome man caused wonderful sensations to fill her chest, and not because of his intoxicating smell. Where men were concerned, she used caution, but Lucy and three women broke through the barriers and forced her to look at James beyond the badge. She liked what she saw. She almost hated the thought of leaving.

Arriving at the clinic, Carmen thanked James and alighted from the vehicle. When she closed the car door, she expected him to be on his way.

But he hopped out and smiled.

She lifted a brow. "You're coming in?"

"Sure. I want to see the doctor in action."

With any other cop, those words would bother her,

but judging from the attitudes of the mountain residents, James was a straight arrow. She returned the smile. "All right, then. In we go."

Once inside the small emergency room, she stopped. The facility gleamed with state-of-the-art equipment and every conceivable necessity to care for a patient—from intubation apparatus to digital monitors. Even a portable X-ray machine was tucked into the corner, and those machines cost a pretty penny. The four stretchers were the latest in design with foot levers to flatten or raise the bed in seconds. She hadn't expected to enter such a well-stocked facility.

She zeroed in on the four-year-old boy sleeping on one of the beds.

An elderly woman fidgeted on a nearby chair, dabbing a tissue to red, swollen eyes.

No monitor hook-up on the child, which wasn't a surprise. Given a chance, children yanked leads, IV lines, and pretty much anything connected to their bodies. They also verbalized their dislike by screaming off their little heads.

A nurse, sitting at a small desk, stood while raising a finger in a wait gesture, and hurried through a door beyond the beds.

James leaned close. "I'll wait here."

Nodding, she approached the boy's bed.

Alex appeared. On meeting Carmen's gaze, she smiled. "Hi, thanks for coming. This here is Becca, my right hand." She gestured to the red-headed nurse to her left. "I hate bothering you, but visiting pediatricians are a rare breed on the mountain." She stopped alongside the old woman in the chair and rested a hand on the woman's shoulder. "This is Maggie Taylor, Joey's grandmother. She watches him while her son and daughter-in-law work. The parents have been notified. I told them to stay put until I talked to you." Reaching behind the boy's stretcher, she handed Carmen a clipboard. "Joey ate an entire bottle of Vitamin D gummy tablets."

The grandmother dabbed her nose with the tissue. "I just bought the bottle. Didn't even tear off the cellophane."

Taking the clipboard, Carmen chuckled. "Never underestimate the determination of a child and the challenge of child-proof packaging." She glanced between Alex and the grandmother. "I see this sort of thing at least once a week. All these chewable tabs look and taste like candy and are totally irresistible to a child." She read through the information on the clipboard. Two hundred gummy tablets each containing one thousand international units of Vitamin D plus five hundred milligrams calcium. Blood pressure elevated, heart rate accelerated, dehydration, and vomiting upon arrival. As expected, the child's calcium level was off the chart. She cocked a brow at Alex. "May I?"

"By all means."

Carmen turned to the red-headed nurse. "Let's get a line in him and start with furosemide to lower his BP." She turned to Alex. "Do you have calcitonin?"

Alex shook her head. "It's not a medication we stock, but I'll make a phone call and have some delivered in an hour."

"Helicopter?"

Alex grinned. "You bet."

"Okay. Place an order for an IV drip, and I'll start his line."

While Becca laid out the paraphernalia for the IV, Carmen patted the grandmother's frail shoulder. "Your grandson will be fine once the proper medication arrives. This particular drug will knock his calcium level to a more manageable level. After that, he'll stay on a low calcium diet until his blood work looks good."

The old woman sniffed. "I'm so glad you're here."

"Oh, Doctor Colter could have handled him." She shot Alex a one-eyed glare.

With her cell phone to her ear, Alex winked.

Sneaky little devil. A phone call to any pediatric hotline would give Alex an answer. Smiling, Carmen shook her head. She turned to the nurse. "Joey's lethargic, but as soon as I insert a needle, he'll be hell-bent on getting away. Let's wrap him tight in a sheet with his left arm exposed."

She loved her profession. As a partner in one of Richmond's biggest pediatric practices, she worked with children every day, and not a second passed when her heart didn't tug to create offspring of her own. At thirty-six and single, she had entered the time in her life when conceiving a child took medical intervention—unless she was lucky to be fertile into her forties. Judging from her choice in marriage material, luck wasn't something she had in abundance. With Enrico still in the picture, any chance for male companionship put her and her beau in a dangerous situation...even a mountain sheriff.

****

James stood off to the side, thoroughly enjoying the vision of a woman confident with her chosen field. Carmen was so damn easy on the eyes. Even her voice sent chills straight up his spine. Evidently, she had the same effect on her patient. As she crooned to the boy, the little guy hardly fussed and stared at Carmen's face. Before he knew what hit him, the boy had an IV line inserted and secured.

I know how you feel, pal. James couldn't shift his gaze from Carmen either. For some strange reason, a sense of pride swelled within his chest. Damned if he understood why. He had no claim on her, but deep down, he liked Carmen. She intrigued him, and no woman—visitor or resident—activated a yearning for a permanent mate. *I'm a goner.* He chuckled to himself.

While slipping her phone into her lab coat pocket, Alex strolled to his side. "The copter will be here in forty minutes."

He checked his watch. "I'll run to the field. Should I have the copter wait in case you need to fly Joey to a hospital?" Getting no answer, he nudged Alex, whose face beamed as she watched Carmen. "You never needed her help, did you?"

Grinning, she stuffed her hands into her coat pockets. "Call this tactic an evaluation. And no, let the copter go." Receiving a furtive Okay sign from Becca who worked alongside Carmen, Alex winked in return. "I'd love to have a pediatrician on staff. Look how she inserted the IV and calmed the boy."

"Don't belittle yourself. You're damn good."

"Thanks, but I have little pedie experience. I took a few courses in Roanoke before I opened the clinic, but I can't call myself an expert." She sighed. "She'd be a great addition to my staff."

Gaze narrowed, he pursed his lips. "What do you have up your sleeve, woman?"

"Oh, you know, if you and she…"

"Uh-huh. I'm stuck in the middle of a feud, remember?"

She faced him. "And speaking of the jackass, I heard he's out. The speed even surprised Charles." She jerked a nod in Carmen's direction. "Does she know?"

He shot a quick glance toward Carmen to see if she overheard, but she was busy talking to the grandmother. "Only if she's been to the cafe. Marion hears everything."

"Not to mention how Harry stops in several times a day. I'm glad Charles restricted Enrico's access." She joined Carmen at the boy's bedside.

For what good restrictions would do. Other than posting sentry guards at the base of the mountain, James would have no other option but to charge Cruz with trespassing. Big deal, a misdemeanor.

After rechecking his watch, James headed for the door. "Be right back, ladies."

He needed a reprieve. Watching two beautiful doctors head-to-head stirred all his dormant hormones. And Becca wasn't bad looking either. Before stepping into the cruiser, he sucked in a deep breath of the cool mountain air.

Over the years, a lot of residents pushed a woman his way and waited for sparks to fly. Nothing ever happened. Sure, he dated but never took a woman to bed. He used Lucy as an excuse, and to be honest, she meant everything to him now. After her mother died, she lived with Henrietta because he wasn't man enough to admit Lucy was his. Alex, being an astute physician, uncovered the truth and convinced him to accept his responsibility. By that time, Lucy was six. So, he threw his bachelor life to the winds and gave the girl a permanent place in his heart and home.

For the first time, Carmen forced him to question his self-imposed single fatherhood. He couldn't shake the woman out of his head. What to do with her ex played in the back of his mind. Men like Cruz believed themselves all-powerful. In truth, James thought Carmen exaggerated about his connections. But when a judge ordered his release, reality slapped James's face. What the hell was he supposed to do, pat Cruz on the wrist and say, be a good little boy? Hitting the gas, he took off for the elementary school.

At the end of her two-week stay, Carmen would once again be vulnerable to Enrico's machinations. Somewhere along the way, Enrico could succeed with Carmen's accident. What the hell could a small-town cop do? His jurisdiction ended at the Billings' boundary line, which was the county highway at the base of the mountain. He had a few friends in the state police and some stationed in the valley, but how could he trust them to stay on the straight and narrow? *What a damn dilemma.*

Pulling to a stop near the helipad, he jumped out and popped the hatchback while the sounds of the helicopter vibrated the air. Dragging a box from the back of the trunk, he dug through the necessities for a red smoke flare, ignited the flame, then placed the stem in its holder on the helipad corner. The pilot had a good day for flying with calm winds, but the smoke always made for a safer landing.

Seconds later, the helicopter flew over the trees and began its descent.

After fifteen minutes, with medicine in hand, James returned to the clinic and handed the packet to

Becca.

Carmen glanced over her shoulder and flashed him a smile.

Her brown eyes glowed, and his breath hitched. Damn, she tied his gut into knots. Sad to say, he enjoyed every second.

After a brief conversation with Alex, she shook hands with both Alex and Mrs. Taylor then squeezed Becca's arm.

Until this second, he hadn't noticed how graceful Carmen moved. Fluid would be a good word with no exaggerated sway of her hips, despite long legs. If she dressed to the nines, she'd melt him into a puddle of goo.

"Can you drive me to the cabin?"

Her words broke his trance. Like she had to ask. "Absolutely." The one word nearly stuck in his throat. He coughed.

"If Joey doesn't respond to the medication, I told Alex to call. She'll know in about an hour."

He waited for Carmen to settle onto the seat before closing her door and hurrying to the driver's side. After fastening his seatbelt, he started the ignition. "You must love kids to do this kind of work." He pulled onto the roadway.

"I do." She gazed out the side window. "Funny how you think your life is moving at a nice even pace, and all of a sudden, you're in a free fall." She shifted her gaze forward. "I fell for Enrico's big-family speech like a sap." Sucking in a deep breath, she rotated on the seat. "Lucy's a darling child, James. Did you ever want more children?"

Nodding, he rounded a curve. "Next time, I'll do it

right, like marry first."

"You don't want to wait too long. Otherwise, you'll need a walker to attend a college graduation." Chuckling, she tugged on her jacket. "Becca's interested."

He shot her a glance. "How do you know?"

"She asked if you and I were an item."

"And your response?"

Straightening in the seat, she pulled the seatbelt away from her neck. "I'm a woman with too much baggage, and you deserve better."

Talk about baggage. Now was as good a time as any. Before rounding the next curve, he gripped the steering wheel. "Enrico's out."

She grunted. "I'm not surprised."

"Since Billings Mountain is private property, Charles issued orders to keep him off the mountain."

She fussed with her seatbelt. "No one gives orders to Enrico. He'll defy you and Charles. You'll throw him in jail. He'll make his phone call, and you'll have no choice but to release him. Even if you do keep him out, he'll have his PI reporting."

The woman lived with constant fear hanging over her head. Lucy's mother lived that way, and he was powerless to help her.

"How does a man own an entire mountain, James?"

Grateful for the subject change, he loosened his grip on the wheel. "Way back in the 1800s, the Billings family ran a mining and lumber operation and amassed a fortune. Several generations later, with mining depleted and lumber too arduous, the family invested in the stock market and tripled their money. Charles is rich, but he still walks around in jeans and flannel shirt.

With Charles's mega bank account, Alex could stay home all day with the kids, but she loves being a doctor, and we needed one. Before Alex arrived, we believed Charles would be the last of the Billings. In short order, he produced two heirs, and I don't think they're done."

She laughed. "A fairy tale romance. I love it."

Her laughter was like music to his ears. She deserved so much happiness. He cleared his throat. "Ever since Alex opened the clinic, she's done her best to entice other doctors to join. As our sole doctor, she has no relief and is on call 24/7. When she had her babies, she relayed orders to Becca who, I might add, is very capable. For assistance with surgical procedures, she calls a nurse anesthetist in the valley."

He turned onto the Mallotum drive and stopped alongside her car. After killing the ignition, he looked her way. "What are your plans for the rest of your stay?"

She released her seatbelt and faced him. "I'll spend the time relaxing, knowing you and Harry are on the lookout for Enrico." Without waiting, she alighted.

Her confidence in his small police department stoked his ego, but who would help her once she left? *If she left*. The germ of the possibility took root in his brain. In his haste to get out of the car, he fumbled with his seatbelt and hurried to catch up. "I worry about you."

Turning, she arched her brows with a flutter.

Hadn't anyone ever said those words before, or had she struggled on her own for too long with a madman always two steps behind?

Gaze soft, she placed both hands on his cheeks.

"You are a wonderful man, James. You restored my faith in law enforcement."

His ego swelled, and somewhere along the way, his chest puffed. He took her chin in his hand. "How about men in general?"

Oh so slowly, she wrapped her arms around his neck and kissed him.

Having a need for her to be even closer, he wrapped his arms around her waist and deepened the kiss. Heat flushed from his core and traveled through every cell in his body. With her so close, smelling of flowers, tasting like toast and jam, and feeling so soft in his arms, hell, he wanted a bed—a really big bed. The shoulder mike crackled. "Sheriff?"

James groaned into Carmen's mouth and broke their lip-lock. "I'm still on duty." Loosening his hold, he clicked his mike. "Yes, Harry?"

"I blew a fan belt, and I'm due to stand-by for cable repair by Smitty's place."

Sometimes, he cursed the narrow mountain road. A cable truck meant another traffic hazard. "All right. I'll head to Smitty's. Is Jenkins giving you a hand?"

"Yeah, he's on the way with the tow truck."

"Good. Keep me advised."

Giving Carmen one more squeeze, he rested his forehead against hers. "You make me feel good."

She kissed his nose. "You make me feel safe."

He gazed at her swollen lips. This woman ignited a desire he hadn't felt in years. Carmen had to stay on this mountain, and by golly, he would find a way. "Come over for dinner tonight."

Without loosening her arms, she drew back, brows high. "You're serious?"

"Of course. I'll throw together something. Nothing special. Just the three of us."

She gaped then bit her lower lip. "Wow. I don't know, James."

"Do you have other plans?"

She laughed. "Not a one. Okay then. What time?"

"Six." He might be making the biggest mistake in his life, but he enjoyed every second with her. Even at the risk of getting burned, come hell or high water, he'd deal with the scars later.

Chapter Twelve

I'm officially out of my ever-loving mind. Carmen slapped her forehead like she'd knock some sense into her brain. Why did she agree to dinner with James and his daughter? Was she so desperate for her own family that she set up herself for disaster? One catastrophe in a lifetime was enough, thank you—namely marriage to the wrong man. She debated canceling, but Lucy already called, full of excitement. The girl gave directions—twice, as if Carmen couldn't follow the path in front of the cabin to the next house. She chuckled at the thought.

After grabbing the flashlight from the kitchen drawer and checking for brightness, she stuffed the device into her jacket pocket, locked the cabin door, and followed the worn track in front of her cabin—the path to James's place. *Oh, God, help me.*

Why couldn't the people on this mountain be a bunch of isolationists? No, they had to be wonderful, outgoing people who welcomed strangers with open arms. In a few short days, Lucy, Henrietta, Marion, and Alex embraced her like she was some long-lost cousin. And James...well, he had a different reason to stop by. Legal capacity or not, she enjoyed his visits. Probably why she agreed to dinner. *Stupid, stupid, stupid.*

Since the sun wouldn't set for another two hours, she had enough light to see her way through the trees.

The scents of forsythia and pine wafted through the forest, and she sucked in a large breath. The pine she understood since her feet crunched a blanket of needles along the footpath. The forsythias, however… Looking in all directions, she spotted nothing yellow to indicate a blooming plant.

A short distance later, the path opened into a large clearing where a cute log cabin stood. There, she spotted the source of the elusive flower scent. Surrounding the front porch, blossoming yellow forsythias brightened the entire clearing and created a stunning accent against the brown of the house logs. She smiled.

The cabin was medium in size, a rancher in style, and built high off the ground with four wooden steps leading onto a full-length porch. A child's pink bicycle rested against one of the wooden posts—a mountain bike by the look of the tires. James's cruiser sat close to the cabin, tail in first. No garage, but a sizable shed stood tucked into the trees with a wood pile alongside.

Single fatherhood, especially for a cop, presented a load of challenges. First and foremost, what became of Lucy when an emergency arose in the middle of the night? An eleven-year-old was a trifle too young to be left alone. Sucking in a calming breath, she climbed the steps.

Before her foot hit the porch deck, the front door flew open.

Wearing a big smile, Lucy stood behind the screen door and bounced on her toes. "Carmen's here! Hi, Carmen. Dad's almost ready, and I'm starved."

Like earlier, Lucy gushed the words in one breath and then waved in Carmen like a fire trailed behind her.

Her open, unassuming nature could cure anyone's surly mood, and the girl tugged on Carmen's heartstrings. Chuckling, Carmen entered the cabin.

A rustic-styled living room stretched before her, complete with an overstuffed sofa, large screen TV, and a beautiful stone fireplace. In front of the sofa, an oval throw rug covered the wooden floor, but the rest of the floor had a distressed look with some spots more worn than others. The cabin wasn't new by any stretch of the imagination. Although, to be honest, she hadn't a clue how a structure aged when sitting in the middle of the woods.

Several framed photos of Lucy occupied the space on the fireplace mantel, the majority of her in a red sport uniform, but nothing hung on the pine-paneled walls except for a gold-plated clock. Aside from the curtains covering the front windows, the room—while clean and well-maintained—lacked a woman's touch. No pillows for accent, no plants or flowers, and in truth, no bright colors to offset the browns dominating the room. Carmen stood in a true bachelor's home who so happened to have a daughter.

After tossing Carmen's jacket onto a living room chair, Lucy led the way through an archway, which opened into a wide kitchen.

Standing at the stove while stirring a big pot, James glanced over his shoulder and smiled. "We're having chili, my specialty. Hope you're hungry."

"I'm always hungry for chili." She felt awkward coming empty-handed, but he said nothing fancy. Besides, where would she buy something appropriate on short notice? She hadn't thought to run to the general store before it closed for the day. She hadn't worn anything special either—her regular blue jeans and sweatshirt. Approaching the stove, she sniffed. "Smells good. Can I do anything?"

"Nope, not a thing." Using a spoon, he tasted his concoction. Then, without measuring, he dumped in more chili powder.

Oh dear. She might need a ton of antacids tonight. She took a good look around the kitchen.

Avocado appliances told of a room in need of an upgrade. Several linoleum tiles had corners chipped out, and the pattern was barely detectable from years of scrubbing. A four-chair dinette table sat in the corner near large French doors opening onto a wooden deck with a spectacular view of the valley. The scene stretched for miles—just like from her bench, but here, the deck's overhang framed the picture like a canvas. Walking over, she gasped at the sight. "James, this view is beautiful."

"Thank you. My parents built this cabin and positioned it perfectly to catch the sunrise. I often stand outside with my coffee."

"I don't blame you." Looking to the left, she spotted a plastic table with four chairs and beyond that, a barbecue grill. "How are the winters here?" She turned away from the doors.

He placed his spoon on a holder. "For the most part, mild. Fog is our biggest problem. When the mist rolls in, hikers find themselves disoriented and often get lost."

Lucy hopped onto a chair and leaned across the table. "I broke my leg on ice last year. Alex fixed me."

Smiling, Carmen meandered toward the table. "From what I see, Alex did a good job." Still smiling, she faced James and met an intense gaze, one every woman recognized—full of heat. Her smile slipped, and she shifted her gaze to his lips. God help her. Drifting lower, she took in the muscles showing through a black T-shirt. Before she did something she'd regret, she stuffed her hands into her jeans front pockets and tried her best to appear nonchalant. "How about air conditioners? Do you need them?" She needed one now, but hey…

Chuckling, he switched off the burner. "Normally, no. The woods keep us cool." He handed Carmen a serrated knife. "How about cutting the bread?"

"Sure." Anything to keep her mind off his tight jeans. The man had a nice tush. She took the knife. "Got a board?"

Lucy jumped from the chair and grabbed a wooden cutting board from the counter. "The bread's from Mrs. O'Reilly. She makes all kinds."

"Yum. Bread is my absolute favorite. Homemade is even better." She could make an entire meal with bread as a main course. Plain—no butter, no cutting. She'd simply rip off a piece and indulge.

"Okay, we're ready." With the pot in hand, James turned to the table and ladled chili into the bowls already on the table. "Lucy, get the sour cream and shredded cheese from the fridge." He replaced the pot on the stove. "Carmen, what would you like to drink? I'm having beer."

"Beer sounds good." Finished with the bread, she placed the knife by the kitchen sink.

Unsure of where to sit, Carmen waited until Lucy tugged her onto the chair opposite James. Carmen didn't know what was worse, facing James or sitting beside him. Either way, she'd be hyper-aware of his close proximity.

"Okay, I think we have everything." James flopped onto a chair then nodded toward Lucy.

Lucy said a simple prayer of thanks.

At the softness of the little girl's voice, something gripped Carmen's heart. She'd gone a long time without sitting at a family meal—two years last Christmas, in fact. The casual conversation between James and his daughter conjured images of home with family gathered around the table. Because of her busy practice, she rarely scheduled a trip to see her parents, and she had no one to blame but herself. Fighting a wave of sadness, she dug into her meal.

The chili was on par with her father's—hot, hot, hot. Thank God for cold beer. Lucy ate two helpings, not in the least bothered with the heat buildup about to explode her intestines. Carmen preferred filling the rest of her stomach with the delicious homemade bread.

After cleanup, she followed James and Lucy into the living room.

"Can we watch a movie, Dad?"

James caught Carmen's gaze. "What do you say? Have you had enough of our company?"

What a question! She cherished every second. Rather than admit the comfort he instilled, she gave a half shrug. "I've nothing planned tonight." She faced Lucy. "What's on the billboard?"

Lucy shot her brows halfway into her hairline. "What's a billboard?"

Oops. Carmen just showed her age. She chuckled. "A list of movies."

"Okay. How about *Stones of the Jungle*? It's my

favorite."

James rolled his eyes. "I've seen this movie a hundred times."

A children's classic, full of songs and mayhem. Carmen laughed. "Then, I guess you're seeing it again."

She settled on the sofa—James at one end, her at the other, with Lucy in between. Carmen wasn't interested in the movie. She'd rather watch James. He watched her back with a gaze like a slow caress. Heat traveled the length of her neck, and she fought the urge to tear off her sweatshirt. Where was a fan when a woman needed one?

Lucy elbowed Carmen's side. "Sing with me."

Huh? Oh, the movie. Gaze-lock broken, she stroked Lucy's hair and smiled. "You're doing a fine job, honey." Even if the girl sang off-key. So funny.

When the final credits flashed onto the screen, James stood. "All right, Lucy. Time for bed. Say goodnight to our guest."

After a tight good-bye hug, Lucy disappeared down a hallway.

Not wanting to overstay her welcome, Carmen retrieved her jacket from the side chair.

"I'm glad you came." He helped her with the jacket.

"I'm glad you invited me. It's been fun." And stimulating. Nice to know a man's gaze still activated her dormant hormones.

He followed her onto the porch. "I'll walk you to your side of the woods."

"No, you won't. I'll be fine. I've my flashlight." Removing the light from her pocket, she flashed the beam across the clearing. Holy cow! Blacker than black. She clicked the Off switch. "What do you do with Lucy when a call drags you out in the middle of the night?"

He rubbed the nape of his neck. "Late-night runs don't happen too often, but if Harry can't handle it alone, I have a grab bag in the closet with some of Lucy's things. Then, I take her to Mrs. O'Reilly. She lives in the next house above us." He took her by the shoulders and turned her to face him. "If you don't mind, I don't want to discuss Lucy."

Arms wrapping her in an embrace, he lowered his lips, and she met him halfway. She tasted chili and beer. Not a bad combination—tantalizing and a bit tangy. She slipped both palms onto his chest, and his muscles rippled beneath her fingers. *Dios mio.* She wanted more and slid her hands to his neck to deepen the kiss. Tongues danced and explored. She almost dragged him into the woods to have her way with him. Lifting her head, she gazed into a pair of sparkling blue eyes. "I had a wonderful time."

"I'd like it to be better." Loosening his hold, he rested his forehead against hers. "I wanted to kiss you from the moment you entered the kitchen. I'm almost sorry the night has to end."

"Don't you dare apologize for being a great dad." Patting his chest, she stepped from his arms. The cool night air hit like a freezer blast, even through her jacket.

He stuffed his hands into his jeans' back pockets. "I should walk you. Enrico might not be on the mountain, but the PI probably is."

A warm, fuzzy feeling filled her chest. When was the last time a man worried about her safety? Smiling, she stroked his cheek. "I'll be fine. After a whole year of being followed, I never once saw the man. I don't expect him to break his pattern."

Nodding, he released a long breath. "All right. Call me when you lock yourself inside the cabin. If I don't hear from you in five minutes, I'll come running."

She flashed him a wry grin. "Now that, Sheriff, is a tempting offer. I might forget to call."

Giving him a quick peck on his lips, she descended the steps and whirled to give him a wave. His pants had a noticeable bulge in the zipper area. Too bad she couldn't ease his urge, but her pride sure swelled.

****

After checking the time on his watch, James followed the glow of her light until it disappeared within the trees. As a Southern gentleman, he'd insist on walking her to her door, but with Lucy alone in the house, he shoved his manners onto a back burner. The pedophile from the other day reminded everyone on the mountain of the dangerous world beyond their boundaries. If anything happened to his little girl...no, mustn't spoil the mood of a wonderful evening. He jammed a hand into his hair and tugged.

He had to admit Carmen forced him to think about his static lifestyle—like maybe he should look for a wife and give Lucy the mother she always wanted. The women on the mountain were willing, but really, ever since Carmen entered the picture, no one else would do. Should he ask her to extend her stay? Would she even consider such a suggestion?

At the five-minute mark, he reached for his cell just as the device rang. "I almost sent up a flare."

She chuckled. "I'm in."

Her sexy chuckle flushed him with a warmth he

hadn't felt in years. He shook himself. "And you checked around first, right? No one hiding in the bathroom?"

"All clear. Thank you for a lovely evening."

"I wouldn't mind doing it again."

Silence.

"We'll see. Good night, James."

He disconnected and stared at his phone. The woman was too beautiful to let go, but how could he convince her to stay?

"I really like her, Dad."

Lucy stood behind the screen door in her pajamas.

He entered the house and closed the door. "She is special, isn't she?"

"You never invited anyone else to dinner. I'd say it's about time."

Yeah, his little matchmaker. He couldn't blame her. Losing her mother at the age of two didn't allow for an accumulation of pleasant memories. With two hands, he nudged her shoulders. "You're up way too late for a school night. Off you go. Want me to read you a bedtime story?"

She smacked her lips. "Gosh, Dad, how old do you think I am? I can read to myself, you know."

Yes, his little girl was changing. Soon, she'd be on dates, and he'd pop antacids like candy. Over the years, Alex and Mrs. O'Reilly helped with Lucy's hair, but God help him on the day when Lucy asked to wear nylons and put on makeup. And what about that thing called a training bra? What in the world would he do then? Just thinking about the challenges ahead gave him a headache. If, by chance, a delayed growth pill was invented, he'd stick it in her hamburgers.

Chapter Thirteen

Carmen tossed and turned all night. She couldn't blame the bed since the mattress was beyond comfortable, nor could she blame the chili. After what felt like hours, she drifted into slumber. Dreams of passionate kisses filled her mind and drove her to the brink of climax. She awakened with a gasp and a smile. Never in her life had she dreamt of something so erotic. In truth, James's soft lips seared the very depths of her soul. His warm embrace, the touch of his hand, and even the caress of his gaze forced her to wonder what the hell she'd been missing all her life. If she wasn't careful, she'd fall for that handsome sheriff and live to regret it.

At the crack of dawn, she stepped under a cold shower, but all the water accomplished was to give her shivers, because boy, the mountain water flowed straight from a freezer. Since a shower failed to clear her mind, a brisk walk through the woods could do the trick. Determined to get a grip on her emotions, she ate a quick breakfast, tied on her hiking boots, and threw on her canvas jacket. As an afterthought, she slipped a bottle of water into her pocket and also her phone.

She headed for the main road until coming to a well-worn footpath leading up the mountain. Since she hadn't explored much beyond her cabin, she turned left and headed uphill.

Well, okay, a brisk ascent on uneven ground wasn't a great idea for someone who did little more than yoga. Slightly breathless and with heart pounding, she unzipped her jacket to allow cool air to hit her body and slowed her pace. Besides, an easygoing walk was a nicer way to take in the various colors of rhododendrons. Not all the flowers were in full bloom. She saw peeps of yellow and purple and even some white. Nearing an overlook, she paused to study the horizon. She stood much higher than her cabin's view and faced more northwest. Deciding this was a wonderful place for a break, she sat on the stone parapet, took a large swallow of water, and then sucked in the crisp mountain air.

The scenery was unbelievably serene. She could sit for hours with the beauty of so much green surrounding her. Off in the distance, cities sprouted above the trees, and even farther, an interstate highway cut through the landscape with heavy truck traffic heading north or south.

After finishing her water, she checked her watch. Holy smokes, lunch passed hours ago, and her breakfast was a simple piece of toast washed down with pineapple juice. No wonder her stomach sounded as if she swallowed a lion. She hopped from the parapet and started her descent. To complete her day, she'd make a pit stop at the cabin and then go to the cafe for an early dinner. She could eat a horse. But as she turned onto Mallotum Drive and approached the cabin, she slowed.

Lucy sat slumped on the porch with her cheeks in her hands. The crunch of stones drew her gaze, and she lifted her head and smiled.

Carmen stopped at the step. "Hi. This is a nice

surprise. To what do I owe the pleasure?"

Scrunching her face, Lucy huffed. "Evan Thompson invited me to the dance."

"Okay." Not the typical reaction from most young girls. Usually, a girl bubbled with excitement from a boy's attention. She sat alongside. "Is that bad?"

Lucy hugged her knees. "I didn't tell my dad yet. Evan only asked me at recess this afternoon."

Hmm. Something more serious was going on. Stretching her long legs over the step, Carmen leaned back on her hands. "First date?"

"Yeah."

"Will your dad approve?"

She shrugged her small shoulders. "Evan's twelve. I think he's always liked me."

Which didn't answer the question. Carmen studied her. "So, what's the problem?"

"It's our Earth Day Dance."

Geez. Like pulling teeth. She sat forward. "What's that mean?"

Lucy rocked back and forth. "We dress up a little more. No jeans and stuff." Frowning, she dropped her chin onto her knees. "I need a dress and new shoes. I don't fit in my old clothes anymore."

Ah, and herein laid the reason for her funky mood. Carmen remembered those days. Like the time she was thirteen when her favorite dress broke a few stitches across her chest. Convinced she'd never find another dress as pretty, she cried for hours. Her mother proved her wrong. She nudged Lucy's elbow. "I'm sure your father will take you shopping."

"But he's a man. I need a mother to help me."

"Oh." Her heart ached for Lucy. While not unusual

for a father to raise a daughter, every little girl wanted a mother, like every little boy longed for a father. "How about Alex? I'm sure she'll take you shopping."

"She has to stay on the mountain for some scheduled surgery." Shooting a sideways glance, she shuffled her feet. "She suggested I ask you."

"Me?" *Alex, you conniving little matchmaker.* Carmen almost laughed. Instead, she coughed. "Honey, I'm a visitor here. You should go with a woman you and your father know."

Face bright, she clamped onto Carmen's arm. "We know you."

Oh dear, now what? "But I don't know my way around." Somehow, she had the feeling she'd lose this argument. Probably because the idea of shopping with Lucy appealed more than she cared to admit. She always dreamed of a daughter to dress in frilly clothes and watch her turn into a young lady—unfulfilled dreams from a lifetime ago.

"We can get directions. Please, Carmen? I know." Releasing Carmen's arm, she snapped her fingers, but no sound emerged. "You should come to the dance and be Dad's date. Then, we can both buy dresses."

Unable to contain herself any longer, Carmen burst into laughter. What a precocious child! And so adorable. She wrapped an arm around the girl's shoulder and squeezed. "Your dad might already have a date, Lucy."

"Nah, he never does. He takes me to the dances then stands around like some chump on a log." Brows drawn tight, she pounded a fist into an open palm. "He needs to get serious if I'm ever to have a mother."

Carmen chuckled at Lucy's chump-on-a-log

167

comment. The words were different, but the analogy fit a lot of men. "Lucy, it isn't your responsibility to find your father a date. A man must ask a woman himself."

"Like Evan asked me? Yeah, I get it. But Dad won't. He never does." She again plunked her chin onto her knees. "He said he'll date when I go off to college. I won't need a mother then."

According to James, Lucy lost her mother at the age of two. In nine years, James hadn't dated? But he kissed like he had so much practice. She shook herself and tapped Lucy on the shoulder. "Tell you what. If your dad gives me permission, I'll take you shopping."

Her head shot up, and she whirled, gaze sparkling. "Really? You mean it?"

"Of course."

"Wow!" She jumped to her feet. "I'll go ask him." Reaching for her backpack, she hesitated then, quick as a flash, threw her arms around Carmen. "You're the best."

Backpack flung over one shoulder, she hurried into the woods.

Carmen sighed. She took a flying leap without looking, but knowing James, the sheriff wouldn't let his daughter go with a woman being chased by a crazy man. If anything, Carmen shifted the solution onto James to make him the bad guy. But how could she refuse browsing through clothing stores with an enthusiastic little girl? Fathers never had the patience for going from store to store and searching through rack after rack. A girl needed a woman's guidance to find the perfect dress. Helping Lucy might be her one chance to fuss over a little girl who wasn't a patient.

Using one hand, she squeezed her temples. She had

more to worry about than Enrico. Lucy's shopping invitation was a direct indication of a growing attachment. Other women were available for this excursion. Maybe not Alexandra, but Lucy could ask someone else. A classmate's mother, for example. *I should have my head examined.* Carmen stood, brushed off her butt, and entered the cabin.

She talked herself out of an early dinner at the cafe. Lucy had her heart in turmoil, and if Carmen got any closer to the people on this mountain, she might not want to leave. She had a career in Richmond, friends— no, not true friends. More like colleagues whose main purpose was to advance their career through a series of networks.

All right, so her life in Richmond was a tad lonely. This trip to Billings Mountain proved to be an eye-opener. She had a great career but no real friends. Her social life was nil, but to improve matters, she'd need her pain-in-the-ass ex out of the picture. *Yeah, easier said than done.*

A quick dinner of salad with hard-boiled eggs settled the growl in her belly. She almost stripped for a shower when car headlights glowed through the front drapes. The crunching of tires on stones followed. Peeking around the curtains, she smiled at the sight of the police cruiser with James behind the wheel. Within seconds, her heart rate skyrocketed, and her chest swelled with joy when so often a police uniform had filled her with dread. Without a doubt, he was the most stimulating man she'd met. He looked like sunshine on a cloudy day with a sexy smile that should come with a warning label. Not waiting for his knock, she opened the door.

Brows drawn tight, he stopped on the porch step.

She elevated both hands in surrender. "I made sure who you were."

Chuckling, he tugged on his ear. "Good."

"Come on in." She waved him through the door. "I've a hankering for a beer. Want one?" She headed for the kitchen.

He followed. "I'm off duty, so yeah, I can use a drink." He flopped onto a kitchen chair. "I'll take Lucy shopping, Carmen."

Opening the refrigerator, she extracted two beer cans and handed him one. "I imagine Lucy protested."

He popped the tab and took a swig. Smacking his lips, he grinned. "I needed this." He met Carmen's gaze. "My little girl isn't pleased. I got the strange feeling she'd rather I stay home." He stared at the beer's label. "She's growing up."

Beer can in hand, Carmen settled onto the opposite chair and popped the tab. "Her body is changing, James. Some girls mature earlier than others. Estrogen kicks in. I can't say for sure in Lucy's case, but certainly over the next two years."

His eyes grew wide and showed two blue orbs surrounded by white.

She smiled at the sheer panic on his face. Such a typical reaction from a father, as if the idea of his daughter developing breasts and menstrual cycles was too much to handle.

He shook himself. "Maybe I was wrong for not marrying all these years."

"From what I hear, you have many potential candidates waiting." Still waiting, if Marion and Becca were any indication. "Why the disinterest?"

After a quick sip, he shrugged. "Single father learning the ropes. Too busy with work. Putting Lucy's needs first. A thousand excuses." Grunting, he stared at his can.

"I don't mind taking her shopping, James, but I am concerned about Enrico."

Looking up, he narrowed his gaze. "I won't let you go anywhere off this mountain without an escort. So, the three of us go together."

Okay, she hadn't expected a threesome, but yeah, his added company sounded like fun. She wouldn't have to worry about watching her back. *My own personal bodyguard.* As an added bonus, he'd know his way around better. She inwardly smiled.

Gaze focused on her face, he leaned on the table. "What about the second part of Lucy's request?"

"Second part?" Her mind drew a blank.

"Lucy mentioned you as my date."

"Oh—yeah, that." She sipped her beer. "If I had a dollar for every kid who played matchmaker, I'd be living on the French Riviera sipping champagne."

With a leg quivering enough to vibrate the table, he shot her a quick glance. "I'll be honest. You're the first woman I've kissed in years."

"Coulda fooled me." She smiled because she meant it. His kisses would melt an iceberg. "You flattered my ego."

"And you gave me a taste of what I've been missing." He ran a hand through his hair. "I can't even sleep at night because I can't get you out of my mind."

With those words, her ego soared. After years of being downtrodden by Enrico, she longed to hear she was still desirable. But judging from the grimace and slight shake of his head, the poor man looked downright distraught over the admission. She stretched across the table to squeeze his arm. "I love your kisses, James, but you know I'm not here to stay. You should ask someone else to the dance." She withdrew her hand.

The leg bouncing increased, and he avoided eye contact. "I can't dance." He sucked in a long breath before shooting her a glance.

Forcing herself not to laugh, Carmen rotated her beer can. "So, learn."

"From who? Charles is the best dancer on this mountain, and I'll be damned if I ask him. Can you dance?"

Chuckling, she tossed her hair off her shoulder. "My brother and I danced all the time. We even won a *flamenco* contest when we were teenagers."

"Then, teach me."

Snorting, she lifted her right foot onto her seat. "What type of music do they play at your dances?"

"All kinds. Why?"

She eyed him through narrowed lids. "I don't want to teach you a foxtrot if all you'll do is jump around like a monkey to some heavy rock beat."

Sitting up straight, he grinned. "I can slow dance."

She curled her lip. "Slow numbers don't require fancy footwork." Not to mention, dancing in a man's arms with bodies moving in unison was the ultimate prelude to sexual intimacy. Picturing him swaying against her generated too many X-rated images. She swallowed a swig of beer. "I suppose I can teach you a few steps before I leave." *Oh, Dios mio. What the hell am I thinking?*

"The dance is tomorrow night."

Mouth agape, she thumped a foot to the floor and straightened. "Your little girl needs a dress and shoes, James. That means our shopping trip should be tomorrow, and we could take all day. How do you expect me to teach you to dance?"

He shrugged. "I figured an hour will do. How hard can it be?"

Santa Maria. Men! She shot him a one-eyed glare. "If dancing was so easy, you'd have learned in high school."

"Well then, be my date and teach me at the same time."

And make every woman on the mountain jealous? She shook her head. "I packed all casual clothes."

"So? Wear what you have."

Wear what I have? Was the man out of his mind? She shook her head. "Not for my first dance in eons."

"Then, you're shopping along with Lucy."

The damn man had a victorious smirk on his face. Flopping back against the chair, she laughed. "I didn't agree to be your date."

"Why not? You'll sit here in the cabin while the rest of us have fun. All guests are invited."

Should she? She deserved a little diversion, and if fun meant helping a little girl buy a dress and teaching her handsome father how to dance, then hell, yeah. *But the intimacy...* Again, hell, yeah. She pictured his arms wrapped around her for more than a kiss, and the vision ignited a ball of fire that settled deep inside her core. But doubts surfaced. She caught his gaze. "What about Enrico? He'll follow us on our shopping expedition."

"Let him. The local authorities can lock him away for another violation of the restraining order." He draped an arm across the table to take her hand. "Come on. What do you say? Be my date. You don't have to buy anything fancy."

Since divorcing Enrico, she bypassed all social events, dressy and otherwise. Maybe it was time to get herself back into the social scene. Tucking a strand of hair behind her ear, she chuckled. "All right. I'll be your date."

He stretched his lips into a broad smile. "How about the three of us eat breakfast at the cafe and hit the road afterward?"

"Okay, and I can ask Marion for some good dress shops." She stood. "It'll be fun—for us girls." She walked him to the door.

Pausing with his hand on the knob, he turned. "Just so you know—"

He slipped his arms around her and pulled her close. She should resist. Really, she should, but why fight this undeniable attraction? Her heart urged her to go as far as he dared. Smiling, she wrapped her arms around his neck, being careful not to knock his shoulder mike. "You were saying?"

His gorgeous smile lit up the room as he lowered his lips to hers. *Lord, help me.* Dragging him to her bed looked better and better.

Chapter Fourteen

In the morning, Carmen met James and an over-exuberant Lucy at the cafe.

Lucy hardly sat still for two minutes and, once finished with her waffles, rushed outside to talk to her friends.

Brows high, Marion approached the table. "What set Lucy on fire?"

Carmen chuckled. "Shopping trip. Can you recommend some girls' dress shops?"

"Sure. Right in Halifax." She spieled off a list of names and directions. "Some nice women's shops, too. You should find everything you need." She clucked her tongue. "You three look like a happy little family." She moved on to the next table.

At the words, James grinned, but for Carmen, reality hit like a bitter pill. Ever since she could remember, she longed for her own family, and the familiar ache grew within her chest. *Ah, well.* If she kept her heart in check, she'd survive their excursion to Halifax. Today, she was a friend helping a little girl prepare for her first date. She swallowed a resigned sigh with a sip of her coffee.

James tapped his mug. "You're being too reflective here. Want to bow out?"

"Heavens, no." She forced a smile. "I'm worried about Enrico."

"Don't be. I've got everything planned. Since you and Lucy refuse to ride in my cruiser, I'll wrap aluminum foil around your car's wireless antenna. You left your phone in the cabin, right?"

This time, she did smile. "Yes, sir, as instructed."

No GPS, and no Enrico. Time to enjoy a day of shopping.

Once in Halifax, James parked the car at an outdoor mall. Marion's recommendations hit dead-on with shops galore spanning a two-block area. Cobblestones lined the streets on which vehicles were not allowed. Sidewalks, constructed of red bricks, created an atmosphere of stepping back in time when shoppers wandered city streets instead of malls. Vinyl benches sat alongside the curbs, and young trees planted in huge wooden boxes showed fresh blooms sprouting while daffodils popped from the tree soil.

"Come on, Carmen. Time's a wastin'."

With a death grip on Carmen's hand, Lucy dragged her from one store to another and then pulled her along the racks in her quest for the perfect dress. Tonight's dance was her first real date, and she wanted to look all girly. The child tugged on Carmen's heartstrings as well. She was so cute, and her joy made her a nonstop chatterbox.

Throughout, James moaned and groaned and acted every bit the bored father.

But he couldn't fool either of them. He enjoyed watching his daughter play dress-up. Heaven forbid he should admit it.

"Ooh, Carmen, I found it."

Lucy twirled in a pale-blue chiffon, which accented her gorgeous blue eyes. The garment fit perfectly.

"Honey, it's lovely."

Grin broad, Lucy flared the skirt. "What do you think, Dad?"

She whirled in front of her father, whose face beamed with pride.

Shoes were next. Several stores accommodated adults and children, so she and Lucy hit the selections with gusto. After helping Lucy pick out a pair of cream-colored flats, Carmen tried on heels, even though she had yet to look at women's clothes.

According to James, the Earth Day Dance had no real dress code. Most folks wore something nice but nothing fancy. Men put on a suit jacket with ties optional. Their guests, like Carmen, packed for nature trails and bird watching and were invited to attend wearing whatever they chose.

But she wasn't about to go in jeans. Carmen, like Lucy, had a date. While she refused to wow James with something hot and sexy, she did want to feel like a woman again. Over the past year, throwing on a lab coat was about as gussied up as she got.

James cleared his throat. "High heels with blue jeans work for me."

Pivoting from the floor mirror, she caught his heated gaze. Lord have mercy. No way in hell could she allow him into a women's apparel store. He already caused heat to rise whenever his gaze swept over her. She'd rather not sweat trying on clothes, thank you very much.

By some stroke of luck, she convinced James to wait on a curb bench with their purchases while she and Lucy hit the women's shops. Carmen posed for Lucy who "oohed" with every selection.

With one particular dress, Lucy hopped and clapped. "That one, Carmen. You look so pretty."

Carmen whirled in front of a three-way mirror. The little girl had good taste, but the word pretty was an understatement. The simple black dress hugged her curves without being tight. Flutter sleeves lifted with the slightest breeze, and the V-neckline revealed just enough cleavage to still be modest. The mid-calf length was perfect to accent her new burgundy heels. With a black shawl as an accessory, she was set. No jewelry, of course. All her jewels were locked in a safe deposit box at a Richmond bank. Since this trip was about relaxation, she had no need to carry excess baggage.

Naturally, James claimed not to need any new clothes and no amount of coaxing from his daughter changed his mind. If James fell into the same mold as her father and brother, he'd wear his garments until the seams unraveled and dropped in shreds at his feet.

"Time to eat. Yay! I'm starved."

Lucy took both their hands and led them toward the outdoor food court located right in the middle of the two-block mall.

The weather was perfect. A warm sun coupled with a cool breeze gave them a spring day at its finest. Almost all of the tables were occupied but not too squeezed together to invade anyone's privacy. Being a Saturday, everyone enjoyed a walk through the outdoor mall. After James took her order for ham and cheese on rye, Carmen secured a table near one of several shade trees with their purchases at her feet.

"I never figured you'd suck up to a lawman."

At the familiar deep tone, Carmen stiffened. Years ago, his sexy timbre sent chills of pleasure straight down her spine. Now, the man created chills of regret. *Figures.* Leave it to Enrico to spoil a perfect day. She whirled toward the table behind her. Damn him. He chose one of the few tables blocked by a tree and out of the concession line's view. She glared. "What are you doing here?"

He grinned. "Following you, of course. I'm glad you used your own car."

So much for James's aluminum foil. The urge to knock out Enrico's perfect teeth tempted her. With her luck, she'd break a few knuckles on his shiny porcelain caps and die of a massive infection. She gritted her teeth. "You're in violation again, Enrico."

"No choice, doll. I'm not allowed on the mountain."

Aw, the man sounded a little peeved. The thought loosened her gut, and she smirked. "What's it feel like to encounter a man more powerful?"

"You knew, didn't you?"

She cocked her head. "Knew what?"

"That this hotshot Billings guy is the largest landowner this side of the state. How the hell can one man own an entire mountain?"

Hiding a grin, she grunted. "Actually, I had no idea. Impressive, isn't it?"

"It's downright obscene."

Yeah, after a year in hell, her luck changed. First with a sheriff who couldn't be bribed, followed by a bunch of women whose solidarity warmed her heart. Landing on a mountain owned by a rich man topped the list.

"Have you slept with the cop yet?"

At his tone, she bristled and faced forward, hoping

to catch James's eye, but he and Lucy were too engrossed with the overhead menu. She debated whether to stand and wave her arms to catch his attention, but why let Enrico ruin everyone's day? Lucy deserved to relish her first big shopping trip.

"I'm waiting for an answer."

She huffed. "What I do anymore is none of your business."

"If the man is sleeping with my wife, you bet it's my business." Scraping his chair more toward her, he craned his neck to see around the tree. "He has a cute little girl."

Her gut twisted. She'd not known Enrico to hurt a child, but at this point, she couldn't dismiss any maneuver on his part. Sneering, she hissed through tight teeth. "You hurt a hair on her head, and every person on the mountain will have a go at you."

He chuckled. "You're getting too attached to these people." He leaned closer. "Not what you expected when you lured me here, is it?"

What the hell? The man must be out of his friggin' mind. Eyes wide, she gaped. "You know damn well that isn't true. By the way, what's this I hear about my having an insurance policy on you? That isn't true, either."

"So you say." Snarling, he scanned the crowded sitting area. "You don't belong with these mountain people. Nature isn't in your blood."

His quick change of subject raised the hairs on the back of her neck. She should demand proof that such a policy existed, but she'd rather he get the hell out of her sight. She snorted. "Shows how much you know me."

Once, she lived the life of a full-fledged nature girl,

but a busy career immersed her in city life. Since moving to the east coast, she never took a stroll through a park or even dipped her toes in the ocean. After marrying Enrico, she attended his soirées, usually a hobnob, nose-in-the-air social event, like she was sex on a stick to be paraded before his peers. He selected her clothes, her car, and even the food she ate. In the beginning, she welcomed the reprieve from such simple decisions. The pediatric practice was on a roll with new patients arriving every day. When Enrico demanded she attend even more social events, she fought tooth and nail for the freedom to make her own choices. He treated her like a possession, not a wife, and her eyes opened to the invisible prison walls he erected.

After the divorce, she threw out the majority of his chosen clothes and had a field day buying her own— like blue jeans, sweatshirts, and T-shirts. Sneakers and a canvas spring jacket completed her ensemble and put her on cloud nine. On the first day she stepped outside wearing a pair of jeans, she had flashbacks to her childhood. She lost so much of herself with Enrico. Even though he might follow her to the ends of the earth, she'd retain her newfound freedom.

"When are you leaving?"

His question snapped her mind to the present. She scanned him from head to toe. "Like I'll tell you."

"If you don't want anything to happen to the sheriff's cute little girl, you will tell me."

A rush of anger rose so quickly, she nearly bolted from the chair. How dare he dangle Lucy's safety over her head! Damn, if she only had a gun. She'd put a bullet into his head and to hell with the consequences. Face flushed, she twisted to confront him. "I warn you,

Enrico. You hurt her, and you won't leave the mountain alive."

He waved aside the comment. "Just tell me when you're leaving."

"Three weeks this Sunday."

Frowning, he shot her a one-eyed stare. "I don't believe you."

"Then, why ask? You'll follow my GPS anyway."

"Right you are, babe." With a gaze like fire, he leaned forward. "You can't hide from me, Carmen. You can sell your car or buy a new phone, but my man will find you. Our marriage isn't over until I say so."

He'd said the words so often she hardly let them register. But this time, the prickling on her scalp warned her to take him seriously. Any day now, he would issue his brand of divorce and fire a bullet into her brain.

****

Returning with the food, James sensed the change in the air before he even took a seat. An aura of tension surrounded Carmen so thick he'd need a power saw to cut through. Something happened. Her gaze had lost its beautiful sparkle, and her smile seemed forced. She sat so ramrod straight he'd bet any amount of money she slipped on one of those nineteenth century corsets. Her soul had been ripped out again, and he had a good idea by whom.

Jaw tight, he scanned the area for Enrico Cruz, but the bastard could be sitting in his car anywhere within the large parking lot. *Dammit to hell.*

Oblivious, Lucy chatted during their meal and offered to share her curly fries, but Carmen shook her head and picked at her food. Under the table, James rested a hand on her knee and squeezed. Their gazes met, and a smile curled one side of her mouth.

Anger boiled in his gut at the man who soured Carmen's mood. Would she ever have a moment of peace? Of course, taking Carmen's car was a dumb move, even if he enjoyed maneuvering a luxury vehicle through traffic. With the wireless antenna covered and her phone not in her possession, how did Cruz find her? James made sure no one followed. Could another device be attached to her car, like a homing sensor? Dear Lord, was Cruz *that* desperate to track his ex?

At the first opportunity, he'd ask Harry to comb the car. He was good with all the technology stuff. For the dance tonight, James refused to listen to any argument from his two women. He'd drive the cruiser to the school with Carmen riding shotgun in the passenger seat, and poor Lucy in the rear separated by a security gate. Too damn bad if they complained. Like it or walk.

Once back on the mountain, he parked Carmen's car alongside her cabin and killed the engine.

"Dad, I saw Lizzie enter the cafe. Can I find out what she's wearing to the dance?"

Since he had one foot out the door, he turned to Lucy in the rear seat. "Sure. But don't stay too long. You need a bit of rest before your date."

"Geez, I'm too old for a nap."

He placed a hand over his heart. "All right, *I* need rest before *my* date." He winked at Carmen. "Go on. Go see Lizzie."

"Thanks, Dad. See ya later, Carmen." Lucy opened the car door and ran down the drive.

Carmen released an audible sigh. "I marvel how your kids can run around like the forest is one big playground." She opened her car door and alighted.

He followed and, using the fob, popped the trunk. "The children have been cautioned to avoid visitors. What happened the other day was a lesson learned because Lucy dropped her guard. Like most of us on the mountain, Lucy could walk through the woods blindfolded, but she got a little complacent." After tossing Carmen her keys, he grabbed the packages. "I'll put Lucy's on the porch."

Lucy's run to see her friend afforded him the perfect opportunity to question Carmen's funky mood. She hardly spoke two words on the return trip.

Carmen closed the trunk. "I can carry mine."

"Of course, you can, but I'm a Southern gentleman. Allow me to assist you." He expected an argument, but she unlocked the cabin door. After dumping her bags on the sofa, he faced her, arms folded across his chest. "All right, what did he say? Don't deny his presence, Carmen. He's a man who kills the light in your eyes."

She had an excellent poker face. Nothing showed…for about two minutes. Then, a debate flashed within her gaze. She didn't want to tell him. He knew why. She had fought the battle against her ex for so long she failed to see a friend willing to help. Of course, standing like a lawman in front of a suspect didn't help. Relaxing his pose, he dropped his arms. "Talk to me, Carmen."

The debate continued. Then, her shoulders slumped, and she flopped onto the fat arm of the sofa with her gaze focused on the floor. "I won't let him hurt you or Lucy or anyone else on this mountain."

His chest squeezed, and he damn near threw a fist into the wall. "He threatened you?"

"Not for the first time." She hung her head. "Mr. Billings can restrict Enrico's access to the mountain, but Enrico will hire others to do his dirty work." She met his gaze. "I'm afraid for Lucy. I should pack and leave."

That's it. I'll kill the bastard myself. He tightened his jaw until his teeth hurt. Flexing his fingers, he sucked in a calming breath. "If Cruz touches Lucy, he'll stare into the barrel of a shotgun, and I won't hesitate to pull the trigger."

She shot him a look full of questions, as if she didn't believe him. He wasn't sure he believed himself. He'd sworn to uphold the law, but when faced with imminent danger to family, all bets were off.

All right, enough. She had a great day, and high time she got it back. He took her by the shoulders and urged her to stand. "Tonight, we'll have fun at the dance."

"I shouldn't go, James."

"Sorry. You can't cancel after I endured a torturous shopping trip with two women." He kissed her and meant for a light touch on her lips, but holy damn, she tasted good. As she relaxed against him, he wrapped her in an embrace and deepened the kiss. Thoughts of Cruz flew right out of his head at the taste of ham and cheese on her tongue. Lifting his head, he stared into a glistening gaze. "Tears, Carmen?"

She stretched her lips into a smile. "You're doing things to me I haven't felt in a long time. Thank you."

And she awakened his long-dormant body. Too bad Lucy wasn't old enough to stay home on her own. He desperately needed some alone time with this woman.

Chapter Fifteen

Carmen tried to relax, but every time she sat, she jumped up and flitted around the cabin looking for something to take her mind off that wonderful man. How could she not lean into him when his lips drew her like some magnet? And his hands...*Santa Maria*. Every touch scorched her skin, even through her clothes. She almost stripped naked to allow cool air to hit flesh. How would she survive the night dancing in his arms? She'd need ice down her back...and front.

She glanced at her wristwatch. James said six o'clock. Two hours gave her sufficient leeway for a relaxing shower and a bit of pampering—if she could keep her mind focused. She undressed and headed into the bathroom.

As the clock approached the six o'clock hour, she zipped her dress and rechecked her makeup. She hadn't been this nervous since high school prom. *And please, please, please, don't make me sweat in this gorgeous dress.* With the perfume bottle in her hand, she stared at the label. She only packed the candy scent. Her seventy-dollars-an-ounce bottle remained on her bureau at home. With luck, James liked chocolate, and he'd eat her up. She shivered with the thought and dabbed a bit behind her ears. As an afterthought, she added a few drops to her cleavage. After a quick re-fluffing of her wavy hair, she slipped on her heels then whirled in front of the dresser mirror. *I am so out of practice.*

A soft knock sounded on the door. Sucking in a calming breath, she hurried to the front windows and peeked through the curtains. Her heart did a happy little dance to see father and daughter waiting. She grabbed her shawl, wrapped it around her shoulders, and opened the door.

Her breath caught at the sight of the man on the porch. Casually dressed in a blue sport jacket, white shirt, and black trousers, he was positively drool-worthy. With an effort, she tore her gaze from James to focus on the bouncing little girl by his side.

Beaming with a big smile, Lucy whirled while flaring the skirt.

Carmen returned the smile and nodded her approval. "You'll knock your date right off his feet."

"So will you." She ran toward the cruiser. "Come on, you two. Let's go. Time's a wastin'."

James leaned close. "She's been hyper since we arrived home. She won't even wear her sweater, but I threw it in the rear seat in case she gets cold."

Since words stuck in her throat, Carmen nodded in response. He smelled of clean man and spice, and that blue jacket emphasized the color of his eyes. Swooning, she caught the doorknob to hold herself steady, but dear Lord, his gaze glowed like blue flames with a slow perusal shooting bolts of fire straight to her core. Swallowing hard, she locked the cabin door.

On the drive to the elementary school, Lucy chatted through the partially opened metal gate separating her from the front. For Carmen and James, a console with computer and two-way radio divided their bucket seats. The whole environment felt weird, like she rode in some futuristic vehicle. No way should a police cruiser be a date car. Intimacy was impossible with all the gadgetry in the way. Even the console forced her to keep her hands in her lap. Not as if she'd try anything with Lucy on board, but a stolen kiss or two would be nice—especially since she struggled to listen to Lucy when her gaze constantly drifted to the man behind the wheel. Damn, she yearned to fall into his arms—and stay.

"What do you think, Carmen?"

Oh, shit. Lucy asked a question. What the hell was she talking about? "I don't know, Lucy. What do you think?"

"I'm old enough."

Huh? *Fess up, girl.* She cringed. "Old enough for what, honey?"

"Nylons. Didn't you pay attention? Dad won't let me wear them."

James flashed Carmen a smile.

The cop missed nothing, and heat flushed Carmen's cheeks. She squinted at James but smiled at Lucy. "Your dad has final say, Lucy."

"Drat. Us girls are supposed to stick together." She craned her neck. "We're here!"

Saved by a timely arrival.

Cars packed the school's parking lot and overflowed in and around the soccer field's bleachers. People milled about, some smoking and others talking.

Maneuvering the car to where grass met asphalt, James cut the engine.

With a quick "see-ya-later," Lucy dashed across the parking lot.

By a set of double doors, a cute redheaded boy

greeted her. They clasped hands and ran inside. Carmen smiled. "They look adorable."

James grunted in answer then hurried around to her side of the vehicle. Yanking open the door, he offered his hand.

Electricity filled the air. She had never experienced such intensity from any man. The thought of skipping the dance and dragging him to the cabin ran through her mind. Someone at the school could watch Lucy, right? Gazes locked, she slipped her hand into his.

Without bothering to close the door, he wrapped an arm around her waist to draw her close. "You look beautiful." His lips lowered to hers.

Her body ached to take him, here and now, on the scant stretch of grass near the cruiser. So what if anyone saw them? People should be inside the school enjoying the festivities, not filling their lungs with cigarette smoke. Nudging James closer, she opened her mouth to taste his tongue. God, help her. He was a feast waiting to be savored.

A loud wolf whistle broke the spell.

"Get a room!"

After biting her lower lip, he lifted his head, gaze twinkling. "Sorry, but the sheriff is with a date. Talk will flow."

And envy. At the soccer game, women eyed him with stars in their eyes. She patted his chest. "Come on. Let's go inside. Oh, wait." Since she was already overheated, she threw her shawl onto the front seat then handed him her cabin key. "Hold this for me, will you? I'm not carrying a purse." She hadn't thought to buy a clutch, and her shoulder bag was out of the question. No comb, no lipstick, and no worries. All left behind.

Time to relax and enjoy a night with a hot man. Smiling, she hooked an arm through his. "Lead on, Sheriff."

Once entering the building, James stopped at a small table positioned in the hallway and greeted the two elderly men.

"Finally brought yourself a date, eh, Sheriff?" The man on the right winked at Carmen. "You know the rules, James. Five bucks apiece. Not even the sheriff gets in free." He snatched the money from James's hand then grinned. "Ain't ya gonna introduce us?"

Chuckling, James spieled off their names.

Carmen nodded her hellos. She half listened. The rhythm of the bass beat vibrated through the walls and filled her with memories of carefree days so long ago. High school dances, dates, and pep rallies were a few thoughts coming to mind. Pre-med studies changed her whole life...and tied her down. Small wonder she'd made such a poor decision to marry Enrico. Like a fool, she was desperate for love. *A hard lesson learned.* With a warm hand on her lower back, James guided her through the entrance.

The gymnasium was alive with activity. Couples danced. Children played tag. Old codgers relaxed on folding chairs and tapped a foot in time with the music. Along the far right wall, food, desserts, and drinks covered cloth-draped tables, while close by, people sat at long, fold-out tables digging into plates of food.

Henrietta swayed behind the dessert selection, sampling as she arranged platters.

Away from the refreshments and stuck into a corner, a DJ sashayed in rhythm to the beat.

The atmosphere was loud and boisterous with

everyone shouting to be heard. She expected to be deaf within the hour.

Lucy and her redheaded date danced in the familiar fashion of bobbing heads and flailing arms—no particular pattern or dance style. Neither looked at each other nor touched. Heaven forbid they should make eye contact. Carmen smiled. "Did Lucy's date pay her way?"

"Children under fourteen pay a dollar. I gave Lucy the money in case she had a cheap date."

Carmen laughed. She'd been down that road, too.

On the dance floor, Marion from the cafe executed some fancy moves with Harry. A big, bear-like man—whom she recognized as Charles Billings—whirled a laughing Alexandra. He was a striking man and the complete opposite of James. Charles had dark hair and eyes in contrast to James's blond hair and blue eyes—a night-and-day comparison. Kinda how Carmen felt standing next to James.

Clamping onto her hand, James urged her onto the dance floor and wrapped her tight about the waist.

Laughing, she slipped her arms around his neck. "This is not a slow number, Mr. Sheriff."

"I don't care. If you must know, when you opened your cabin door, I damn near hit the floor. You look gorgeous in your new dress, and if I wait for a slow song to hold you in my arms, I'll die."

Her pulse quickened at his darkened gaze, and earlier thoughts about dragging him to the cabin resurfaced. Thanks to this man, she was ready to conquer dating with a renewed gusto. Even if their relationship ended after the dance, she'd still thank him for an awakening long overdue.

The music stopped. Everyone applauded—except her and James. He swayed as if they were the only two people in the entire gymnasium. Then, an easy ballad flowed through the overhead speakers. No man could go wrong with a slow song, and he nudged her closer. Too close for the crowd. But hell, she didn't care. Tearing her gaze from his, she rested her head on his shoulder with her nose close to his neck. His spicy cologne clouded her senses. She lost all track of space and time, and every muscle in her body relaxed against him...until a not-so-subtle pressure hit her belly. Lifting her head, she raised a brow.

He growled. "Don't you dare step away."

Chuckling, she lifted her lips to his ear. "Your jacket should hide the bulge." Oh, how she'd love to spring him loose. But too many children were about. Sighing, she replaced her head on his shoulder.

She shouldn't be here and shouldn't have started an affair. Yet, she hadn't expected to be attracted to a man within a few short days. Was she so starved for a man's arms she lost every ounce of reason? Without the slightest push, she could fall in love with James. She already loved his daughter. But then what? She still had to leave. With Enrico alive, she'd have no peace.

The song ended. This time, she loosened her hold and smiled. "Is it safe to separate?"

"Hmmpf."

But he smiled in return and guided her toward the food tables.

Alexandra and Charles, hand in hand, met them halfway.

Carmen extended a hand to Charles. "I'm officially meeting Charles Billings. Thank you for your help the other day."

He grasped her hand. "Anytime, but I have a different way for you to thank me. James told me you won a *flamenco* contest as a kid."

"Teenager to be precise." She dropped her hand. "That was eons ago."

"Then, how about I ask the DJ to play an appropriate number, and you show me your stuff."

Mouth agape, Carmen blinked at Alexandra.

The small woman shrugged. "Charles dances very well. I do not." She waved a hand. "You have my permission."

Brow arched, Carmen glanced at James.

He grinned. "Don't look at me. I can manage a slow number. After that, you're on your own."

Charles slapped James on the shoulder. "Great. Let me talk to the DJ."

Furrowing her brows, Carmen shot a glare from James to Alex. "You two didn't help me at all. What if I trip over my own feet?"

"Oh, pfff." Alex crossed her arms over her chest. "Charles is good enough to draw everyone's attention."

Carmen started. *Draw—what*?

Breaking through the crowd, Charles returned and held out his hand. "Ready?"

"Hell, no." But she slipped her hand into his and followed, all the while saying a silent prayer that she didn't make a complete fool out of herself.

****

James sighed. Whenever Charles escorted a woman onto the dance floor, he had a habit of showcasing his partner as a signal for an impending show. He twirled Carmen now, and the spin flared Carmen's dress to expose shapely legs, long and toned.

The crowd reacted with smiles and eager clapping as a large circle formed around them.

Glancing over her shoulder, Carmen caught James's gaze and cringed.

Every feature on her face said *what the hell?* Containing a laugh, James blew her a kiss. She was so damn cute.

He leaned toward Alex. "I told Carmen Charles was a good dancer. I never mentioned how the crowd stops to watch."

Gaze riveted onto the couple, she chuckled. "You're in for it, James."

He hoped so. Punishment from a beautiful woman? Hell, yeah!

The music started. A Latin beat. Carmen took all of three seconds to follow her partner's lead.

She looked stunning in her simple black dress. Curves galore filled the material. Her high heels gave her legs endless length, and long, dark hair bounced as she danced. Her moves were agile and smooth with hips swaying and heels clicking. She was a sight to behold, and every muscle in his body tightened at the carnal thoughts drifting into his mind.

Alex nudged his side. "I'll bet she hasn't been this happy in a while."

Speechless, he nodded. Carmen's face absolutely glowed.

"She's perfect for you, James."

He grunted. "I have nothing to offer her."

"How about love and security? She's living in hell with that ex of hers." She clutched his arm and tugged. "You're a great catch, but you need to remove your blinders. She is not pass-up material."

He frowned. "Get real, Alex. I'm a man who doesn't make a whole lot of money. Plus, I have a daughter, and we live in a two-bedroom rancher. Carmen's a doctor. She has plenty of opportunities to make a ton of money."

"Hey, not all doctors are interested in making money. Look at me." She hip-bumped him. "I arrived for two weeks of relaxation. I met and married Charles, created two wonderful children, and never once considered leaving."

True. Because she was a New York surgeon, Alex had the potential for making a lot of money, but she chose to stay and be the mountain doctor. Folding his arms over his chest, he snorted. "You married a man with money. Different story."

"So? You can marry a *woman* with money." She squeezed his arm.

Frowning, he narrowed his gaze. "What kind of a man do you think I am? I can't live off her money."

"She might be more than willing to share." Mouth twisted to the side, she toyed with her diamond necklace. "You can work a pre-nup into the conversation. This way, you'll both be comfortable." She hip-bumped him again. "Talk to her about staying. I could use a partner."

Lips pursed, he shook his head. "I don't think Carmen and I will move as fast as you and Charles. Carmen's recovering from a bad marriage, and I have a child to consider. Besides, she might not want to leave her Richmond practice." Even if Carmen was the most extraordinary woman to cross his path, he couldn't ask her to stay. Her career entitled her to so much, and she'd live to regret the move.

The song ended, and the crowd cheered. "More, more, more!" The chant continued along with wild applause.

James laughed from the wide-eyed look Carmen shot him. He should have warned her about Charles's performances, and knowing Charles, he wouldn't release a good dance partner too quickly.

After leaning toward Carmen's ear and receiving a nod in answer, Charles signaled to the DJ, and another Latin beat blared through the speakers.

Alex chuckled. "Oooo, the *samba*. Think Carmen can keep up?"

"I have a feeling she will."

Carmen matched Charles step for step, and she performed a few shimmies that raised his friend's brows. Damn, she could move. Her glowing face and sparkling dark eyes mesmerized, and James couldn't look away. She was beautiful. He nudged Alex's arm. "She's good."

Alex chuckled. "I have a feeling Carmen's Spanish heritage gives her a one-up on Charles."

If Charles wasn't his best bud, James would bash in his face without an iota of regret. But Charles loved Alexandra, and he also loved to dance. Still, jealousy surfaced, and he flexed his fingers. Maybe he should learn to dance.

With the show over and followed by another round of applause, Carmen and Charles returned, both faces flushed and beaming.

Charles kissed Carmen's hand. "Thank you."

She flashed a wide smile. "For such a big man, you're remarkably light on your feet." She faced Alex.

"You're a lucky woman."

Alex grunted. "Yeah, well, despite all his efforts, I still can't do anything fancy. I have two left feet."

"As do I." James leaned toward Carmen. "You danced like a pro."

"Thank you. I haven't done the *samba* in years."

He'd love to have her samba in the privacy of a bedroom. The sway of her hips in rhythm to the music did a number on his imagination. For the first time in years, he wanted a woman in his bed. All night, if possible. But he had Lucy to consider. A sexual romp in his small house was out of the question.

A slow number began. James glanced from Alex to Charles. "Excuse us. My turn." He grabbed Carmen's hand and led her onto the dance floor.

She pointed toward the food tables. "I could use something to drink."

"After this." He wrapped her flush against his chest. After her physical exertion, her body radiated heat and intensified the scent of her candy perfume. In his book, she smelled downright delicious. "I love your perfume, Carmen."

She lifted her arms to circle his neck. "It's a new fragrance. I bought it to soothe my little patients. I never considered its effect on a grown man."

On her, any perfume would work. He gazed into her sparkling eyes. "Your gyrating was a complete turn-on, you know."

"Oh?" She fussed with his jacket collar. "The *samba* can be classified as an erotic dance, but Charles kept it clean." With a subtle smile, she slipped her fingers into his hair. "I can teach you."

He shook his head. "Waste of time. My gyrating

isn't done on the dance floor."

She widened her eyes. "Is that a fact? Think you can prove it?"

Damn, yeah! Somehow. Where and when were the questions. He'd be a fool to let her go one more night. But what the hell could he do with Lucy?

Chapter Sixteen

Carmen was having the time of her life, and her heart sang with the joy of freedom. When had she ever had this much fun without worrying about how others perceived her actions? Ever since obtaining her medical degree, she followed strict guidelines about how to dress and act, what words to avoid, and what parties to attend. Networking became the norm. Doctors' balls and fundraisers, along with retirement parties for the upper-crust members of the hospital board, joined a long list of social obligations with boring conversations.

At one tedious fundraiser, she met Enrico. The man swept her off her feet with his wide smile and sophisticated charm. Then, of course, her nightmare began. Mister Charm reverted to Mister Harm. She was so damn stupid.

Here, on Billings Mountain, from the moment of her arrival, the people welcomed her with no expectations or demands. Even while she danced with Charles, the crowd cheered her on, as if she and Charles danced together for years. The night couldn't get any better. *No, let's retract that.* Sex with a gorgeous man shot to the top of her to-do list. As she swayed with James, she loved the feel of the bulge pressing against her belly. When their gazes connected, questions flashed across his face. Did he see the answer in hers? Was he looking for permission to finish the night with a bang? But what about Lucy? The girl had a long day and would soon collapse from exhaustion. Sighing, she rested her head on James's shoulder.

He kissed her hair. "I hope the whispers aren't bothering you."

"Nothing will bother me tonight." Not even the soft words about what a handsome couple she and James made. The bachelor sheriff and the pedie doctor sounded nice even to her ears. Lifting her head, she smiled and slipped all ten fingers into his hair to toy with the strands.

With his arms tightening around her waist, he moaned. "I'd like to take you home with me."

"A little too obvious considering how everyone is watching us." With strong arms around her, the smell of spicy cologne swirling her senses, and slow music to set the mood, she was in heaven. Releasing her fingers from his hair, she returned her head to his shoulder.

Two songs later, James loosened his hold. "How about something to eat?"

Food, water—yes! Stepping away, she tugged on his sport coat. "I thought you'd never ask." She could have kept her head on his shoulder all night, but dear Lord, she was truly falling for this handsome man, and the realization shook her core.

He squeezed her hand. "You seem reflective."

Yeah, he was Mister Right dancing with Miss Wrong. She'd cause him nothing but heartache. Forcing a smile, she looped a hand through his arm. "Let's eat. I'm starving."

With paper plates loaded with sandwiches and salads, she chose two available seats at a long table. Every person seated turned and smiled...well, except for the two elderly men with cheeks full of food. Like earlier, James spieled names, and she half listened. Some other day. Tonight was about James.

He leaned close to her ear. "I'll grab some drinks. Iced tea?"

"Perfect."

A minute later, he returned with two cups of iced tea.

She took a bite of a juicy roast beef sandwich. The meat melted in her mouth, and she groaned. "This is fantastic." She took another bite, chewed, and swallowed while scanning the dance floor. "Where's Lucy?"

Cheeks full, he chewed and swallowed then jerked his head in the direction of the food tables. "She's on her second piece of pie. I hope she doesn't overdo the sweets and get sick on me tonight."

She patted his hand. "You're a wonderful father."

After polishing off the sandwich along with potato salad, two deviled eggs, and four chunks of tomato, Carmen leaned back and rested a palm on her stomach. "I haven't eaten this much since forever. I might actually gain weight on this trip."

James wiped his mouth with a napkin. "Any room for dessert?"

Gaze flitting to the food tables, she cringed. "I almost skipped the potato salad to save room for the wonderful brownie dessert near the cherry pie. But I shouldn't. Help yourself."

Alexandra wandered to their table and placed a hand on James's shoulder. "Can I steal Carmen for a few minutes?"

Grinning, James jumped to his feet. "Go right

ahead. I'm raiding the dessert table." He winked at Carmen and hurried off.

Alexandra hooked an arm through Carmen's and urged her to stand. "I want you to see the playroom."

Grateful for a reprieve from the loud gymnasium, Carmen followed to an open door on the far side of the folded bleachers. Toddlers of all sizes—from crib-age to perhaps three to four years old—ran around the room. Five elderly women surrounded a large oblong table with food and drinks before them. Two women held infants with bottles. As Carmen and Alex entered, all five turned toward the door and smiled.

Alex patted Carmen's arm. "Ladies, meet one of our guests, Doctor Carmen Santiago, a pediatrician."

One older woman with blue hair waved. "You're the one who helped Joey. That was so nice of you."

The others chimed in with equal thanks.

Geez, she was only doing her job. She scanned the children's faces. "Where is Joey?"

Another woman answered. "Sitting with his parents. They're watching everything he eats."

Alex chuckled. "As you can see, we have our own babysitting squad. This room has soundproofing, but if the door is left open, the ladies can still listen to the music. The dark-haired four-year-old is mine. Charles the fourth." She pointed to a little boy immersed with a toy train.

"He's gorgeous." No lie either. The child with his curly black hair was the creation of two beautiful people.

A little, dark-haired girl ran forward, arms outstretched. "Mommy, Mommy!"

Alex hefted the child onto her left hip. "This is

Maria, our two-year-old."

She kissed the girl who fussed to be released. Smirking, Alex lowered her, and off she ran. "The kids love the dance, but they get underfoot and tired. We designed this room specifically for them with toys and sleep mats."

"It's a thoughtful concept." As her gaze drifted from one young face to another, she felt the familiar tightness in her chest. How had her life taken such a wrong turn? She concentrated so long on her career she failed to keep her eyes open at the men in her life. Enrico charged after her like a bull in a china shop, and she ignored the subtle clues, like how he never let another man near her or how he stressed salads over burgers. He demanded to know where she was every minute of the day. In the beginning, his possessiveness flattered her. When his demands grew and grip tightened, he awakened a part of her that rebelled. Because of him, she wasted several good, child-bearing years. *So friggin' blind.*

"As you can see, we have a lot of children on the mountain."

Carmen laughed. "You're not too subtle, Alex."

Shrugging, Alex cocked her head. "Just saying. Come on. Let's return to the party."

An elderly woman snagged Alex outside the door.

To allow the two women privacy, Carmen continued toward the tables where James and Harry stood with their heads huddled together.

Harry slipped something into James's palm, and James slipped his hand into his trouser pocket.

Her instincts shot on high alert. *Please, don't let him use drugs.* She wasn't into that shit and prayed

James wasn't either. She pegged him as a wonderful father and an honest lawman. Drugs would tarnish his image.

The two men separated with a handshake.

What should she do? Ignore what looked too obvious? A good cop in New Mexico once told her to believe half of what she saw and nothing of what she heard—good advice, even now. She'd question James later. Squaring her shoulders, she approached.

Turning, James locked onto her gaze and smiled.

Her pulse quickened. Every single time he smiled, he toyed with her insides, like she swallowed a mouthful of jumping beans.

Catching up, Alex nudged Carmen. "James hasn't worn a big smile in quite a while. You've changed him."

He changed her, too. She trusted a man with a badge, and because of him and Lucy, she opened her heart. But her ex hung around her neck like baggage with no intention of leaving any time soon. She shook her head. "I'm not here to stay, Alex. My ex will make everyone's life a living hell."

Alex huffed out a breath. "Oh, I don't know. Charles has his connections."

But were his friends more powerful than Enrico's? How many lawmen did Charles have in his pocket? She shook her head. "Enrico is my problem, not his."

"With you being part of our mountain family makes Enrico everyone's problem." She squeezed Carmen's arm. "I could sure use a backup at the clinic." With a wry smile, she disappeared into the crowd.

The offer was tempting. The pace would be slower than a busy pediatric practice, but the question from earlier resurfaced. Where would she live? She hadn't seen any *For Sale* signs on any houses. Even more important, what about Enrico? Even if Charles Billings banned him forever, what about Enrico's paid cronies? No, with Enrico still in her life, she could never stay.

As a rock beat blared through the speakers, James approached with a finger plugging each ear. "Can I talk to you outside?"

"Sure." She took his offered hand.

He led her through a side exit and into the parking lot. The cool night air hit her warm skin like she wandered into a freezer, and she sighed with relief. All the dancing, food, and being with this stimulating man raised her body temperature. She looked around at the still-full parking lot. "Are we leaving?"

"Not yet."

She didn't think he'd leave Lucy. "Where are we going?"

"You'll see."

Apprehension surfaced. With Enrico and his many surprises, at this stage of her life, she needed something more straightforward than a "You'll see". She tugged on his hand. "James—"

Glancing over his shoulder, he stopped. "I'm sorry. I wanted to surprise you. I can tell you now."

"Tell me wha—"

Without giving her a chance to finish, he whirled her into a tight embrace and crushed his lips against hers.

Dios mio. The man tasted good, like lemon meringue pie, which he probably ate while she was with Alex. Strong hands caressed her sides and tingled every nerve along the way, until his fingers cupped her bottom and pulled her against his erection. Fire ignited in her belly and traveled straight to her core. *Did the earth just move?*

He lifted his head, gaze ablaze. "I had to get that out of my system."

"Wow! Anytime." She barely found her voice. His blue eyes held such a glow she swore they reflected an overhead light. Except a light wasn't anywhere nearby. To regain some control, she sucked in a shuddering breath and exhaled. "What are you up to, James?"

He continued across the parking lot. "We need to talk."

Stopping, she tugged on his hand. "Okay, talk." She stood behind someone's large SUV. The vehicle was huge and protected her from prying eyes. Grateful for a little privacy, she slipped her arms inside his suit jacket and around his waist. The warmth of his body matched her own, and she sucked in his tantalizing scent.

"Lucy's staying with Alex and Charles tonight."

At the implication of his statement, a flood of moisture hit between her legs. Never before had such a powerful urge for sex ricocheted through her body with lightning speed. Since he held her so close, he had to feel the obvious message from her hardened nipples.

He brushed his lips across hers, lifted his head, and smiled. "I think of you night and day, Carmen. You invade my dreams and interfere with my work. I want to discover everything about you. Above all, I want to make love with you."

Stunned speechless, she gaped. James talked about lovemaking and not a quickie in the closet. Where had this man been all her life? She cleared her throat. "You want to spend the whole night together?"

"If you're willing. I've arranged to pick up Lucy around noon." Gaze gentle, he flicked a finger under her chin. "What do you say?"

"Before I answer, I saw Harry slip you something. I don't do drugs, James. Never have and never will."

He grinned. "Nice to know." He dipped a hand into his trouser pocket and extracted five packets.

Condoms! She laughed.

He shot her a sheepish look. "I hadn't one to my name, but Harry, being a little more active, ran home and came back with five." He replaced the condoms to his pocket. His brow cocked. "Is that a yes?"

Uncertainty filled his gaze. Did he think she would refuse? He couldn't know how much she longed to spend a night in his arms, but she'd show him. She gave her answer by plastering her body against his and used her tongue for a deep, probing kiss. His arms tightened, his erection swelled, and her hands itched to feel his skin. She broke away with a gasp. "Let's go."

****

Thank you, Lord, for giving me good friends like Alex and Charles.

James mentally repeated the mantra on their drive to Carmen's cabin. If conniving Alex hadn't dragged Carmen to the playroom and then Charles suggesting a sleepover for Lucy, hell, he'd be relieving his hard-on in a cold shower. Thanks to them, he would have this sultry woman with the smoldering gaze in his arms all night. Damn, he was a lucky man.

He parked alongside her car and cut the engine.

Reaching across the cluttered console, she stroked his jacket sleeve. "I'm having a guilt trip about leaving.

How many people witnessed Harry giving you condoms?"

"Probably too many. With Alex taking Lucy tonight, the mountain gossips will have a field day."

"Oh God." She threw her head onto the headrest and closed her eyes.

"You can still change your mind." Heaven help him.

She met his gaze. "Not on your life." Grabbing the door handle, she grinned over her shoulder. "Race you to the cabin door."

Of course, he beat her. Her high heels dug into the dirt and impeded every step. Since he still held the key to her cabin, he unlocked the door and practically dragged her inside.

Not two seconds after he closed and bolted the latch, he pinned her to the wall. God, he couldn't wait to get her alone. She was curvy and soft with dress material smooth enough for easy hand gliding. With her candy-shop scent and the taste of Henrietta's potato salad on her tongue, he was beyond controlling his appetite.

Lips fused together, she slipped off his sport coat while he lowered the back zipper to her dress, but whoa, he was moving too fast. And the cabin was way too dark. The scant light from the kitchen appliances didn't do shit to help him see. Breaking the lip-lock, he held her at arm's length.

She blinked. "What?"

"If you think I want a quickie, you are much mistaken. We have all night, and I intend to savor."

Wide-eyed, she smiled. "You won't hear an argument from me."

"Good. I want you to moan and cry out my name, and I'll continue until you beg for mercy."

She chuckled. "You shouldn't have told me. I'll bite my tongue and keep my lips sealed." With shaky fingers, she unbuttoned his shirt. "You might have to get real inventive with your limited number of condoms."

Oh, he'd be inventive, all right. Not all maneuvers required a condom. She'd cry uncle before the night was through, or his name wasn't James Thomas. Releasing her, he turned on a lamp by the sofa. "This light should allow me to see you. And I *do* want to see you, Carmen." Talk time was over. He swept his arms under her legs and carried her to the bed.

Chapter Seventeen

Carmen had no illusions about her size. At five-foot-eight and average weight, she was no feather in his arms, but James swept her off her feet. The incredible floating sensation thrilled her like nothing before in her past. For the first time since her divorce, she welcomed a man's dominance. James wouldn't hurt her. She trusted him with her body—but not quite with her heart. No man deserved her heart just yet.

After slipping her onto the bed, he stripped her of what clothes remained and caressed her naked skin with calloused hands. Despite the toughened skin, his fingers stroked with a gentleness that tingled, and the possibility of those fingers entering her core... *Lord Almighty*. Nothing calloused about his lips, though. Their softness possessed her breasts, and her body came alive in full force with every nerve firing at once. For a man supposedly out of circulation, he knew how to please a woman. Too bad Harry hadn't given him the entire condom box.

By morning, after a wonderful night of nonstop sex, Carmen popped open an eye to see James rummaging through the refrigerator. He wore his dress slacks but no shirt, and muscles rippled on his chest as he moved. Stimulating as hell. The man hadn't an ounce of fat on his body. Oh, and yes, nice tush.

Heat flowed from the gas fireplace to help dispel

the cabin's morning chill. She glanced at the nightstand clock. Almost ten. Wow. She never slept this late. Then again, their sexual exploration with each other's body didn't leave much room for sleep. James handled her like fragile porcelain, yet his thrusts shot her to the moon. When she floated to earth, she again found herself on the launch pad, even though she tried to turn the tables. *Santa Maria.* What a man! If she wasn't careful, she'd slide into a love pool—love for him and his daughter and for the mountain and its people. All of them lifted the heavy weight around her heart and allowed her the freedom to do anything she damned well pleased.

The thump of a drawer closing returned her attention to the kitchen.

Catching her gaze, he smiled. "Morning. I'm making breakfast."

She propped onto one elbow and stifled a yawn. "You don't need to cook." Although, she had no desire to dress and head to the cafe, not with two more hours available before he left to retrieve Lucy.

The wonderful aroma of fresh-brewed coffee forced her to swing her legs over the side of the bed. As was her morning ritual, she stretched. Bad move. She was completely naked. A loud clang shot her gaze toward the kitchen floor where a fry pan lay.

Ignoring the pan, James stared, his gaze dark. "You're beautiful, Carmen."

Whoa. The air in the cabin rose ten degrees from the heat of his gaze. She'd like nothing more than to skip breakfast and continue lovemaking but best not to press her luck. Grabbing her robe from the bottom of the bed, she stood and slipped her arms into the sleeves.

"Don't dress on my account."

He had a noticeable bulge in his pants. Yep, to hell with eating. She licked her lips. "Did you start breakfast yet?"

"No. Why? Got something else in mind?"

As if he had to ask. Turning toward the night table, she retrieved the small packet by the lamp. Using two fingers, she dangled it. "One condom left." She dropped the robe to the floor, exposing herself fully. "How about we save on water and take a shower together?"

He had his pants off before he passed the sofa.

Yanking the packet from her hand, he ripped the top open with his teeth, fitted the latex onto his swollen shaft, and then hurried her into the shower.

She hadn't a chance to grab the soap bar. With the water spray on his back, he pinned her to the shower wall, held both her hands overhead, and entered her with a full thrust. She climaxed within seconds. He followed soon after but remained inserted, breathing hard against her neck.

How could she let this man go? He restored her shattered womanhood and made her feel whole again. Would she stay if he asked? *Not until Enrico is out of the picture*. The thought just about broke her heart.

****

Still glowing from the aftermath of great sex, Carmen flitted around the cabin to straighten the mess. According to the rules, housekeeping visited once a week on Saturday and after every person's stay. So, last night, she and James slept on fresh sheets and a perfectly made bed, which at the moment resembled a cyclone blast. Nothing like sex on clean linens, but today, the mess fell on her shoulders. She found one high heel under the bed and the other under the luggage holder. Her dress fell in a heap alongside the sofa, and she searched high and low for her panties. She almost suspected James stuffed them in his pocket until she found them hanging by a magnet on the side of the refrigerator. The rascal. Laughing, she plucked them before someone surprised her with an unexpected visit.

Finally alone with her thoughts, she analyzed the feelings tumbling within her chest. All her life, she'd had so-so sex, but for some reason, being with James was a whole other ballgame. He caressed her skin in a slow, torturous pattern. His gaze glowed with a combination of gentleness and heat while scanning her body as if she was the most beautiful creature on the planet. He thrust her to new heights and forced her to reconsider her choices in men. She had none. James was the one. So, how in the world could she return to Richmond without leaving behind a piece of her heart?

Her cell phone chirped with a text, and she tensed. Over the past year, she'd gotten leery whenever a call or message arrived via an unfamiliar ringtone. Three times, she changed her phone number, and three times, Enrico found her. Disposable phones, too. Enrico paid one damn good PI. Wincing, she peeked at the ID. Caller unknown. Gee, what a surprise.

—You have one hour to leave the mountain, or I will guarantee you lose your medical license and never practice medicine again. I will also ruin the sheriff's reputation and recommend his daughter for foster care. You know I can do this, my dear. The choice is yours. I'll be watching the mountain road for your inevitable departure.—

Gut twisting, she wanted to scream. If she were

back in her condo, she'd throw something, but here...what could she throw? She grabbed one pillow and tossed it across the room. The other pillow, she punched—repeatedly. Damn him. During divorce proceedings, he threatened to destroy her career with child pornography unless she agreed to no alimony. Little did he know, she had no intention of touching any part of his money. Now, he threatened the two people she'd come to love, and she would kill Enrico before he separated James and Lucy. He could do it, too. He ruined the careers of a Richmond judge and two small town police chiefs with just innuendo. Bribing someone in social services would be a piece of cake, and they'd yank Lucy from James faster than water flowed through a sieve.

Carmen paced the small cabin. Her breakfast turned sour in her stomach, and she swallowed several times to control the rising bile. What should she do? Should she tell James? No. He'd talk her into staying. He had no idea about the scope of Enrico's influence. Her ex was evil, plain and simple. And she had no delusions about why he wanted her off this mountain. He was setting the stage for her accident.

She should be biting-nails frantic, but a round of pillow punches calmed her. The confrontation so long anticipated was upon her and was the precise reason why she never made plans for tomorrow. Only through death would her troubles cease—his death or hers. More likely, hers.

Not wasting another second, Carmen tossed her clothes into the suitcase without a care about folding. Next, she grabbed the non-perishable food staples and stuffed them into plastic bags. The perishables she threw into the kitchen trash bin then tossed the bag into the metal container alongside the cabin. Jerking into her canvas jacket, she checked for secure latches on her suitcase and hurried outside. Using her key fob, she popped the car's trunk.

"Carmen."

At the sound of the voice, she gasped. Dropping the suitcase into the trunk then slamming shut the lid, she whirled and willed her heart to slow. She should have known Lucy would visit. No little girl missed the chance to talk about her first date. Carmen forced a smile. "Hey." So much for slipping off the mountain.

Gaze narrowed, Lucy jammed her fists onto her hips. "Where are you going?"

She never lied to children, but should she make an exception, like her mother needed her or her brother broke a leg? *Oh, God, what should I do?* Her heart wanted to break in two. She loved this little girl so much. Sucking in a calming breath, she took Lucy by the shoulders and gazed into her beautiful blue eyes. "Honey, I have to leave."

"Why? I thought you liked it here."

"I do, but I can't stay." Lucy would never understand the real reason for leaving. How could a child comprehend the malevolence of one man?

"Don't you like my dad?" With her face scrunching into a frown, she folded her arms across her chest. "What did he do?"

If her gut wasn't in such turmoil, she'd laugh. Carmen swallowed the lump in her throat. "Your dad is wonderful, Lucy." She bit her lip. *Dammit.* She almost burst into tears, but what purpose would it serve except to upset Lucy more? Blinking to control the accumulating moisture, Carmen used one finger to lift Lucy's chin. "Honey, I like you *and* your dad very much."

"Then, stay."

"I can't." She hurried to the cabin to snatch the bags of food by the door. Since she already slammed the trunk shut, she again used the fob. She dropped in the bags.

"Take me with you."

Carmen's hand froze on the trunk hood. Dammit. Lucy, in her desperation for a mother, attached herself to Carmen. A rejection at this stage could have long-lasting effects on a young heart. Fighting to control the ache in her chest, she eased down the trunk hood until the latch clicked shut. Taking Lucy's hand, she urged the girl toward the porch. Carmen slipped onto the edge of the deck and patted the space to her right.

Silent, Lucy plopped her butt onto the boards.

Carmen wrapped an arm around the girl's shoulders. "Honey, I'm running from a bad man. He wants to hurt you and your father. I can't let him touch either one of you."

She whirled to latch onto Carmen's arm. "But my dad's the sheriff. He can stop him."

"Not this man. He refuses to obey the law." *Damn, this is so hard.* She cleared her throat. "I don't expect you to understand, but I'm leaving to protect you and your dad."

Tears swam in Lucy's eyes. She sniffed. "What about you? The bad man can hurt you, too."

"Yes, he'll try, but protecting you and your dad comes first." Carmen patted the hand gripping her arm.

Tears slid down Lucy's cheeks. The sight officially

broke Carmen's heart, and she fought back her own tears.

Releasing Carmen's arm, Lucy wiped her nose with her jacket sleeve. "Will you come back?"

"I—don't know. I'll deal with this man first." She wasn't sure how, but she would fight. To the death, if necessary.

On impulse, more to ease the ache in her own chest, Carmen lifted Lucy onto her lap and wrapped her tight in her arms. The girl buried her head on Carmen's shoulder and sobbed. Her whole body shook, and Carmen felt her heart break into a thousand pieces. Oh, how she wanted to hug this little girl forever. She kissed Lucy's hair. "Be brave for me, honey." A sob stuck in her throat. Sucking in a deep breath, she hugged Lucy one last time, kissed her teary cheek, and shifted her onto the porch. Carmen stood. "Go home, sweetie. Say good-bye to your father and tell him thank you."

Turning to hide the tears ready to free-fall, Carmen grabbed her purse inside the cabin door, closed and locked it, and then hurried to the car. Waging a losing battle to clear her vision, she let the tears fall as she started the engine and drove off, leaving a crying little girl in the rearview mirror.

What choice did she have? Leaving ensured everyone's safety. She cursed herself for coming to Billings Mountain and for falling in love with the sheriff and his daughter. *Oh, shit.* The realization hit her like a brick. Yes, she fell in love with James. She loved both of them. How could she let her guard slip? These two wonderful people didn't deserve to have their lives disrupted, and she'd do everything in her power to protect them. If Enrico set his trap, then she must willingly walk in.

She stopped at the office to turn in her key. After parking, she dabbed her eyes with a tissue and blew her nose, all the while praying James wouldn't drive by. Holding her head high, she alighted and entered the office.

Henrietta stood behind the counter staring at the computer screen. She shifted her gaze and smiled. "Hi, Carmen. What can I do for you?"

"I'm checking out, Henrietta." Holy crap, her voice cracked. She coughed. "I need to leave."

"Oh dear. Nothing serious happened, I hope."

Something flickered in the woman's gaze, but she maintained a professional air.

"Serious enough." Carmen slid the cabin key across the counter.

Henrietta studied her. "You've been crying. Did James do something?"

If Carmen wasn't so sad, she'd laugh. Poor James. No one would believe how special he made her feel. She shook her head. "Lucy caught me packing. She's upset."

"Oh." Head cocked, Henrietta gave her a long look. "That little girl loves you."

"Yes, and I love her."

"And her father."

She swore Henrietta saw into her soul, but she admitted nothing. She couldn't. James deserved a woman without baggage. She squared her shoulders. "If you don't mind, Henrietta, I'd like to be on my way."

"Of course." Henrietta frowned. "You realize mountain policy won't allow a refund for your unused days."

"Yes, I know." Like she cared. The cabin committee earned every penny for their first-class accommodations.

Sighing, Henrietta flipped through a file folder and extracted a sheet of paper. "Give me a minute to finalize your bill." She turned to the computer. While typing on the keyboard, Henrietta shot Carmen a sideward glance. "Does James know you're leaving?"

"No, I—huh…" She lifted her chin. "I'm in a hurry, Henrietta—please."

A flash of light struck the wall behind the registration desk. The momentary intensity reminded Carmen of sunlight hitting a car window. Silently praying the glare wasn't from the sheriff's vehicle pulling into the lot, she strolled to the front windows. Nothing. Her car stood alone in the lot.

"Here you go, dear."

Carmen hurried back.

"Just sign on the line." Henrietta handed her a pen.

Tears accumulated. She couldn't see the paper let alone the line. She was really leaving. Forcing her eyes to focus, she signed then slid the paper to Henrietta. "I'll never forget my time here. Thank you…for everything." She headed for the door.

"Carmen."

With a hand on the doorknob, she stopped.

"Look at me, dear."

Carmen forced herself to meet Henrietta's gaze.

The older woman gave a small smile. "Sometimes, we can't fight our battles alone."

But alone was her safest option if it meant protecting the two people she loved.

Chapter Eighteen

On the drive down the mountain, Carmen glanced at the dashboard's clock. Five hours of daylight remained. That was more than enough time to reach Richmond. She'd hole up in her condo, and the first chore Monday morning would be to call her lawyer— provided Enrico didn't snuff the life out of her before then. His plan might include the car. Hmm. A car crash would suit him. Quick, easy, and no questions asked. Maybe she'd use a different route home to foil the plot. What was an extra hour or two driving? *All right, that sounds like a plan.* The logical route to Richmond was east via US460, the way she arrived. Once off the mountain, she'd head north.

"Choo."

Startled by the muffled sneeze, she jerked the steering wheel and nearly lost traction on the curve. With her heart beating like a runaway freight train, she slowed the car to a crawl and peeked into the rear. Empty behind the passenger seat. The sneeze wasn't a figment of her imagination, and she had no doubt who the culprit was. "Lucy?" Not like Carmen expected an answer, but without a full body twist to see behind the driver's seat, she couldn't confirm her suspicions. With little choice, she eased the car into the first available clearing—the boulder field, the first overlook she passed on her arrival onto the mountain. She braked and shifted the gear into Park. After praying for guidance, she unclipped the seatbelt and turned to inspect behind her.

Lucy sat huddled into a ball, head on her knees.

Carmen pinched the bridge of her nose to control the chest ache coming back in full force. She dropped her hand. "Lucy—"

Lifting her head, the little girl pouted. "I want to go with you."

Could Carmen's departure be more heartbreaking? She almost reached the main road with Lucy on board. What if she drove halfway to Richmond? To hold back the flood of tears threatening to fall, she sucked in a shuddering breath. "Honey, you can't come. What about your father? He'll miss you so much."

"Then, stay with us."

"Lucy, I—" Squeezing her eyes tight, she counted to ten, not because anger surfaced but because she loved this girl. She handled children every single day of her life, but Lucy touched a part of her heart that would never heal.

"If my dad asked you to stay, would you?"

Carmen opened her mouth then snapped it shut. Honestly? Yes, without a second thought, but she'd be a fool to think any man would consider such a suggestion so early in a relationship—if she called what they had a relationship. Shaking away the vision of a wonderful night and morning, she scanned the road for Enrico's car. If he came with Lucy on board... *I'm wasting too much time.* She threw open the car door.

"I'm not getting out! I'm going with you."

Nor could Carmen force Lucy to walk home alone regardless of how well she knew the forest. To ensure

221

her safety, she'd drive her and take the chance of running into James. And then what? *Santa Maria.* Getting off the mountain proved to be a task unto itself. Carmen opened the rear door and held out her arms. "Come here, honey."

"No!"

"You know you want to."

A mere second passed before Lucy unfurled from the floor and leapt into Carmen's embrace. The girl released a torrent of tears and clung to Carmen's jacket.

Feeling her heart break all over again, Carmen carried the child to the stone parapet and sat with Lucy on her lap. She kissed the girl's hair. "You can't come with me, honey. It's too dangerous. I need to handle this bad man without anyone else getting hurt. Do you understand?"

"No." She sniffed. "Dad will help you. So will Charles." She pushed away from Carmen's chest. "You don't have to do anything alone. Let us help you."

Lucy's words echoed Henrietta's. Ever since her divorce, Carmen fought a solitary battle against Enrico. Her lawyer could only do so much and often hit a brick wall fighting Enrico's connections. What did Carmen have? Big deal, a bunch of doctor friends who were half afraid to stick out their necks. Should she take the advice of a little girl and a wise, older woman? Could this mountain community be the answer to her prayers? With a sense of calm lifting her spirit, she patted Lucy's leg. "Dry your eyes, honey. Let's go find your father."

Using her jacket sleeve, Lucy wiped her nose. "You mean it?"

"Yes, I'm tired of fighting alone."

A flash of light caught Carmen's eye. Snapping her

gaze toward the road, she muffled a curse as a silver car rounded the curve.

Struggling to suppress the wave of panic for Lucy's safety, Carmen forced the girl to her feet and gripped her shoulders. "You remember the bad man from the soccer game? Lucy, look at me." Carmen shook Lucy's shoulders. "That's him, honey. I want you to run and find your father. Don't turn back for any reason. Can you do that for me, Lucy?"

Eyes wide and lips trembling, Lucy shook her head. "I won't leave you. He's gonna hurt you."

But Lucy's safety was paramount. To protect a child, she would face the devil, despite shaking limbs. She swallowed hard. "Yes, he'll try, but I don't want him to hurt you. Do you understand? You're very important to me."

The silver car crunched to a stop inches from her front grill, filling the overlook's stoned parking area.

With her heart jumping into her throat, Carmen tightened her grip on Lucy's shoulders. "Honey, this is not a time for heroics. Please, go find your father." Whirling Lucy, she pushed on her back. "Run—now!"

With a wide gaze flitting from Carmen to the second vehicle, Lucy nodded and sprinted up the road.

What friggin' luck. Like she believed she'd slip off the mountain or, for that matter, expect help from anyone else. Her solitary fight never ended. And what better place for her to have an accident than a cliff? *Dammit, dammit, dammit.*

Enrico stepped from his car with a snarl on his lips, his gaze riveted on the running child.

Standing while silently praying her knees would hold, Carmen squared her shoulders and faced her ex.

"Let her go."

He stopped alongside the passenger side door of her car. "Of course, I'll let her go. I don't want witnesses any more than you do." He looked around. "Are we off Billings Mountain?"

"I have no idea." She narrowed her gaze. "Why didn't you wait for me to reach the main road?"

Squinting, he stared uphill. "I'm guessing this Billings guy can't own the ground all the way to the highway."

He didn't answer her question, so obviously, he planned her accident to coincide with the mountain. She should be scared to death, but for some reason, she welcomed this confrontation. Death would be preferable rather than spending the rest of her life avoiding this man. But she refused to go down without a fight. He caught her off-guard once and put her in the hospital. Never again.

Enrico nodded toward the parapet. "How steep is the drop?"

She scanned the surroundings. No houses were in sight, and the overlook sat on a tight curve. Across the road was a thick forest and, over the parapet, sat the boulder field. Meeting him at this point couldn't be a coincidence. "You wanted me to stop here."

He shot her a wicked grin. "Sure. I waited for your car to turn around the bend. You just happened to have the little girl with you, and that's a damn shame. She's got a long uphill run."

Knowing Lucy, she'd cut through the woods, but he didn't have to know how the children played in the forest. What Carmen needed was to stall for time and allow Lucy to find her father. She lifted her chin. "Why here on this mountain, Enrico?"

Tugging on his jacket, he sneered. "I'm in a hurry for some money, and I have a two-million price on your head. Double indemnity should you slip and fall. Four mil total. What better place than a mountain cliffside?" He waggled his eyebrows.

Four—what? She gaped. "You have *me* insured?"

He chuckled. "Just because we're divorced doesn't negate the beneficiary. Take a look over the side."

The bastard planned to kill her for money? Then, her best defense was *not* to die in an accident. She'd be damned to let him win.

She scanned the area for life. Did the entire mountain hibernate on a Sunday? Why weren't some cars driving in for the day? The weather was beautiful and perfect for a walk in the woods. Where the hell were all the hikers when she needed them? She gritted her teeth. "Did you lie to the sheriff about me insuring you for two million?"

"Of course not. A buddy of mine suggested the two policies. Less suspicion. Clever, huh?" He again nodded toward the parapet. "Look over the side, Carmen."

Since ten feet separated them, she edged closer to the stone wall and peeked. The boulder field sloped downward with the initial drop of about fifteen feet. A survivable fall—barring a few broken bones.

He slipped a hand inside his jacket, pulled out a silver gun, and waved the barrel. "Stand on the wall."

She curled her hands into fists. A gun, eh? Death from a bullet was blatant premeditation, but he had to scare her somehow. The man must peg her as an idiot. "No, thanks. I'm afraid of heights."

A flush rose from his neckline and covered his face within seconds. *Yeah, Enrico. Have a stroke. Make my day.* Maybe his fatty diet would kick in and clog a few arteries.

Jaw twitching, he glared. "I'll tell you again, Carmen. Stand on the wall."

So he could pull her feet from under her and plunge her head-first into the rocks? *No, thank you.* She could run. A bullet to her back meant Murder One, but would the bastard go to prison? She studied the boulder field. She could survive the fall, but running across a rocky terrain full of various size obstacles made for one dangerous feat, especially for a woman in horrible physical shape. No, she would not run or hide anymore. This showdown would be their last. Lifting her chin, she stood her ground. "I'd rather die right here by my car with a bullet hole in my chest, Enrico, but you can't call that an accident, can you?"

Scowling, he clenched his jaw and glared. "You used to be so obedient, too. I can still claim you had the gun, and in defending myself, you took a bullet." While waving the gun, Enrico stepped closer to fill the gap between them. "Move. We don't have all day."

She must allow Lucy the time to find her dad or for someone to drive by so she could flag them down. If anything, Enrico was heading over the side with her…somehow.

His gaze flashed, soon followed with the deepening red of his cheeks. She knew him well enough to recognize the imminent explosion. She jammed her hands onto her hips. "Screw you, Enrico."

"Arggh!"

Enrico charged, gun raised overhead in a striking

position.

Instinctively, she swung her left forearm to block his downward sweep. Metal impacted against bone. Excruciating pain shot through her forearm and straight to her eyeballs. Ignoring the fiery ache, she threw a right fist into his face and connected. Pain radiated through every one of her fingers, and she winced.

He staggered, regained his footing, and clutched her jacket. Growling like some animal, he again swung the gun toward her head.

Gritting her teeth to control the pulsing throb of a broken bone, she gripped his gun hand with both of hers and jerked him off balance as a shot blasted close to her ear, deafening her. Heat seared her left shoulder. Another shot fired, missing her head by inches. Gun oil and powder wafted close to her nose and even his God-awful spicy cologne.

"You can't win, Carmen. I'm stronger."

He shoved until she abutted the parapet.

Still latched onto his gun hand, she swung the gun's tip toward the ground. A third bullet discharged. Buckling, she groaned.

He cursed. His foot slipped on a stone.

Both off-balance, she clamped onto his arm and tugged. "No more, Enrico."

I'm so sorry, James. She threw herself over the parapet and took the bastard with her.

****

With the sounds of gunfire echoing through the woods, James snapped his head in its direction while freezing with his grip on the school's door handle. That shot was the third and close to the other two. Who the hell was shooting on a Sunday? Every mountain

227

household stored a firearm to handle black bears, snakes, and the occasional rabid animal, but these shots reverberated from the valley. Another non-resident teaching a kid how to handle a gun? Wouldn't be the first time an outsider practiced shooting on Billings' property. Frowning, he cocked his head to listen to the silence of the forest. No more shots. Good.

Yanking on the handle, he checked the security of the entrance door. After every school party, some of the older kids liked to wedge a door to gain access for a private little soiree. They should know he or Harry checked every opening to the building, even the small bathroom windows. Under the bleachers was another go-to spot. Stupid kids always left condoms and beer bottles as evidence.

"Dad, Dad!"

Startled, he whirled as Lucy barreled across the helipad. *What the hell?* Where in the world had she come from? Meeting her halfway across the parking lot, he squatted and took her by the arms. "What are you doing here? I thought you went to see Carmen." My God, the girl was breathless.

Gulping air, Lucy pointed into the trees. "The bad man from the bleachers has Carmen. I think he's shooting at her."

Lucy had to be wrong. Cruz wanted to stage an accident. Bullets meant murder. He tightened his grip, inadvertently squeezing her small arms. "Where?"

She again pointed into the trees. "Down by Wilson's Overlook. She told me to run without looking back, and I did, Dad. You gotta help her."

His heart raced. Wilson's Overlook was a quarter mile from the main highway and another mile from the school. Why was Carmen so far from the cabin? And where was she taking his little girl without his permission? *Dammit, Carmen.* One night of lovemaking did not allow liberties with his daughter, especially with a madman on her tail. Straightening, he placed one hand on Lucy's back to hurry her toward the road. "Go to Henrietta. Stay with her until I come for you. Understand?" He nudged her.

"Don't let anything happen to her, Dad." She ran off.

While taking long strides toward his cruiser, he clicked his shoulder mike. "Harry, where are you?"

"By Swanson's place. What's up?"

"Cruz has Carmen. I heard shots. Meet me at Wilson's Overlook, pronto, and put on your vest." Opening his rear hatch, he grabbed his protective vest, slipped it on, and then jumped into the driver's seat. Once on the main road, he hit the gas pedal and flipped on the lights.

All right, stay focused. Enrico wanted Carmen to die in an accident. Why would he use a gun? No jury would call a bullet an accident—unless he fired a few shots into the air to scare her into submission. But gunshots echoed for miles through the woods. Anyone could hear. What if Carmen lied about having a gun? Suppose she planned all along to kill Cruz for the insurance money and played the sheriff for a friggin' sap?

But why take Lucy? She had to know he would never let anyone take his little girl from him ever again. He should be furious Enrico finally caught up with Carmen, but he was angrier at Carmen for endangering Lucy. Despite the feeling he might be falling in love with the woman, he hardly knew Carmen. If she survived her encounter with Cruz, she better have some damn good answers. With a heart pounding out his ears, he tightened his grip on the steering wheel.

Screeching to a halt behind Carmen's car, he jumped from the cruiser with a hand resting on his weapon. Not a soul in sight, not even a sound except the thumping of his rapid heart. Enrico's car faced the white vehicle's engine so Cruz drove in from the valley. Was this a chance encounter or a planned meeting? The former, he understood, but a planned meeting with Lucy on board? Hell, no.

Harry's vehicle skidded to a stop behind the cruiser. He ran alongside. "Where are they?"

"Don't know yet." James scanned the area. Over the decades, Wilson's Overlook became the dumping ground for all the boulders found on the mountain. He leaned over the parapet.

His heart thudded. Below, roughly thirty feet away, a bloody Enrico lay sprawled face-up across the rocks. About fifteen feet to Enrico's right, Carmen sat on her heels while pointing a silver thirty-eight special at Enrico. "There they are, Harry. Activate EMS." She was okay, and his tight muscles eased.

Fighting the urge to hop over the parapet and run toward her, James used the small path off the left side of the wall. Not too many visitors hiked this particular area. The more adventurous ones, determined to conquer the treacherous terrain, arrived in the ER with a twisted ankle. Even the gravel footpath, with all its loose stones, often sent a hiker tumbling.

Careful not to scare a woman holding a gun, James took cautious steps and stopped ten feet to Carmen's left, his right hand ready on his weapon. Dirt and weeds covered her, and her face had lost every ounce of color. The hand holding the gun shook while her left hand dangled by her side. "Put down the gun, Carmen."

With her gaze riveted on Cruz, she sobbed. "Is he dead?"

An unmoving Cruz lay across the rocks with his eyes wide open. Even from his position, he saw no chest movement from Enrico's broad chest. "I can't check him until you lower the gun."

With a blank look, she stared at the shaking weapon then eased the firearm to the ground.

Harry slid to a stop alongside. "EMS is on the way."

"Good. Check Cruz for a pulse. Put on gloves, Harry."

"Right." He extracted a pair from his rear pocket.

James followed with his own pair. Out of habit, he and Harry carried latex gloves in the event of something major occurring on the mountain. Since James had a forensics degree, he taught his deputy whenever possible. This crime scene was a definite test for Harry.

Still moving cautiously, James approached Carmen and picked up the thirty-eight. Releasing the cylinder, he checked the bullets. Four shots spent. Odd. He heard three.

Harry straightened from Cruz's body. "He's dead. I'll notify the county coroner."

Sucking in a calming breath, James squatted on Carmen's left. Emotions slammed him—hate for Enrico, anger at Carmen for endangering his little girl, but most of all, disappointment for a relationship that could never be. Not anymore. Hell, he spent the best night of his life in her bed and didn't know what to believe. Struggling with the urge to hit something, he clenched his jaw and shifted closer. "Is this your gun, Carmen?"

She shook her head.

Yeah, at this point, she'd say anything. The other witness was dead.

A tear in her jacket's left shoulder caught his eye. The frayed canvas edges had a singed look, like a bullet scorched the fabric. Bruises swelled the knuckles on her right hand, and a bloody knee poked through a rip in her jeans. Overall, she fared better than Enrico. He'd bet any amount of money her ex had a bullet in his head.

Carmen turned her blank stare toward him. "Is Lucy okay?"

The wail of sirens echoed through the woods.

"Yes, she's fine." *No thanks to you.* Regardless whether she was in shock or faking, he needed the answer for one very important question. He fought to control his voice. "Why'd you take her?"

Frowning, she blinked. "Take her?"

"You heard me. I want to know."

With a grimace, she slipped a shaky right hand inside her jacket.

Just in case she was reaching for another gun, he clamped onto her wrist. She cried out with…pain? Yanking her hand from her jacket, he gasped. Her hand emerged covered in blood.

His heart stopped. She was hurt after all. He lifted her unzipped jacket and sucked in a hard breath. Blood covered the entire left side of her sweatshirt. All this time, he debated whether to cuff her and haul her sorry ass to jail, and here, she really was in shock. Looking closer, he found the bullet hole in her jacket. How the hell was she shot if she held the gun? "Harry, ETA on EMS?"

"Pulling in as we speak, Sheriff."

Carmen met his gaze. Tears clouded her eyes, but he hardened his heart. He thought he loved her, had even considered proposing, but the law was clear. She committed a crime and had some serious questions to answer.

She sniffed. "I'm so sorry for causing all this trouble."

Bloody hell. She caused trouble, all right—with his heart and his daughter. Even though her voice rose barely above a whisper, he ignored her statement.

Two ambulance crew members hurried along the narrow path. Mick Richie carried a large shoulder bag. His partner, George Jones, followed while hauling the basket stretcher.

Getting out of the way, James watched as Mick exposed Carmen's wound by lifting her shirt. A bullet hole, all right. His gut clenched. Unable to stomach the amount of blood oozing from the abdomen he thoroughly kissed, he joined Harry by Enrico's body to take one long, last look at the man who couldn't leave his ex-wife alone. From the position of the body, Cruz had several broken bones under his ripped clothes—and one massive head wound. Without question, the bullet ripped off half his skull. He turned to Harry. "Search for another weapon."

Not like he expected Harry to find one. The silver thirty-eight in Carmen's hand was a testament to only her being armed. Even with a restraining order in place, she anticipated her ex's arrival and used the opportunity to profit from his death. Two million bucks became one hell of a motive. What irked him more was her lie about having a weapon.

Carmen's stare remained blank as the crew secured her into the basket stretcher and carried her uphill. Could she have shot herself on purpose to render a self-defense plea? As a doctor, she'd know what angle would make the wound convincing.

Harry rejoined him. "So far, negative on another weapon. I'll go to the office and grab the metal detector. This way, I can comb the area between the rocks." He nodded toward the parapet. "I found brain matter and a piece of Enrico's skull on a boulder below the wall. I'd say it's Cruz's point of impact, and both of them rolled to where we found them."

"Cruz could still have a bullet hole in his head. We'll see what the coroner says. Any ETA?"

"One of his assistants is coming."

Lifting his gaze, James watched the ambulance pull away. Damn. He should feel something for the woman on the stretcher—like sympathy or even sadness—but instead, an emptiness filled his chest. He thought she was the one. Lips in a thin line, he patted Harry's shoulder. "I'm putting you in charge. I've too much of a personal investment in this case. Keep in mind our conversation about Carmen's two-million-dollar insurance policy on Cruz. Do a full investigation and file a report. Leave no question unanswered, hear?"

His cell phone rang. Caller ID showed Joe Miller, the owner of the general store. Calls from Joe meant petty theft of a sort. He punched the Accept button.

"Hey, Joe, at the moment, I'm kinda busy."

"No problem. I want to report an abandoned vehicle in the visitors' parking lot across from the store. I saw it last night after I closed and thought someone carpooled to the dance, but it's three in the afternoon, and the driver is still a no-show. Any hikers reported missing?"

"Not to my knowledge. What type of car?"

"A black sedan. It's the one in the far-right corner."

"Okay, Joe. I'll check it out as soon as I can."

Just what he needed, a lost hiker. Could this day get any worse?

Chapter Nineteen

Leaving Harry in charge of Cruz's body, James climbed the incline to his cruiser and sped off for the general store. Five minutes later, he drove into the public parking area where a few cars occupied some of the spaces. The black sedan in question sat alone, and judging from the amount of pollen covering the car, it hadn't moved in over forty-eight hours. Not good.

Before exiting his vehicle, James typed the Virginia license plate into his computer. Within minutes, the ID showed the owner as Rafael Durante, a private investigator from Richmond. His gut twisted with the news. Coincidences didn't happen in law enforcement. The car *had* to belong to Cruz's PI. Frowning, he approached the sedan.

After slipping on another pair of latex gloves, he pulled on all four handles to the doors. Locked. Cupping his hand to the tinted glass, he peered inside. No one in the back or front seats. He contemplated the trunk, but without a viable reason, he couldn't just pop the latch. What if the PI…whoa, wait a minute. The PI would have followed Carmen, and he'd need his car. Hmm. Bending, James sniffed the trunk seam and jumped back. The unmistakable stench of bodily fluids emanated from within. *Okay, there's my reason to pop the trunk.*

He returned to his SUV for a crowbar. While

sifting through the various tools, he scanned the parking lot for tourists. If what he suspected proved true, he'd need the fire department to create a secure perimeter. People gawked, no matter how gruesome the sight. Returning to the sedan and finding the coast clear, he jammed the tool into the trunk crevice and, with one twist, freed the trunk hood.

The concentrated odor of urine and fecal matter escaped and turned his stomach, forcing him to cover his nose. Holding his breath, he bent to inspect the body.

Aw, shit. The victim's black hair and mustache along with the pale gray jacket was unmistakable—the Hispanic from the cafe. After snapping some pictures with his cell phone, he searched the victim's pockets. Finding a wallet, he extracted a photo ID for a private investigator license. Rafael Durante out of Richmond. *Yeah, surprise, surprise.* James clicked his shoulder mike then reconsidered. Since the mountain wasn't on the county's radio trunking system with scrambled frequencies, anyone could listen to his voice. Gawkers would come out of the woodwork like cockroaches.

Stepping away from the open trunk, he slipped his cell phone from his breast pocket and hit speed dial. "Harry, I'll need the coroner here first. We have a dead body in a trunk, and the car's parked in the public parking area. I'm activating the fire department to secure the scene."

His second phone call went to the fire chief. After explaining the purpose of his call and disconnecting, James waited by the body—not too close since the man stunk to high heaven. How could a day that started so well come to a screeching halt? Could Durante's body contain the fourth bullet?

His gut said yes.

One fire truck arrived. James waved to Dan Hansen who set up a roadblock into the parking lot.

His shoulder mike clicked. "Medical examiner is here, Sheriff. I'm sending him your way."

"Thanks, Harry."

Several minutes later, the county van crunched onto the stone-covered lot. A younger man with red hair hopped from the driver's seat.

While tugging on a pair of gloves, the young man nodded. "Titus Turner, assistant ME. You must be Sheriff Thomas. Let me see what we have here." He leaned into the trunk and began his preliminary exam by rolling the body to and fro. "One bullet to the back of the head. Death likely instantaneous. He should have bled more than this so I'm saying he was shot somewhere else and placed in the trunk after death." Bending over to open the case by his feet, he retrieved a thermometer, stuck the tip into the body, and read. "Liver temp suggests he's been dead for approximately eighteen hours." He extracted the probe, wiped the stem, and slipped it into a plastic baggie.

Eighteen hours. James estimated the time of death smack dab in the middle of his lovemaking. The timeline eliminated Carmen. Of all people, *he* was Carmen's alibi. He cleared his throat. "Anything else?"

Straightening, Titus turned. "No other wounds on preliminary inspection. The coroner will send you a full report. Here, I found a key fob." He pressed one of the fob buttons. The door latches clicked open. "I'll bag the fob along with whatever else I find. I assume you want a forensics team for this one. Want me to give them a call?"

He nodded. "I'll inspect the inside of the vehicle and take pictures as I go."

The young man cracked a smile. "We never receive calls up here, and now, you have two."

"Trust me, it's unusual."

Walking to the passenger side of the car, James opened the door and waited for the stench to escape. Then, he stuck his head inside. He looked for signs of a struggle but only found a mess of fast food wrappers on the rear floor. He opened the glove compartment. A gun clunked and caught on the compartment lip. James snapped pictures with his phone before lifting the weapon for inspection—a 9mm, full cartridge. Carrying it to his vehicle, he inputted the serial number. Within seconds, the owner registration showed Durante.

No way in hell could he investigate this murder when the main suspect spent the entire day—and night—by his side. The big question loomed—call in the state police or let Harry handle both cases? Was he ready? He speed-dialed his deputy. "Harry, we have a problem."

****

The soft murmur of a woman's voice woke her. Carmen opened her eyes to see daylight seeping through shaded windows. She lay, slightly inclined, in one of two hospital beds within a large room, the opposite bed being empty.

By the door, Alexandra sat at a desk with a phone to her ear while tapping on a computer keyboard and staring at a screen.

The scent of lavender filled the air. The fragrance reminded her of a visit to the lavender fields in

Delaware, but…when did those purple flowers bloom anyway?

Twisting her head to the right and wincing from the pull of sore neck muscles, she lifted her chin to scan the IV pole with two hanging bags—saline and an antibiotic. The fluid line ran to her right wrist. She checked out the bruised knuckles on her hand. After opening and closing a fist, she felt only stiffness, so nothing broken. A cast covered her left forearm and wrist, and her exposed fingers resembled breakfast sausages. Her arm throbbed like crazy. Using her right hand, she palpated the left side of her abdomen. A large patch covered the area. Bruises colored her arms and, after a quick peek under the sheets, her legs as well, with a gauze pad over one knee.

She vaguely remembered what happened after James arrived, but her memory stayed crystal clear of every detail at the overlook. When she and Enrico tumbled over the parapet, he dropped like lead weight. Gravity smacked him onto a huge boulder where the sound of his splitting skull would remain forever in her memory. Because of his death grip on her jacket, she landed on top, and his overweight body acted like a cushion. Then, they both rolled for God knows how far, and she scrambled for the gun. He never moved. If he so much as breathed, she was ready to pump him full of bullets. Even while recalling the horrible experience, she felt a powerful sense of relief. The friggin' bastard was dead.

Finished with her phone and tossing it onto the desk, Alex glanced across the room and did a double-take. "You're awake!" Wearing a white lab coat over a pair of pink scrubs, she walked close and dragged a chair to the right side of the bed. "You've been out for two days. I expect you have lots of questions." She slipped onto the cushion.

Grunting, Carmen used the buttons on the bed rail to elevate the head. Even with a slow rise, every muscle protested. Satisfied with the position, she met Alex's steady gaze. "Okay. Give me the bad news."

Alex crossed her legs. "You have two gunshot wounds. The one on your left shoulder is a graze. The other shot did a through-and-through in your lower left abdomen. That bullet nicked your descending bowel and took a chip out of your left hip. I repaired your bowel and extracted the bone fragment, but overall, you were damn lucky."

Yeah, some luck. She pointed to her left arm.

"Your ulna bone is cracked near the wrist. Considering the location of the break, I'd say you held your arm in a defensive posture. We x-rayed you from head to toe and found no other fractures. Now that you're awake, I'll have Becca remove the bladder catheter. Carmen—" Lowering her gaze, she toyed with the edge of her lab coat.

Carmen waited...and waited. She tapped the bed rail. "What? Am I riddled with cancer?" She almost let out a hysterical laugh. Cancer would be the crowning touch to a year in hell.

After another minute of silence, Alex straightened in the chair. "The graze on your shoulder has an upward trajectory while the abdominal wound goes downward. Residual gun powder appeared on both areas of your jacket indicating close-range shots." She paused.

Carmen's skin itched like crazy. From the tone of Alex's voice, she prepared herself for something very serious to come out of her mouth. "Go on."

The woman hissed through her teeth. Then, after a quick shake of her head, she met Carmen's gaze. "James suspects your wounds are self-inflicted."

Her heart lurched. Nothing prepared her for such a statement. Loss of a kidney, cardiac arrest during surgery, and even a drop to the floor shifting from the operating table to the stretcher, *those* three were common. Gut twisting, she gaped. "Please tell me he's joking? Of course, the shots were close range. I struggled with Enrico." Why would he even consider...*oh*. She blinked at Alex. "He believes I lured Enrico and set up myself for a self-defense plea. And as a doctor, I knew exactly where to aim." The very idea turned her stomach. Carmen flopped her head onto the pillow and closed her eyes. "What do you believe?"

Alex cleared her throat. "I like James and always considered him a great sheriff, but in my opinion, you didn't self-inflict. The evidence he presented could be interpreted both ways except for one glaring detail. I don't believe him. For one, you could have bled to death from the abdominal wound. Two, a fraction of an inch to your right would have taken a larger part of your bowel, and we'd be dealing with massive infection from bowel bacteria. Unfortunately, I couldn't convince him."

A heaviness fell over her body. She should have known. Their wonderful night together meant nothing to him. Why else would he make such wild accusations? Over the past year, she dealt with one disappointing man after another and truly expected James to be different. *Wrong again.* Lifting her head, Carmen met Alex's gaze. "Thank you for trying." She shifted her gaze to the shaded windows. "I can't believe James thinks I'm capable of something so low."

"I have more." Alex cleared her throat. "He's forbidden Lucy to see you, and I can say we have one unhappy little girl on our hands. Why'd you do it, Carmen?"

Shifting her gaze to Alex, she cocked a brow. "Do what?"

"Take Lucy. James wants to charge you with kidnapping."

Mouth agape, Carmen stared. "Kidnapping? Is he out of his mind?" Where was the man she slept with and, even worse, stole her heart?

"Then, why were you leaving with Lucy?"

"I wasn't." She shook herself and winced. "I found her hiding behind my driver's seat. Lucy should have told her dad."

"She isn't talking to him."

"Well, that's swell." Returning her head to the pillow, she stared at the ceiling. If Lucy talked, she might clear the air about kidnapping, but the self-inflicted idea? Not so much.

"What did your ex say to get you to pack and leave?"

She released a sick laugh. "He threatened to destroy my career along with James's." She looked at Alex. "He could do it, too."

Alex sighed. "I'm to call Harry so he can come by for questions. Are you awake enough for an official deposition?"

"Not James, eh?" She wasn't surprised. He probably hated her, and the emptiness in her chest intensified.

Alex patted Carmen's leg. "You're staying in the clinic for a few days until we get your hemoglobin up. I'll start you on liquids. In a few days, we'll see how your bowel handles semi-solid foods. Before you know it, you'll be on the mend."

And on her way to a new life—or jail. The outcome depended on James. She managed a feeble smile. "Thanks, Alex, for everything."

How could James consider self-inflicted wounds? Even worse, how could he believe she'd put Lucy in danger? Oh, hell. *Can't think right now.* Too much pain. Everything ached...even her empty heart. She'd deal with questions later. For the time being, she'd revel with the realization that Enrico Cruz was finally out of her life. *May he rot in hell.*

****

Over these past few days, nothing went right. He hadn't eaten or slept. Lucy refused to talk and sulked in her room. To top his morning, he tripped coming through the office door and nearly fell flat on his face. James threw his cell phone onto his desk with a little too much force. The device slid across his desk pad, and he lunged before it crashed to the floor. Lucy lost enough phones—the current one included. He didn't need to add a broken one to an already strained, family budget.

The whole damn situation boiled down to a matter of opinions. So what if he disagreed with Alexandra's medical diagnosis? The scene spoke for itself. Enrico was dead, and Carmen held the gun. Until proven otherwise, he'd go with self-inflicted. He was damn good at his job, and no one should tell him otherwise. He flopped onto his desk chair and sighed.

Oh, who the hell was he kidding? His sullen mood soured even more after Harry's phone call to the PI's office. The guy's secretary confirmed Enrico hired the firm to shadow Carmen. All James needed was a ballistics confirmation on the bullet in the PI's head. If the shot came from the thirty-eight in Carmen's hand, she had a lot of explaining to do.

Harry entered through the front door and headed for his desk. "Okay, I have Doctor Santiago's statement. You have any questions, or will you read my report?" He pulled his glasses from his face and held them to the overhead light. Grimacing, he used his shirt to clean the lens.

James huffed. "I'll read your report." He turned to his computer.

"Right." Returning the glasses to his nose, Harry settled in his chair then shook his mouse to activate his computer. "I need three faxes before I can finish."

As if on cue, the fax machine hummed. James turned to snap the paper from the tray and read. He grunted. "A single thirty-eight slug killed Rafael Durante. He was shot from behind approximately eleven to twelve Saturday night. Close range." About that time, he and Carmen were on their third round of some heavy body exploration. He could still hear…

"I showed her the photo of the guy. She didn't know him."

He shook away the thought of Carmen's moaning and cleared his throat. "So she says. You need to substantiate her claim."

"How? The guy's dead."

"Yeah, lucky her."

The fax machine again hummed. James swiveled

and grabbed the sheet. Reading, he released another grunt. He should feel something, right? Like maybe some sadness for the evidence piling up against Carmen? But damn, he felt empty. "The thirty-eight was reported stolen out of Miami four years ago." He glanced at Harry. "Can you believe she bought a stolen gun?"

"She said she doesn't own a gun."

Ignoring Harry's comment, he focused on the report. "Ballistics matches the slug in Durante's head to the gun." He tossed the paper onto his desk and rocked his chair. "Carmen can say anything she wants, Harry. Until we have proof of proper ownership, she's still suspect. What did she say about Lucy?"

Harry craned his neck over his computer screen. "What about Lucy?"

Swiveling his chair, he faced his deputy. "She was kidnapping my daughter."

Brows rising above his eyeglass frames, Harry met James's stare. "Until this moment, I knew nothing about Lucy. Carmen started her deposition at the point where Cruz confronted her at the overlook. Where does Lucy come in?" Gaze narrowed, he leaned forward. "It's bad enough you believe she self-inflicted, and now, you believe she took Lucy?" Slamming a palm onto the desk, he glared. "What the hell is wrong with you?"

"Then, why was my daughter in her car?" He explained how Lucy ran to him at the school. "Carmen placed her in a lot of danger, and I'd like to know where they were going. If Carmen planned to use Lucy as some sort of shield against Cruz, I can book her for kidnapping and child endangerment."

While shaking his head, Harry shot to his feet. "I'll have another talk with Carmen. Then, I'll talk to Lucy."

"Yeah, you do that. And good luck getting my daughter to talk. While you're at it, ask Carmen why Wilson's Overlook. I can think of better places for a trap."

Grabbing a pen, Harry scribbled on a notepad. "You withheld information, James. That isn't like you." He threw the pen onto the desk and ripped off the note paper. "This incident has you twisted into knots."

And every day, the knot pulled tighter. Harry was right. James neglected to mention Lucy. Why? Law enforcement was all about details, and he just made Harry's job harder. Avoiding his deputy's glare, James returned to his computer. "My conflict of interest is the primary reason why you're handling both cases, Harry. I'm in no position to write an objective report."

The fax machine whirled then beeped three times in rapid succession. *Of course.* He meant to reload the paper tray before he left last night. Opening the cabinet beneath the fax, he refilled the compartment and hit Ok. The paper printed, and he snapped it from the holder. "Coroner's report." He read. "Cruz's death is officially ruled accidental. He died as a result of a fall with no evidence of a bullet wound. Strange."

"Why?"

"I heard three shots. If two hit Carmen, the third must have gone wild."

Harry grunted. "Why don't you say she fired the third bullet for good measure? Oh, and by the way, I searched the area with a metal detector and found no second gun. It's in my report—when you get around to reading it." While pursing his lips, he tugged on his duty belt. "She could have snatched the gun after the fall, you know." He ran a hand through his crew cut. "Did the coroner perform a GSR test as requested?"

James read. "GSR positive. Enrico's right hand. Probably deposited during a struggle, and the gun fired."

"Well, I got news for you. Carmen is also GSR positive. Both hands."

Dammit. More evidence against her. He hissed. "That proves she fired the gun."

Approaching James's desk, Harry leaned on his knuckles and sneered. "No, it proves she struggled with Enrico's gun hand while the weapon discharged. The evidence works both ways."

James taught his deputy too well. One day, he'd pass on his sheriff's badge without regret.

Straightening, Harry snatched the fax sheets from the desk pad. "I've never met anyone fall out of love so fast." He cocked his head. "FYI, I believe her."

"Then, you're gullible." He glared at his deputy. "For the record, we aren't in love. We had a nice night together, which I'm certain was planned on her part. Hell, I'm her damn alibi for the PI's murder."

"Yeah, right, pardon me." He returned to his desk and slipped the papers into a file folder. "I'll head over to the clinic. I'm not waking her if she's asleep." He left without waiting for a reply.

The coroner's report cleared Carmen of Enrico's death, but the policy on her ex's life left too many unanswered questions. As of now, when discharged from the clinic, she'd leave the mountain and never look back. She'd collect the death benefit and live two million dollars richer. No doubt she'd fabricate her statement regarding Lucy. What James needed was Lucy's side of the story.

Squeezing his eyes shut, James pinched the bridge of his nose. He lied to Harry. After one night of fantastic sex, Carmen clutched his heart and never let go. He considered asking her to stay, despite their financial differences. Man, was he glad he kept his yap shut. Her taking Lucy without permission was a deal breaker.

Not in the mood to wait for Harry to return from the clinic, James drove to the cafe for a bite to eat. The restaurant bustled with noontime activity. Patrons, mainly locals, occupied the tables and booths, most in for Marion's soup day.

James never appreciated the simplicity of soup. Give him a sandwich loaded with condiments, and he was a happy man. Today, he needed a little happiness. The entire world worked against him. He fell in love with a woman who might be a cold-blooded killer. His daughter sulked morning, noon, and night, and every time a resident passed, he or she shook their heads. A man couldn't win to save his soul. James strolled to his usual spot at the far end of the counter and flopped onto the stool. He flipped the coffee mug.

Marion meandered over. "What can I get you, Sheriff?"

"The usual."

Brow cocked, she leaned on the counter. "Which is?"

Surprised by the coolness of her tone, he straightened his spine. "Ham and cheese on rye with a side of fries and a cup of coffee."

She slapped a menu on the counter. "Your order

got a number?"

What the hell? He narrowed his gaze. "What's wrong with you?"

Glaring, she jammed one fist on her hip. "Me? I'm serving an idiot. Self-inflicted, my ass."

The mountain grapevine was alive and well. He should tell Harry to keep his mouth shut. Forcing himself not to shout, he leaned against the counter. "Look. Until convinced otherwise, I'm sticking to my opinion."

"Alex thinks it's far-fetched. Did you ask Carmen?" Placing a open palm onto the counter, she leaned forward. "No, of course not, because you're an idiot."

Damn, everyone in the cafe had their heads turned in his direction. He squirmed on the stool. "Carmen was leaving the mountain with Lucy. She's lucky I don't file kidnapping charges." There. Take that, eavesdroppers.

Straightening, Marion huffed. "Carmen wouldn't dare take Lucy without permission."

In the back of his mind, he knew her statement was true, but damned if he'd admit it. Without a glance in her direction, he toyed with the menu. "You don't know her well enough to make such a claim."

Jutting her chin, she tapped on the menu. "It seems I know her better than you. She belongs here, James. How many times has a visitor felt so right for our small community?"

Not since Alexandra, but he refused to give Marion the satisfaction of an answer.

She snapped a towel off a hook. "What about Lucy's side?"

For some reason, he felt overheated, as if the cafe's

thermostat was set a little too high. Maybe he should avoid coffee for a while. Sighing, he rested both elbows onto the counter and rubbed his temples with his fingers. "She won't talk to me."

"I guess because you've forbidden her to see Carmen. Overnight, you changed into an asshole."

The dining room erupted with applause.

Slapping his palms onto the counter, he sneered at the crowd. "Hey, why am I the bad guy all of a sudden?" He stood. "I can see I won't be served today. I'll eat at home." He didn't give a damn about Marion's opinion. Under no circumstances would he forgive Carmen for taking Lucy. Period.

He no sooner slammed his car door when his console radio crackled.

"Yo, Sheriff."

James yanked the mike from the holder, loosening the clip in the process. "Yes, Harry?"

"Jenkins and I delivered Carmen's car to the clinic, but he wants to know how long Cruz's car will stay in his lot."

He fingered the loose clip. "Can't answer that. We haven't found any next of kin. From his wallet, I found a lawyer's name, but the guy went on a month-long cruise. According to the secretary, no one handles Cruz's affairs except the boss." He started the car's engine. "Tell Jenkins to keep a storage tab handy in case the lawyer wants some numbers. And make a list of the contents in the car. If Cruz has family, they might want an inventory."

"Right."

Not like he gave a shit.

"Yo, Sheriff."

James sighed. "Yes, Harry?"

"I popped the trunk on Cruz's car and found a briefcase. It's locked."

"Combo or key?"

"Key. Something small."

"Then, we should find one on the key ring we have in his bag. Take the case to the office, and we'll look inside after I eat something—at home." He jammed the mike back onto the clip. Carmen had more motives for murder than anyone, but what he needed was substantial evidence to prove Harry wrong. Maybe the briefcase held the answer.

Chapter Twenty

Since he hadn't a drop of mayo or mustard in the house, James shoveled in a dry cheese sandwich then returned to the office. His mood hadn't improved, but once he opened the office door, he swooned at the wonderful aroma of coffee. He'd give his right arm for a cup. Call him a coward, but he refused to stop into the cafe and face another inquisition. What he needed was a single-serve coffee maker for his home kitchen. This way, he'd skip the cafe and not mooch off Henrietta every day. Right now, he could kiss Harry's feet. He smiled at his deputy. "Smells good in here."

Harry looked up from his computer. "I made you a fresh pot. Figured you'd need it." Leaning back, he folded his arms over his chest. "Word is Marion gave you a hard time."

"To put it mildly." Unwilling to see a smirk on Harry's face, James headed to the coffee maker and poured a mugful without so much as a glance in his deputy's direction. After taking a large gulp and burning the roof of his mouth, he turned to his desk to see the briefcase on his desk pad. Above the simple lock, the initials EJC were engraved in gold. "Did you find anything else of interest in the car?"

"Not really. Want me to get the keys from Cruz's bag?"

"Yeah. Let's see what he's carrying."

Several minutes later, Harry emerged from the storage room jingling a set of keys.

While sipping his coffee, James waved him to the case in a gesture of "all yours."

Fumbling through the ring, Harry found a small key and slipped it into the lock. The latch popped. Sucking in a breath, he cringed. "Let's hope Cruz hasn't rigged the inside with a bomb." With one eye shut and wincing, he eased open the case.

James laughed. "You're watching too many spy movies." Placing his mug on the desk, he surveyed the contents in the case. "Gloves, Harry, just in case."

After snapping on a pair of latex gloves, Harry reached into the case and extracted a pile of papers— legal-looking papers. One, a thick, folded document, he opened. "Here's a life insurance policy on Enrico Cruz with Carmen as the sole beneficiary." He waited for James to slip on a pair of gloves then handed him the document.

James flipped the pages. "Two million, double indemnity if by accident." He whistled. "That's four mil, Harry. A clear motive to kill him." He muffled a curse. "I should have asked Cruz for a copy and confronted Carmen. We could have avoided this mess days ago by asking them both to leave." Avoided falling in love, too. The thought gnawed at his gut.

Shuffling through the papers, Harry lifted a number ten white envelope, opened the unsealed flap, and extracted two sheets of paper. Reading, he snorted. "Then, how do you explain this?"

James took the papers. They were copies of two insurance policies—Cruz's and—*holy shit*!—one on Carmen. "Two million, double indemnity for her, too."

"This doesn't make sense." Harry nudged his glasses up his nose. "Why is Cruz carrying the original policy on himself?" He frowned. "My mom has me insured, but you won't find her carrying the policy."

"Good point, Harry. Important documents are best secured in a safe, not a briefcase." Why was Cruz carrying his own policy? As proof of Carmen's intentions? But a similar policy on his ex with him as the sole beneficiary meant...damn!

Gritting his teeth, he flipped through the documents. "Look at the dates, Harry. Carmen said they've been divorced for a year, and court records confirmed her statement. These policies were written a month ago." He chewed the inside of his lip.

Carmen wanted nothing more to do with Enrico. She refused alimony and even left the house carrying only her possessions. Their divorce went through a simple process where assets were not divided. With the passage of so much time, why did they meet to open life insurance policies? James tapped the papers in his hand. "I know what's going on, and to prove my theory, we need to head to the check-in office."

Harry raised his brows. "Why?"

"I'll show you. We'll take my vehicle. Here, carry the policies."

The drive to the check-in office took all of three minutes. An out-of-state car sat in the parking lot so James pulled alongside. "Let's wait for some privacy, Harry." He cut the engine.

Seconds later, a couple emerged from the building. Nodding a greeting, they hopped into their vehicle and left.

James stepped from his cruiser. "Let's go, Harry."

As the door opened, Henrietta glanced up from her computer and smiled. "Well, to what do I deserve the honor of two lawmen at once?"

Pointing toward her pile of paperwork, James leaned on the counter. "I want to see Carmen's signature on the check-out sheet."

Harry gasped. "Man, smart move. You're thinking she had nothing to do with this whole shebang."

Blinking, Henrietta shifted her gaze from one man to the other. "What shebang?"

James nodded toward her pile. "Later, Henrietta. Let's see the sheet."

Leafing through several papers, she found the one in question and slid it onto the counter.

Holding his palm outward, James waggled his fingers. "Let's see Enrico's policy, Harry."

Comparing the sheets side-by-side, the signature difference was as plain as night and day. A feminine signature for sure but definitely not Carmen's.

Harry gritted his teeth. "He forged her name."

James bit his tongue to contain a string of curses. The lying bastard set her up big time and put enough doubts into the sheriff's thick skull. *Sonofabitch.*

After obtaining a copy of Carmen's signature for their files, James and Harry left the office and approached the sheriff's SUV. Yanking on the door, James stopped and looked over the vehicle at his deputy. "I'll bet any amount of money Cruz needed fast cash and what better way than to insure his ex with a double indemnity clause. Durante discovered his scheme and paid the price with a bullet to his head."

Harry leaned on the hood. "Are you telling me you finally believe the gun belonged to Cruz?"

"Not yet, but we need proof Durante blackmailed Cruz. Since the forensics team took Durante's car, I'll give them a call to see if they found anything to help us. I could fast-express these documents so that they can be dusted for prints." Pursing his lips, he drummed his fingers on the hood. "You should check bank records to see if Durante deposited any large sums of money, but I'm willing to bet he was murdered before any transaction took place."

Somewhere, in the inner recesses of his mind, he recognized the facts clearing Carmen of any wrongdoing. But he couldn't rule her out where Lucy was concerned.

****

Another two days passed and still no visit from James or Lucy. Carmen forced the pieces of her heart together and accepted their rejection as a fact of life. Even though Harry cleared her of any criminal charges, he couldn't convince James on all aspects of the incident—in particular, Lucy. So, Carmen Santiago would return to Richmond, explain to her partners why the vacation turned into a disaster, and then forget how she fell in love with a man and his daughter.

According to a visit from Marion and Henrietta, Lucy refused to talk to everyone, and her silence failed to corroborate Carmen's statement. The poor girl probably blamed herself for what happened. But nothing was Lucy's fault. James needed a way to break the silence. Perhaps in time, he would—like when Carmen left the mountain. She became attached to the place in the span of a week, but this time, she'd leave knowing she'd worn out her welcome.

The next morning, Alex redressed Carmen's

abdominal wounds, all the while mumbling about Carmen's haste to return home.

Really, what choice did she have? She'd be better off in her condo rather than take the chance of seeing James again or—God forbid—have him lock her away for hugging Lucy.

With her suitcase near the bed, Carmen dressed in a sweatsuit, grateful for the foresight of packing loose clothing. She could nudge the waistband to rest just below her bullet wound and be more comfortable for her long drive home.

Alex walked to the bed. "James wants to know if Enrico has any next of kin."

Gee whiz. He couldn't ask himself? Zipping up her suitcase, she shook her head. "As far as I know, most of his relatives are still in Cuba. He's been estranged from them for years. Why?"

"Jenkins, who owns the gas station, wants Cruz's car off his lot. Also, the coroner needs to do something with his body."

"Oh." She owed Enrico nothing, not even a proper burial. Easing her butt onto the edge of the bed, she stopped for a minute to catch her breath. Dressing with a cast on her arm proved awkward, but at least, she had the use of her fingers. However, bending was an absolute bitch.

"You're basically next of kin, Carmen, even though you're divorced."

Carmen fingered the pair of socks by her thigh. "I don't give a damn what the coroner does with his body. Have him cremated as a transient or find Enrico's lawyer and have him pay for burial." She met Alex's gaze. "As for the car, Jenkins can consider himself the new owner of a luxury vehicle."

"Okay, I'll tell James." Brows coming together, Alex folded her arms over her chest. "I'll say it again. You're leaving against medical advice. I'd feel better if someone was home to take care of you." Dropping her arms, she stuffed her hands into her lab coat pockets. "Henrietta kept the cabin available. Why not take advantage of a few more days?"

Carmen smiled. "We've been through this, Alex. I won't stay. I'm leaving because I have to. James will be thrilled to see me gone. I've brought nothing but trouble to this mountain."

"Carmen?"

Startled, Carmen turned too fast and winced.

Lucy stood in the doorway, biting her lip.

Oh, God. She thought she'd never see her again, and her heart soared.

Grinning, Alex waved the girl toward the bed. "I don't care what James said. This girl wants to see you, and if you leave, she won't have another chance."

Lucy ran in and threw herself into Carmen's arms.

The jostling sent jolts of pain throughout her body, but so what? A precious kind of sweetness pierced her heart, more so than all her young patients combined. She loved this little girl so much.

"I'm sorry, Carmen."

Carmen urged the girl onto the bed but kept her right arm around her shoulders. "Sorry for what?"

"Because of me, you stopped, and that bad man hurt you."

I knew it. Lucy blamed herself. Carmen slipped a finger under the girl's chin to stare into her blue eyes. "He was determined to hurt me, Lucy. It wasn't your fault. I want you to talk to your dad and tell him what happened. He won't be mad at you." *I hope.*

She balled her little hands into fists. "He's being mean."

"Oh, I doubt that. He's concerned. Don't you agree, Al—oh."

Alex had disappeared. The little devil defied James's orders and snuck in Lucy. *Thank you, Alex.* Carmen squeezed the girl's shoulders and kissed her forehead.

Lucy sniffed. "Don't leave. You can stay with us."

"I can't, honey. Your father thinks I took you without his permission. He loves you, and the thought of losing you made him angry. If you explain why you were in my car, he'll understand."

Using her jacket sleeve, the little girl wiped her nose. "Yes, I'll talk to him." She hugged Carmen then jumped to her feet. "I'll run to the office right now. Will you promise to wait until I get back?"

Her heart broke all over again. She took Lucy's hand. "I can't promise, honey. My home is in Richmond, and I need to return."

"Then, you can visit."

"Maybe some day." Oh, God, her chest ached.

Lips tight, Lucy nodded, kissed Carmen on the cheek, and ran from the room.

Alex strolled in. "James is acting like a stubborn mule. He's got some bug up his ass no one can knock free. One of these days, he'll kick himself for letting you go." She shot Carmen a one-eyed glare. "You look exhausted already. At least, spend one night in the cabin." With both hands, she clamped onto the bed's footboard. "Look, before you do anything else, lie back and relax. Your face is a little too pale."

Yeah, well, she felt like shit. Dressing took all her energy, and she still had her socks and shoes to put on. Maybe a ten-minute rest would help. Besides, no one waited at home. She could wander in at any hour, and no one would care. Giving Alex a small smile, Carmen lifted her legs onto the mattress and rested her head against the pillow.

"Would you stay if he asked?"

Earlier, she considered the possibility. Now, not so much. Wincing, Carmen adjusted her body for a more comfortable position. "He won't ask." No sense denying. She fell in love with James and Lucy, along with the mountain community. But James hated her, and even Harry's report wouldn't change his mind.

****

With the peacefulness of a quiet office surrounding him, James stared at the picture of Lucy on his desk. Where had he gone wrong? He never claimed to be the best parent in the world. From the moment Lucy moved into his house, he struggled to emulate his father, but raising a daughter without a mother was a challenge beyond his experience. Over the years, every woman on the mountain threw him wise words of wisdom. Some advice he disregarded as being too strict or way too lenient. For the most part, he used his own judgment. Right now, he'd welcome any helpful hints, because obviously, his judgment was flawed. No amount of coaxing loosened Lucy's tongue. The girl absolutely refused to discuss what happened at Wilson's Overlook, not with Harry or even her best friend, Alex.

What in the world could a father do? The poor girl cried herself to sleep every night and ate so little he worried she might get sick. She refused to do her homework or clean her room, and she even reneged on an impromptu soccer game with her friends. When she wasn't silent, she was surly and argumentative.

Pretty much like him these days. Between struggling with the ache in his chest over Carmen and his disappointment for a relationship that could never be, he bit his tongue more than once while out on patrol. His so-called friends called him hardheaded and too set in his ways. He'd known the mountain residents for eons, but everyone took Carmen's side. Hell, she was a visitor...*yeah, one who crept into everyone's heart, including mine.*

Outside, the sound of a slamming car door caught his attention. He swiveled in his office chair only to slam his knee into an open drawer. *Ouch.* Damn, that hurt. While rubbing the sore area, he kicked shut the drawer.

Harry strolled through the door. "Did you read my report yet?"

"Yes." He turned back to the computer.

"Do you agree Durante met his fate before money was exchanged?"

"The evidence is clear, Harry, especially when Durante's secretary found copies of both policies in her boss's safe." He looked at his deputy. "Good work."

He snorted. "Don't congratulate me yet. Since you're not convinced about the gun's proper owner, I contacted the county lab and requested a fingerprint check on the bullets. This way, we can prove once and for all who owned the weapon."

"Smart move." Why hadn't he considered something so basic? He needed to screw in his brain a little tighter. But he trained Harry well, and for that, pride seeped into his chest.

Harry marched over and slid a pink cell phone onto James's desk.

Lucy's phone. Cocking a brow, James fingered the device. "Where'd you find it?"

"Under the driver's seat in Carmen's car. I remembered you asked me to check for a homing device. I found the phone first and then this." He tossed a plastic bag onto the desk.

Inside the bag was a black, rectangular box with a wireless symbol on the face. James frowned. "If I'm not mistaken, a person can track the signal using a phone app."

"That's right." Harry shoved his thumbs into his duty belt and grinned. "I found it stuck to the underbelly of the car. Did you know you can buy these homing devices anywhere?"

And follow the victim to the ends of the earth. His gut twisted.

"I have more." Unbuttoning the pocket closure on his shirt, Harry extracted his cell phone. "Carmen forwarded this message for my report." He swiped his finger across the screen then handed the phone to James.

A text message from Cruz, sent on Sunday forty minutes after James kissed her good-bye. Scanning the message, he flashed a heated gaze at Harry. "He threatened to put Lucy in foster care?"

"Along with ruining your career and hers. Carmen was more concerned about you and Lucy than herself."

No wonder she left in a hurry. She'd had an entire year of fighting her ex and knew his capabilities. Damn.

"So, we have the reason why she took Lucy."

Scowling, Harry placed two fists on the desk and leaned over. "You read my report. Lucy hid behind the seat. FYI, while I was in Carmen's car, I sat in the driver's seat and looked over my shoulder to see behind me, but the seats are too wide. After I parked, I twisted in the seat, just like Carmen described. Only then could I see the floor where a little girl might hide." He straightened. "Sorry, James. I believe Carmen." He ambled to the coffee maker on the table by the wall and poured a cup. "By the way, I received a truant report from the school. One child today." After a quick sip, he faced James. "Lucy cut out at recess."

Inevitable. Why go to class if homework wasn't done? An overwhelming helplessness hit, and his shoulders sagged. Where had his fun-loving little girl gone? He sucked in a heavy breath. "Do you know where she is?"

"Last sighted about ten minutes ago near the clinic."

"The clinic, eh?" Chest tight, he gritted his teeth. "I hope Alex doesn't let her see Carmen."

"Too late."

At the sound of his daughter's voice, James swiveled the chair to see Lucy standing in the doorway.

She entered. "I said good-bye to Carmen." She marched toward the desk, fists tight by her sides. "Carmen's leaving, Dad. Doesn't that bother you?"

Hell yeah, but he refused to admit his regret to his daughter. To anyone, in fact. Not like he really wanted to know when she left...maybe...sorta. He cleared his throat. "Harry, take a break."

"Right." Retrieving his cell phone from James's

desk, Harry plunked his mug on a side table by the door and hurried out.

Frowning, Lucy came around to his side of the desk. "Why don't you like Carmen anymore, Dad?"

What a loaded question. He loved Carmen—at least, he thought he did. But now was a good time to have a few questions answered. Lucy was talking. "Come here, honey." He urged her onto his lap. One day soon, even this simple maneuver would pass. She'd be too big for his lap. "Tell me what happened the day Carmen got hurt."

Resting her head on his shoulder, she toyed with his badge. "Everything was my fault. Because of me, the bad man caught up."

He mentally kicked his own ass. How friggin' stupid. Lucy blamed herself for Carmen's injuries. He should have known the girl would revert back to her prior behavior over the death of her mother. Because of guilt, she spent years in silence. He swallowed the lump in his throat. "Whether here or in the valley, Lucy, he was determined to find Carmen."

Pushing away from his chest, she met his gaze. "But don't you see? It was my fault she stopped."

"Why? Did you want out of the car?"

She hung her head. "No. She said I couldn't go with her." She wiped her nose on her jacket sleeve before replacing her head onto his shoulder. "I hoped she liked us enough to stay, but I found her packing her trunk. She said she had to leave to protect us. She wouldn't take me, so when she stopped at the office, I hid behind the driver's seat."

Emotions slammed his chest. Harry wrote Carmen's exact words in his report, and of course, he called Harry gullible. He owed his deputy an apology. While holding his breath, he said a silent prayer she'd keep talking. "Then, what happened?"

She sniffed. "I sneezed and gave myself away. She hugged me real tight, Dad, like she didn't want to let me go. It felt nice. I don't know how I did it, but I convinced her to get your help. We were about to find you when the bad man came. She told me to run."

His heart felt as if it lost its place in his chest. What a damn fool. He didn't deserve Carmen, not after the way he doubted her. He stroked his daughter's hair. "Why didn't you tell me this earlier, honey? I accused Carmen of taking you from me."

Again, pushing on his chest, she rubbed her nose on her jacket and met his gaze. "Don't you see, Dad? She got hurt because of me. We were almost to the highway, but she stopped, and that bad man caught us." Lips pressed into a thin line, she shifted on his lap. "I hated you, Dad. I almost ran away but was afraid Carmen would die." With a slight smile on her lips, she placed a hand on his cheek. "I don't hate you anymore." She dropped her hand and frowned. "Maybe when I'm old enough, I can visit Carmen." Fingering the open collar to his shirt, she tugged. "How come you won't talk to her?"

He released a long breath. "Because your father is an idiot." He slid Lucy off his lap and stood. "Since school is almost over, I'll take you to Mrs. O'Reilly. I've some serious groveling to do."

"What's that mean?" She again wiped her nose on her jacket sleeve.

Mental note—wash Lucy's jacket. The sleeve was looking a little used and abused. Meeting his daughter's steady gaze, he smiled. "I'll ask Carmen to forgive me." If she listened. Maybe with luck, he'd get his foot in the door.

With Lucy safe under Mrs. O'Reilly's care, James drove into the clinic's parking lot. A small surge of happiness circled his heart to see Carmen's car still in a slot. She hadn't left yet. His phone rang. *Harry.* "Give me some good news for a change."

"Depends on your perspective. Prints came back positive on the bullets. All Cruz's." A pause. "Satisfied?"

"That I'm a total ass? Yeah, Harry, and to put together all the puzzle pieces, Lucy confirmed Carmen's story about why she was in the car. I'm at the clinic to see if I can straighten out my mess. After this, I might consider another line of work."

"Don't you dare. You're entitled to one mistake—even if it is a doozy. Let me know what happens."

"Listen, Harry. I'll be off radio for a while."

"Roger that. Good luck."

Stepping from the SUV, James unclipped his shoulder mike and duty belt and placed everything into the trunk. He was visiting Carmen as a friend, not a lawman. He couldn't do anything about his uniform except run home and change, but he'd lose time. She might leave. Straightening his shoulders, he entered the clinic and ran smack into Alex in the hall.

She narrowed her gaze. "Glad you graced us with your presence. I guess you heard she's leaving."

He grunted. "I expected a phone call."

"Why?" She slipped her hands into her lab coat pockets. "It's not like you care."

He ran his fingers through his hair. "I feel like such

a jerk."

"Well, forgive me for agreeing, but yeah, you are a jerk." Sighing, she patted his arm. "Look, James. We often find ourselves blindsided in our careers. We think we know everything until someone comes along and throws a wrench into our logic. All too often, personal feelings creep in when they shouldn't, but we're human. We make mistakes. How we correct those mistakes is the important part."

How did this woman get so wise? Years ago, she visited the mountain and displayed a naiveté that endeared her to everyone. She might have been medically brilliant, but she needed a good slap in the face to recognize all the love around her...especially from Charles.

He stared out through the entrance doors. "I have no idea how to correct all I've said and done, Alex."

With one step, she moved into his field of view. "You made some serious accusations. You ignored my medical opinion and also Harry's investigation. I'm not sure what you can do either. Your biggest problem is you were the sole believer in your own words."

A sinking feeling hit his chest. He had no one to blame but himself. *Nothing but damn stubborn pride.* Not willing to meet Alex's gaze, he again stared out the front doors. "She'll never forgive me. I disregarded all protocols because I was angry. I saw her pointing the thirty-eight at Enrico and assumed the worst."

"Do you love her?"

He huffed out a short laugh. "I couldn't eat or sleep from the moment she got shot." Stuffing his hands into his trouser pockets, he hung his head.

She elbowed his arm. "I don't want her to leave the

mountain, but she won't stay with Charles and me. Henrietta kept her cabin ready, but she wants to go home. The drive's too long, James."

He met her gaze. "What should I do?"

Studying him, she pursed her lips. "If you ask, she might stay, but you, sir, have an awful lot of explaining to do. If anything, you should apologize for turning into the world's biggest jackass." She stared in the direction of the post-surgical ward. "She fell asleep while getting dressed and has been out for over an hour." She returned her gaze to James. "Convince her to stay for at least another day. If she leaves now, she'll arrive home after dark."

But would she listen? Even more important, would she consider staying on the mountain even if he lost her heart forever? He had to try. Squaring his shoulders, he gazed in the direction of the post-surgical room. "Here goes nothing."

Chapter Twenty-One

Yawning for the umpteenth time, Carmen dragged her socks across the bed and stared as if they would miraculously slip onto her feet. She could wear her sneakers without socks and avoid bending altogether. That sounded like a good idea. At the moment, her body was being uncooperative. The stitches in her side pinched, the skin under her cast itched, and every bruise screamed with the slightest movement. Sighing, she lifted her foot onto the mattress.

As a doctor, Carmen knew the hazards of doing too much post-surgery. Two more days of rest would be the sensible course, but how could she stay? Sure, several of the mountain residents expressed their desire for her to remain, but one important person wanted her gone. She'd take the nice memories created here on the mountain and store them. As for Enrico, he was out of her life. If she could, she'd jump for joy, but the weight of what happened left her emotionally and physically drained. She no longer wanted to think or feel. Too bad her heart refused to listen.

Maybe she should say good-bye to Virginia, pack her possessions, and return to New Mexico. Over the past year, she'd often thought about relocating. Albuquerque had pediatric practices to investigate. She'd be near family. Her mother would love to have her home again. This alone shit was for the birds—like now. God, she hadn't left yet and already missed the community feeling of the mountain. Once she reached Richmond, she'd be just another face in the crowd. Wincing, she stretched toward her foot.

"Let me help you."

At the familiar male voice, she froze. *Now what?* Straightening, she braced for an onslaught of new accusations. Why else would he come? He ignored her for an entire week, and she wasn't about to welcome him with open arms. He hurt her, and if he came to dig the knife a little deeper...

Oh, hell. Despite everything, something deep inside her chest grew. Why? He was the man who left her high and dry at a critical time of need.

Lifting her chin, she watched him stride across the room, happy to see a slight hesitation in his step. Maybe he wasn't here to slap on the handcuffs. With dark circles under his eyes, he had the appearance of a man who hadn't slept. For some reason, his lack of sleep gave her hope. Swallowing hard, she diverted her gaze.

Dragging a chair closer to the bed, he sat and lifted her leg onto his lap. "Give me the socks."

She didn't argue. The sooner she had on her shoes, the sooner she'd leave. She already lost a lot of daylight with her extended nap.

"Alex tells me you're in no condition to drive. I'm offering my services."

What the hell? Why play nice now? She eyed him through narrowed lids. "I'm heading home."

"Yes, I know." Finished with one sock, he lifted her other foot to his lap. "I'll deliver you to your condo and then hitch a ride back."

Talk about an awkward ride. She tucked a loose

hair strand behind her ear. "Look, James—"

He held up a palm. "I have a lot of explaining to do. It might take our entire trip." Bending, he picked up her right shoe. "Right foot, please."

Resisting the urge to kick him, mainly because she didn't have the energy, she obeyed. His hands sent a shot of warmth across her skin, even through the sock. Damn him. He still affected her.

With her foot in position, he slipped on the sneaker and tied the laces. "I handled this incident like an amateur, Carmen. I assigned the case to Harry but dismissed his findings because I had my own assumptions. All wrong, of course." He shot her a glance. "I'm sorry."

And like that, she was supposed to forgive? Dammit. The pain in her heart didn't have an Off switch. She stared at her foot on his lap. "A little too late, don't you think?"

Easing her foot to the floor, he snapped his fingers. "Other foot, please." Finished with the second sneaker, he lowered her foot and pointed toward her cast. "What are your plans for tomorrow?"

She stared. "I have no plans. I'm going home to fall into bed."

"You'll be doing everything one-handed."

"Not really. The cast doesn't restrict my fingers." To prove her point, she wiggled her digits in his face.

Nodding, he shifted his gaze to the windows. "I want you to understand why I reacted so strongly about Lucy." Facing her, he rubbed his palms along his thighs. "I told you about the car crash that broke Lucy's back. What you don't know is Lucy spent the next three years in silence. When Alex rented one of our cabins,

Lucy latched onto her, and they became fast friends. Somehow, Alex coaxed Lucy to talk, and after all that time, we discovered how Lucy blamed herself for the death of her parents. Right then, I promised that little girl I would never let anyone take her from me." He huffed out a loud breath.

Using her good hand to push on the mattress, she repositioned her butt. "I can understand your promise, but you should know me better, James. Turns out, I'm the one who was fooled."

Shoulders sagging, he cringed. "I deserve that. I have no excuse for jumping to conclusions." He jabbed his fingers through his hair. "After our night together, I struggled with too many conflicting emotions, ones I've never felt before. When Lucy came running, all breathless and scared, all those emotions turned negative. I flashed back to Lucy's accident and the promise I made. I was wrong, and I'm sorry." Sucking in a large breath, he dropped his chin to his chest. "I'm not worthy of the sheriff's position anymore. I'll give notice to Charles and move on."

If she didn't feel so empty inside, she'd have something significant to say. Like *You can't quit. You love it here.* But words failed her. She was too tired to care. No, that wasn't true. Despite his actions, she did care. She stared at her feet. "What would you do?"

Clearing this throat, he leaned onto his knees and intertwined his fingers. "Don't know yet. I have a criminology degree, but I just failed Forensics 101." He tapped his thumbs together. "I should return to school to take refresher courses."

She almost agreed, but why add fuel to the fire? Unfortunately, his leaning forward drifted his cologne a little too close to her nose. Memories collided. Rather than watch his strong hands fidget, she lifted her gaze to his face.

Straightening, he released a short, stifled laugh and met her gaze. "I'm so stupid. I damaged the one relationship with the woman who made life worth living. I also hurt my little girl by keeping her away. I was so wrong with everything, but I'm not wrong about you." He reached for her hand but froze in mid-air. Jaw tight, he dropped his hand to his thigh. "I love you, Carmen. If you leave, you'll take my heart. If you tell me to go away, I will, but I'm asking for another chance. In the meantime, we'll head to Richmond. I'll get you home safe then make arrangements to return to the mountain."

Even without his touch, she could feel the pull of this man, like a magnet attracting its mate. But the pain ran too deep. She shifted on the bed. "I've nothing to say to ease your guilt, James. If—" *Wait—what?* Her belly fluttered, and she snapped her gaze to his face. "You love me? How can you say that after you practically threw me to the wolves?"

He curled one side of his lip. "I should have told you at the dance. To be honest, I fell for you the first day we met at the elementary school."

Again, his hand reached and, again, retracted. Grasping both knees, he leaned forward, his gaze locking with hers. "I want us to make a life together—you, me, and Lucy. Wherever you desire. I'll sell my house, and Lucy and I will follow."

She blinked. Was he joking? He'd quit his job and follow her to the ends of the earth? With her heart pounding, she gasped. "You'll uproot your entire life for me? But you grew up on the mountain. How can you leave?"

"I can, and I will."

Santa Maria. She was so sure whatever she shared with James was over. "I need to wrap my head around this, James." Should she take a chance with this man? More importantly, could her heart forgive him? She hadn't come to Billings Mountain to fall in love, but she fell hard, and yes, despite everything, she still loved the man.

"We should get on the road." He slapped his knees and stood.

"No." She needed time to think. She understood why he had so many suspicions about her encounter with Enrico. What bothered her more was his perception about Lucy. "I'm tired of being hurt, James, and I'm forcing myself to be cautious. At long last, I rid myself of a horrible man, and I'm afraid my judgment might be skewed."

"I'm not rushing you." Reclaiming his seat, he took her hand and stroked a thumb across her knuckles. "You determine how much time you need and let me know when you decide. If you agree to marry me—"

"Marry you?" She sucked in a breath and choked. Coughing, she stared. "I don't recall hearing a proposal."

"Oh." Shrugging one shoulder, he grinned. "The inevitable outcome. I love you too much."

Marriage? Holy cow—and yes, wow! Words eluded her, and she hadn't any idea how to respond. Over the past few days with nothing better to do with her thoughts, she analyzed her life. Her busy pediatric practice drained her energy to the point where she fell into bed at night, totally exhausted. If she joined Alex at the clinic, she'd savor the slower pace. As a bonus, watching Lucy grow into a young lady would be fun. But could mere words repair the hole in her heart?

Aware of his thumb caressing her knuckles, she shifted her gaze from his hand to his face. The man was serious, but he needed to earn her trust all over again.

He chewed his lip, his gaze troubled.

No, she just couldn't stay…not yet. She shook her head. "I'm sorry, James. I need time."

Nodding, he stood. "I'll drive you home and won't take no for an answer. Give me time to change out of my uniform and come back. Just in case, I'll take your car keys. I assume Harry left them in the car?"

"I don't have them."

"Okay, then." He grabbed the handle on the suitcase. "I'll lock your case in the trunk. See you in a bit."

With a glance over his shoulder, he left.

She sighed. She had the power to forgive. He made a mistake, misjudged her, and approached with his tail between his legs. If she didn't forgive, how could she move on?

Alex strolled in carrying a lightweight jacket. "Marion's giving you this to wear home." She helped Carmen slip her arms through the sleeves then stood back. "I hear you're getting a police escort."

Flipping her hair free of the collar, Carmen grunted. "He insists on driving me home. I have no idea how he'll get back."

"Charles will handle it." Standing at the foot of the bed, she folded her arms over her chest. "He apologized?"

"Yeah, and proposed."

Brows high, Alex grinned. "I wondered what took him so long." Her grin faded. "You didn't accept."

A statement, not a question. Carmen shook her head.

Becca popped through the doorway. "Your police escort is here, Carmen."

Rolling her eyes, she acknowledged with a wave, stood, and wrapped Alex in a tight hug. "Thank you for everything."

"You're welcome. I'll walk you out...unless you want a wheelchair."

Carmen chuckled. "I can walk." She should protest the escort. Yes, all right, driving with her injuries would be a bitch, but how could she think with him alongside?

Becca met her and Alex at the main entrance. The two women followed her out the door.

Flashing police lights caught her attention. Surprise turned to curiosity at the sight of Lucy standing in the middle of the parking lot, hands on her hips, and wearing a frown. She was dressed in a Billings Mountain police uniform, complete with badge and duty belt. She even wore aviator sunglasses and looked so damn cute. Carmen choked on a sob.

Behind Lucy, James stood alongside the police cruiser, legs spread and still in uniform with his arms folded across his chest. A pair of aviator sunglasses hid his gaze, but his expression matched Lucy's.

The scene was surreal, and Carmen's thoughts froze.

Lucy stomped forward two steps. "I hear you're leaving against medical advice."

To stifle a grin, Carmen bit her lip. "Yes, ma'am."

"Aren't we good enough to take care of you?"

What a question! She gaped. "I—eh…"

"Just because you're a doctor doesn't mean you can't take orders from someone else." She dropped her arms to her sides. "I'm here to place you under house arrest."

Oh, dear Lord. Carmen was about to burst into tears. Her love for this little girl just about overflowed her heart. If push came to shove, she loved James even more. He was a part of her now and as necessary as her next breath. Deep down, she already forgave him. She needed to say the words, but right now, moisture clogged her throat. Blinking back tears, she nodded.

Smile wide, Lucy removed her sunglasses. "You're on, Dad."

James strolled forward, removed his sunglasses, and slipped them into his shirt pocket. Stopping in front of Carmen, he took her face in his hands and kissed her.

A gentle kiss with no demands. Even so, his lips told her everything, and emotions ripped through her— from love to surprise to overwhelming happiness. Lifting her head, she swallowed the lump in her throat. "I love both of you. For a while, I doubted any love remained, but my heart tells me to grab hold and never let go."

Releasing a long breath, he dropped his hands to her neck. "Be my wife, Carmen. Be Lucy's mom, and however many kids you want, we'll have."

Behind her, Alex and Becca sighed.

Unable to contain the joy building within her chest, Carmen burst into tears, happy tears because she wanted all this—the mountain and people, James and Lucy, to be a part of a community, and to love and be loved in return. So much had been missing from her life for too long. Gazing into James's beautiful blue eyes, she smiled. "I'll marry you under two conditions."

"Name them."

She tapped a finger on his chin. "One, you stay the sheriff, and two, we live on Billings Mountain."

Brows high, he grabbed hold of her finger and kissed it. "You're serious?"

"Of course, I'm serious. I love everything about this place. And Alex already hit me with a partnership proposal."

"Yes, I did," Alex shouted.

Becca shushed Alex.

James grinned. "I don't know where we'll put all our kids in my small house, but we'll figure out something."

Could he get any more handsome with his brilliant smile and bright blue eyes? She patted his chest. "Come on. Take me to the Mallotum cabin."

Lucy ran up and wrapped her arms around Carmen's waist. "I love you, Carmen."

Even though Lucy hugged her incision area, Carmen didn't care. She kissed the girl's head. "I love you, too."

James slapped his thigh. "It's settled. No Mallotum cabin. My house. Lucy and I will take care of you." He held out his hand.

Slipping her fingers into his palm, she squeezed. "I still have to return to Richmond. I have a partnership to dissolve." Smiling, she bumped his shoulder. "And a new partnership to begin."

Epilogue

While she spent the next two weeks recuperating under James and Lucy's care, Carmen pored over the expansion plans for the house. As an engagement present, Charles re-zoned the land adjacent to James's property, and the additional acreage allowed sufficient room to grow. The renovations would start immediately upon her return to Richmond.

After another week, she felt strong enough for the long drive to her condo, but this time, she wouldn't be alone. With Lucy chatting away in the back seat, James drove her car, and all three behaved like a happy little family—which they were. The little girl was ecstatic at finally getting a mother, and Carmen loved every second in the role. The three of them spent a week in her three-bedroom unit and enjoyed some of Carmen's favorite restaurants. Afterward, James and Lucy returned to the mountain via helicopter—another ecstatic moment for the little girl. Carmen stayed behind to finalize her life in Richmond.

James wanted to marry right away, but no way would she rush. She compromised on an October wedding. Waiting several months allowed her time to sell her partnership and also for her family to make preparations to attend. Fulfilling her obligations at the pediatric practice also took priority, so she used the time to pack her possessions and place them in storage.

Once the expansion to the house was complete, her furniture in storage would fill the new rooms.

Several months later, when Carmen arrived to stay, she entered a property pasted with *Welcome* streamers, along with construction equipment and half the house already expanded. The next day, a party was thrown in her honor, and everyone gathered at the cafe. Carmen's heart swelled at their acceptance. She found home.

Carmen and Alex began the legal process for a partnership at the clinic. Within a short time, word spread of a medical facility on Billings Mountain staffed by a New York surgeon and a Richmond pediatrician. Every day, new patients from the valley called for appointments, and Alex made plans to expand the individual-care rooms from two to ten.

As August turned into September, Carmen's cell phone rang while she and Lucy prepared dinner—Carmen at the stove browning ground beef and Lucy at the table chopping carrots. The kitchen was spanking new with space-age appliances, as James pointed out. From the day she arrived, Carmen couldn't get over how happy she was. This house and mini family were the real deal.

"You want me to get the phone, Mom?"

Carmen sighed. She would never tire of hearing Lucy calling her Mom. She glanced over her shoulder. "I'll get it, honey."

Shifting her gaze to the phone on the counter, she recognized the number and groaned. Enrico's lawyer—again. She tapped the Accept button. "Yes, Mr. Vesta, what do you want this time?" She hadn't meant to sound so curt, but even in death, Enrico managed to infiltrate her life.

"Doctor, please. Bear with me. I'm holding your four-million-dollar check from the insurance company. You still want the money, right?"

"Yes, Mr. Vesta, I'll take it. I haven't changed my mind." She'd be a fool to refuse. Enrico owed her big time for all his aggravation. Besides, four million would pay for home renovations and college tuition for their children.

"Thank you, Doctor. I'll deposit the check into your Richmond bank account, and you can withdraw as needed. The other reason I called is about Mr. Cruz's estate." He paused. "I've had some nasty phone calls about money he owes. He probably opened that policy on you to pay off these characters."

Well, well. No wonder Enrico drove all the way to the mountain. He could have arranged her death in Richmond, but with creditors breathing down his neck, he couldn't wait.

"There's more."

Of course, there was. She frowned. "Go on." She added salt and pepper to the beef.

"My investigator found a bank account your ex-husband controlled but is in your name along with your social. It's also a non-interest bearing account so it never got reported to the IRS."

Leave it to Enrico to hide money from his shady lenders and use her in the process. The man was full of devious schemes. "Okay. Take the money and pay off his creditors."

"Oh, no, Doctor. I already told them they'll get their money in full when I sell his estate. This account is yours, free and clear."

"How much are we talking?"

"Another million."

"What!" Spoon clattering onto the counter, Carmen staggered to a chair.

Lucy's eyes grew into saucers.

Poor Lucy didn't know what to think. Patting Lucy's hand, Carmen sucked in a deep breath to calm her racing heart. "I don't want any part of his estate, Mr. Vesta."

"This is not his estate, Doctor. No way can I justify adding it to his holdings. This account is yours to do with as you please. Absolutely no taxes to declare."

Dios mio. A total of five million dollars would solve any financial problems for life. She swallowed. "Transfer the money into my bank account, Mr. Vesta." She terminated the connection and stared at her phone.

The front door slammed. "Honey, I'm home!"

Her heart fluttered. She'd never tire of hearing that particular phrase either.

James walked into the kitchen. After glancing from Carmen to Lucy and back, he raised both brows. "What's going on?"

Lucy pouted. "Mom just got off the phone. I think she's in shock."

Eyes wide, James dropped to his knees in front of Carmen. "Your face looks a little pale, honey. What happened?"

She blinked to focus. "We need to have a serious talk about money."

Leaning back onto his heels, he smiled. "We already know what we're doing with the insurance check, and we have a meeting with Charles's investment adviser on Tuesday. What else?"

"Another million, to be precise."

He gaped then shook his head. "I don't know about you, but I have no plans to change my lifestyle. At the way cost of living is increasing, five mil won't amount to much in the future."

Just what she wanted to hear. Nothing would please her more than to live the rest of her life on this beautiful mountain and surrounded by so many wonderful people. Gad, her heart felt so full.

"Are you taking it?"

She locked onto his gaze. "It's mine, no matter what I say." She stroked a finger along his stubbled cheek. "The money won't change us, James. I love our plans for the house, but maybe we should do a little furniture shopping."

He cocked a brow. "I thought you said you had bedroom sets to fill the new rooms."

"I was thinking of something to fit a smaller person." She took his cheeks in her hands and kissed his soft lips. Lifting her head, she gazed into his sparkling blue eyes and smiled. "I'm pregnant."

A word about the author...

With a growing backlist of books, Jane Drager continues to write mysteries with a strong romantic element, always with a happily-ever-after. An avid reader as well as writer, Jane has lived her life as diverse as her stories. She was a journalist, sports editor, office manager, firefighter, ambulance captain, caterer's assistant, but retired from her long career as a Respiratory Therapist and instructor. She's married to a wonderful organic farmer who keeps her busy with canning and freezing.

Visit her at janedrager.com

Other Titles by the Author

All Chocolate, Extra Cherries

Ask Nothing in Return

Infinite Choices

Memories for a Lifetime

Secrets and Assumptions

Secrets by Necessity

The Riddle Key

Until We Say Goodbye

Thank you for purchasing
this publication of The Wild Rose Press, Inc.

For questions or more information
contact us at
info@thewildrosepress.com.

The Wild Rose Press, Inc.
www.thewildrosepress.com